The INITIATE

Some Impressions of a Great Soul

The INITIATE

Some Impressions of a Great Soul

Cyril Scott

SAMUEL WEISER, INC.

York Beach, Maine

First American edition published in 1971 by
Samuel Weiser, Inc.
Box 612
York Beach, ME 03910-0612
www.weiserbooks.com

First paperback edition, 1977

08 07 06 05 04 03 02 01 00 99
17 16 15 14 13 12 11 10 9 8

Library of Congress Cataloging-in-Publication Data

Scott, Cyril. 1879-1970
    The initiate: some impressions of a great soul / Cyril Scott.
        p.   cm.
    Reprint. Originally published: 1920.
        1. Haig, Justin Moreward. 2. Spiritual Life. 3. Occultists. I. Title.
BF1408.2.H35S3   1990
133'.092--dc20   90-47988
    [B]   CIP

ISBN 0-87728-361-3
BJ

Cover illustration is "Time Travelers" copyright © 1988 Rob Schouten.
Used by kind permission of the artist.

Printed in the United States of America

The paper used in this publication meets the minimum
requirements of the American National Standard for Permanence
of Paper for Printed Library Materials Z39.48-1984.

CONTENTS

PART I.
JUSTIN MOREWARD HAIG.

PART II.

INTRODUCTORY
ON INITIATES, ADEPTS, AND MASTERS

THE story, if so it can be called, of Justin Moreward Haig is a true one, in so far that such a person does exist, although, as explained later, I have been compelled for many reasons to conceal his identity. And I emphasise the fact of his existence because there are a number of people who may doubt the possibility of attaining to that degree of perfection which he undubitably manifested, thus crediting me with writing romance instead of fact. And yet he does not by any means stand alone at his stage of spiritual evolution, for not only are there many more like him living amongst us at the present time, but if world-history is to be accredited with truth, there have been hundreds as great as and greater than he in the past. True it is that the so-called enlightenment of our twentieth century civilisation seeks to negate or explain away the unusual powers of these men, but deeper thinkers who have taken the trouble to penetrate behind the veil of superficial knowledge are coming to the conclusion that the old truism "where there is smoke there must also be fire" is applicable to the case in point, and that this negation and explaining away on the part of so-called civilisation is not the result of real knowledge, but of ignorance instead. Nor must we leave aside the contributions which Romance from the most ancient of times has afforded in this connection; dating from before the period of Kalidisa to the latest works of fiction published in the present year, we have novels, stories, and dramas dealing with mysterious and marvellous beings so far above the ordinary " man in the street " almost., as a human soul is above an animal. Indeed, seeing this is so, are we not forced to ask the pertinent question whether the imagination of creative genius has not somewhere its foundation in Truth? Can all these poets, dramatists, and writers really be weaving the fanciful web of mere fable, and nothing beyond? For if so, why do they still persist, in the face of scientific ridicule, and thus continue to fill the public mind with false-hood and unsubstantiality? And the answer to this question is, consciously or unconsciously, they are stating the truth, and their subjective mind is aware of facts which their objective mind is ignorant of; for these Adepts, Sages, and Masters do exist, and he who knows how to search can find them and become convinced of their reality once and for all.

Now, although I have inferred that Romance is correct as far as the fundamentals are concerned, yet as a matter of truth it is very often incorrect in its details, or at any rate very misleading, in that it blends allegory with fact without notifying the dividing line between the

one and the other. And to begin with, these
great Adepts of Spiritual Science are not quite as
mysterious as writers of fiction and even
supposed fact would have us believe. Although I
am aware that two such Masters (or Mahatmas,
as they are often called) reside in the far distant
fastnesses of Thibet, yet to suppose they all
follow this example is to suppose a fallacy; for I
know there are several such Masters living in
England at the present moment, as well as in
America and in almost all countries of the world.
Nor do they remain in one locality, but often
travel from place to place as any ordinary mortal
might, being to all outward appearance perfectly
human, nay, perfectly normal. They may not
cruise about the world in a marvellous yacht, as
Marie Corelli would have us believe (if that be
her object), nor are they the " morally dried-up
mummies " which Bulwer Lytton depicts in his
prototype Mejnour, to be found in Zanoni, his
occult novel; but as Romance permits itself, and
quite naturally the indulgence of " romancing,"
we must not expect accuracy from its writers any
more than we must expect it from impres-
sionist painters.

I have said that to all *outward* appearance these
Adepts are perfectly normal, perfectly human; but
it is to outward appearance only, and not to the
deeper knowledge which accrues as the result of
a closer relationship with them, and their minds
and faculties. To the casual acquaintance, apart
from an appearance of unusual health, calm,

dignity, and force, there is nothing which might awaken the suspicion that they possessed powers of whose existence he was entirely unaware. Dressing neither in strange garments nor living in ghost-haunted castles, these men, far from wishing to awaken the curiosity or admiration of their fellows, seek to render themselves as ordinary to the casual observer as they possibly can. Many of them even affect some harmless vice of their fellows—such as smoking for instance—in order the more to normalise themselves in the eyes of the world. But this is indeed only to the world, for those who come to them, seeking with the necessary qualifications occult wisdom at their hands, obtain a very different impression; an insight into their marvellous personalities, which to any others is sedulously denied. And it is absolutely essential that in order to find we must know how to seek, only to him who follows the requisite of this maxim is it possible to discover the truth; and that truth is the very quintessence of real romance. In other words, the outer world, not knowing for what to search, finds nothing, or at best very little; so that for any portrayal of an Adept or Initiate, we must of necessity turn to the student or disciple, and to him alone; for through his thirst for occult wisdom he has earned the right to know the Masters as they really are in all their divine possibility.

Let us then try to imagine a human being, devoid of the weaknesses and drawbacks of the ordinary person; a being who is utterly beyond the feelings of selfishness, vanity, jealousy, anger, hatred, and other " vices " of a kindred nature; moreover a being who possesses a consciousness so intense, so infinitely alive as to warrant the expression *super*consciousness rather than *life*. And this superconsciousness of necessity embraces a continual " sensation " of unconditional bliss and unconditional Love, conjoined with which is a supreme wisdom and power. As to the latter, the Adept, possessing knowledge of Nature and its laws as yet not disclosed to Humanity at large, is able to control natural forces in a way which the ignorant cannot even imagine, let alone follow: indeed, were he to exhibit the manipulation of those forces to the uninitiated (which, however, he never *would* do) they in their utter incredulity and ignorance would ascribe the whole exhibition to trickery, and pronounce him at best a conjuror, if not a fraud. In a word, show people what they cannot understand and immediately they will ascribe it to something they *can* understand—for that is ever the tendency of the ignorant.

We have thus attempted a description of the inner man; and now to deal with the outer aspect, the more visible side of the Adept. And to begin with, he manifests perpetual health, and in many cases perpetual youth, or better said, the prime of manhood. Electing to work unceasingly for the good of Humanity, and finding an aged body a hindrance to this, he brings his occult knowledge to bear on the molecules of his physical body, and so prevents the change known as age; finally dying when he chooses to die, and not before. Nor must we omit another point connected with his youthfulness and perfect health, namely the fact of his entire freedom from worry, and his entire immunity from all those jarring emotions which so tend to age the body and upset the bodily equilibrium. Possessing in his mind an eternal Peace, the frets and troubles of life seem to him childish and insignificant, as insignificant as the troubles of infancy to the grown-up man. And yet being possessed of perfect Love, he can sympathise with others as a mother loves and sympathises with her child, and the very frets she knows it will one day outgrow. Indeed, as sympathy to be intrinsically valuable must be untainted with fear—for otherwise it were impotent truly to aid and console—so is the fearless sympathy of a Master the most valuable and help-bringing it were possible to conceive. And at the back of this utter fearlessness is Knowledge, that Knowledge which must ever exist as the only true basis of solace, the balm wherewith to soothe the bleeding hearts of nescient suffering Humanity.

I have attempted this lame description of the Adept in order that my reader may the more easily understand the truthfulness of this book, and not credit me with adding to the large proportion of romance on the subject; for verily, in my opinion, " truth is more romantic than

fiction," whether it be *stranger* or not. Indeed,
should I in the following pages succeed in
depicting one-fourth of the essence of romance
emanating from the magnetism of the personality
of my teacher, then I shall not entirely have
failed—which is all I can hope for in so difficult
a task. I have, in fact, much to contend with,
for the simple reason I am not permitted those
scenic and ceremonial appurtenances which
fiction draws to its aid. An Adept or High
Initiate is so different in respect of greatness to
the ordinary great man; so chary of fame and all
its glamour that to know him in the spirit and
flesh is really the only way to know him at all.
Being devoid of vanity, and thus importuned by
any form of curiosity on the part of the public,
he seeks in every way to draw attention *from*
himself instead of the reverse: and thus if he
lives apart from the " world " it is to hide himself
in solitude, and if he lives amidst the world, it is
to hide himself among the crowd.

PART I

JUSTIN MOREWARD HAIG

———

PART II

THE CIRCUITOUS JOURNEY

CHAPTER I

THE MAN HIMSELF

 HAVE before me the absorbing task of writing my impressions concerning a man who has reached a degree of human evolution so greatly in advance of his fellow-creatures that one might regard him almost as a living refutation of the old catch-phrase: "Nobody is perfect in the whole world." The fact is, like many catch-phrases, the assertion involved is so far incorrect that one of the objects of this book is an attempt to prove its incorrectness.

Whether Justin Moreward Haig (I am not permitted to reveal his real name) was what occultists call an Adept, this I cannot say: for in all honesty I do not know, the reason being that in matters concerning himself he was exceptionally reticent. But I do know that if one could erase the many unsatisfactory associations connected with the word saint, and rid the word "Superman" of its equally unsatisfactory ones, Justin Moreward Haig (I usually called him Moreward) might with perfect right be called either of these, or both. Indeed, my association with this truly wonderful man showed me that a saint could exist without

exhibiting an ultra-devotional temperament, carrying itself almost to a degree of unpleasantness,
and a superman could exist likewise, without that
arrogant love of power which is so characteristic of
the Nietzschean ideal. But there is one thing,
however, without which neither saint nor superman could come into being, and that is an inherent
spirituality; and although the wisdom-religion of
Moreward Haig was as different from the piety of
the average parson as a genius is from a man of
very meagre intelligence, to deny him a religion at
all were to grossly misrepresent a certain side of
his almost unique personality.

All the same, in speaking of religion and perfection we must not forget there are certain
unreflective persons who imagine that to be perfect
means of necessity to be tedious at the same time;
they quite fail to realise that dullness is an attribute
of imperfection rather than perfection, and that
they might with equal lack of rectitude say that to
be white is of necessity to be black, or that to live
in the Nirvana of perpetual bliss would be to live
in the tedium of a perpetual hell. If there was
one thing which Moreward was *not*, it was tedious;
such an epithet cannot apply—he was too unexpected in all his opinions and in most of his
actions. He was not a man who merely talked
poetry (for true poetry always has an element of

the unexpected, otherwise it would be a banality),
but his life itself was a continual poem—the poem
which the highest ethics would demand that it
should be, yet which the most exceptional human
being hardly ever lives up to; for really to live up
to that demand, and without any apparent effort,
would be to do one of the most unexpected things
on earth.

The story, if so it can be called, then, of this so
exceptional man is a true one, in so far that such a
person does exist, although, as explained later, I
am compelled for many reasons to conceal his
identity. But I feel constrained to emphasise the
fact of his actual existence because there are a
number of people who may doubt the possibility
of attaining to that degree of perfection which he
assuredly manifested, and so may regard him as
merely another romantic and improbable creation
of mere fiction. All the same, however much an
actual living person Justin Moreward Haig may
be, I must apprise my readers at the outset that I,
on my part, am neither a species of Boswell to a
present-day Dr Johnson nor a Dr Watson to Sher-
lock Holmes; I never lived in the same house—
except for a day or two now and again—with
Moreward, and therefore I could not follow him in
all his adventures—if he had any—and relate them
afterwards. All I set out to do is to record his

opinions, and the way he lived up to those opinions as far as I have come into contact with them, and no further. I cannot write the story of his life, for the simple reason that I do not know that story; I can only surmise it may have been a very remarkable one, and there the matter ends. As to the description of the man himself: as regards personal appearance, I am requested not to give too much detail; and apart from that request, I think it expedient to allow the reader the full play of imagination: let him, in other words, form his own portrait of this remarkable man from the perusal of his sayings and actions. One has often noticed in life how many personal idiosyncrasies exist in connection with a preference for this or that physical type; and many a hero of a novel has been spoilt for certain people by a description of the very type of personal physiognomy which they happen cordially to dislike. So that, in the present instance, I think such a thing is especially to be avoided; and, although I grant this course is far from usual, my plea is that expediency is weightier than convention. It is not a very difficult matter to establish the connection between what a man *is* and what a man *looks*; and when I present a human being who never indulged in the folly of worrying, and who was moderate in all things, the first supposition concerning him would be that he

presented an appearance of perfect health. In
addition to this, if I say that during the years I
have known him, not once have I seen him sorrowful except with the pleasant and mild sorrow of
perfect compassion, it is not difficult to imagine
that his face was one of serene happiness, with
that beauty of expression which corresponds
invariably to such a state of tranquil mind. As to
the psychic element in his personality, let those
who have the notion that psychic faculties can only
exist with an unpleasant concomitant of hysteria
and the outward appearance which goes hand in
hand with it, rid themselves of a notion so false;
psychic faculties to be entirely *reliable* must be
accompanied, save in very exceptional circumstances, by perfect health and by nothing short of it.

For the rest, I would add that Justin Moreward
Haig entered my life some twenty years ago, and
left it about ten years later for activities in another
part of the world. Although I have his permission
to write these impressions, yet at the same time he
requests me to refrain from any description that
would disclose his identity and the identities of
those with whom he associated. Nor, as to the
latter, could I well do otherwise, since no doubt
many of them are still alive, and my allusions to
some of their weaknesses might not be entirely to
their liking. As to the former being thus

restricted, I can but leave my readers to guess who this remarkable personage is, if in the course of their wanderings they have ever come across one who resembles him in Wisdom and Love.

I may add one word more, explanatory of how these impressions came to be written, for, should I omit this, my readers may credit me with a perfection of memory I make no claim to possess. The fact is, when I realised I had come into contact with a man of such exceptional wisdom—at least in *my* opinion—I made use of certain facilities I had acquired in connection with shorthand, jotting down many of his sayings whenever occasion presented itself.   True it is, I was compelled very often to rely entirely on memory, seeing I could hardly bring out a notebook in the presence of others, but the strain on my memory was at any rate only slight, for, having kept a diary for a number of years, it had become a habit of mine to write the events of each day in the evening before retiring to bed.   For the rest, it is only right I should inform my readers that on certain occasions my memory may have played me false, and therefore the record has proved inaccurate as a result, and possibly I have then put words into the mouth of Justin Moreward Haig which he never uttered. Should this be so, then the fault is mine and not his, and that being the case I prefer to call this

book " Impressions " rather than any more pre-
sumptive title.

As to the anonymity of the Author, I think I
need make no apology respecting this, for were I
to reveal my own identity I should be in great
danger of revealing the identity of its " Hero " as
well. Moreover, in books of a moral-philosophical
nature, the personal is not only uninteresting, but
may often prove an obstacle, in that hardly a human
being on earth is entirely without enemies. Often
have I heard the remark, " If such and such a book
is by *that* man, certainly I shall not read it "; and
through this fact that avowed authorship may
evoke such a reflection, one is constrained to feel
how disadvantageous is the personal element. For
the man who writes alone for his friends, and not
for his enemies as well, falls short of being a true
philosopher, by reason of the fact that all real
philosophy has missed its goal unless it brings us
Peace.

THE AUTHOR

CHAPTER II

THE WISE INNOCENT

IT is quite a mistake to suppose that the romantic can only come into being through a combination of perfectly congruous circumstances, for there is a species of Romance which is born from the entirely unexpected. To find a great sage living on a lonely mountainside is to find the *obviously* romantic, but to meet a great sage in the most mundane London drawing-room is to find the unexpectedly so : the lonely mountainside acts as a frame to the central picture, the frivolous London drawing-room acts as a foil—that is the only difference.

How Justin Moreward Haig came to be in the drawing-room of one of the most worldly women in London is a secret I shall disclose at a later period in the progress of this narrative—suffice it to say, I am indebted to Lady Eddisfield's hospi· tality for the most valuable friendship of my life. Nor have the details of this strange meeting escaped my memory. I can recall how, at the end of the most unmusical of all musical performances, I found myself encumbered with a companion of a far from sympathetic type; a species of ill-fortune which fell to my lot as the result of that pairing

together of people on the part of hostesses, irrespective of whether they be suited to one another or
not. And so it was, we found ourselves at one of
those round supper tables with a party of four
others : the man I have called in this episode " the
Wise Innocent," and three women, who remain in
my memory, because they struck me at the time as
being a sort of trinity of superlatives. One seemed
to me the most corpulent woman I had ever beheld;
the second, the tallest; and the third, the darkest,
outside the category of negresses and Indians.

He was talking what the three ladies, who leant
with enthusiastic curiosity in his direction, seemed
to regard as extraordinary wisdom; as for me, I
merely regarded it as extraordinary at the time—
minus the wisdom.

" A certain point of view," he was saying, " is a
prophylactic against all sorrow " (I could see one
of the ladies had never heard the word prophylactic
before), " and to acquire the right point of view,"
he continued, " is the object of all mature thinking. That being so, mental pain is the result of a
certain sort of childishness, and a grown-up soul
would be as incapable of suffering over the thing
you spoke of, as a grown-up person over the
breaking of a doll."

" You mean, I suppose, by a grown-up soul,"
said the stout lady, " a philosopher ? "

"Precisely: I mean a sage, or a saint or philosopher," was his answer; "in other words, a man who has identified his mind with that unconditional happiness which is *within*, and which is the birthright of every human soul."

I pricked up my ears and looked significantly at my companion for a moment, and then I asked a question.

"You suggest," I said, "that all mental pain is a form of childishness; then why isn't happiness the same?"

He turned his strangely gentle but forceful eyes upon me. "Pain," he replied, "belongs to the illusory things of life; and it is a characteristic of children to like illusions; their very games consist in *pretending* to be kings or soldiers or what not. Contentedness, on the other hand, is one of the qualities of maturity, and . . ."

"I can't see," interposed one of the ladies, "where the illusion comes in if Wilfrid's wife has ceased to love him and fallen in love with another man."

"The illusion comes in," he replied dispassionately and smiling, "in his being upset by the fact."

"Well really?" ejaculated the stout lady.

"Jealousy," he continued, "is also, of course, a form of childishness."

"But Wilfrid never *was* jealous," pursued the first lady.

He smiled upon her with a benign friendliness. "Jealousy exists in two degrees," he said; "one where there is no cause for it, and the other where there is—only he who is unperturbed when there is real cause for jealousy is in truth an unjealous man."

"I should hate to marry a man who wasn't a *bit* jealous," said my companion somewhat hotly, turning to me.

"Yes," he said, casting his benign smile in *her* direction, "and there are many women who say the same thing. You see they think jealousy is a compliment to *them*, but that again is an illusion—the real compliment would only exist if a man loved a woman so much that he always put her happiness before his own."

"I should hardly think there are many such husbands running round," said I.

"And if there were," urged my companion, "they would be more like fish than husbands. At any rate I should hate to have one of that sort."

"That is only because perhaps you have never thought about it very particularly," he replied soothingly. "You see," he continued with a touch of chivalry, "a *noble* woman would never wish her husband to be troubled by both a painful and a rather deplorable emotion—simply in order to gratify her vanity."

At which juncture my companion took refuge in a laugh. "You are certainly very clever," she said.

He waved the compliment aside with a suave gesture. "I am merely one of those fortunate or unfortunate creatures who can't help seeing things exactly as they are," was his answer.

"Then you lack the artistic," said one of the ladies. "You can't, like a modern painter can, see a factory chimney as if it were an old castle."

"Alas! Perhaps you have hit the nail on the head," he admitted. "In fact, I am troubled with an innocence which makes it very difficult for me to realise how people *can* believe things that are palpably untrue."

"For instance?" I queried.

"Why, for one, that a man can never be really in love unless he be jealous."

"It is obvious you are not married yourself," I inferred with a touch of inner maliciousness.

"I *was* married," came his somewhat tardy reply (and for the fraction of a moment the word "divorced" entered my mind and the thought "Now I have put my foot in it"); but he continued, "I am a widower." (And then we all exchanged hasty glances.) "That being so," he

pursued, as if to put us at our ease, " my matrimonial ideas are not of necessity mere theories."

" In fact," said one of the ladies, " you were a
very magnanimous husband."

Again he waived the compliment aside. " I was
merely a practical husband because I have always
felt that it never pays to be anything else but what
you flatteringly call magnanimous. Besides," he
added, " the sense of possession is again a childish
attribute."

" What do you mean by that? " queried my
companion.

" Why, that you might as well try to own the
moon as to try to own another human being: every
human soul belongs to itself, and to itself only."

" Then why marry at all? " said I.

" So that you may live with the person you love
without bringing scandal upon her," came the
ready reply.

And here, somewhat to my annoyance, the voice
of a flunkey interrupted me by the whispered
information that I was desired by the hostess to
complete a bridge quartet. I arose, with the cus-
tomary civilities, and departed.

It was only as I was standing in the hall at a
very late hour, waiting for a cab, that my whetted
curiosity was to some extent gratified, for one of

the three ladies was standing there for the same
purpose.

" Who on earth was that extraordinary young
man ? " I asked in an undertone.

" Young ? " she said. " I happen to know he is
well over fifty-five."

" That makes him more extraordinary still—but
who on earth is he ? "

" Well, his name is Justin Moreward Haig, and
he came from Rome two months ago—that is all I
know about him," was her answer.

But this very meagre bit of information did not
satisfy me, and I felt that this stout lady, who
looked as if an utter absence of curiosity in her
make-up was hardly to be expected, must be with
holding from me, at any rate, what people say, or
what *they* say, as it is colloquially expressed. A
man like that could hardly be seen, and especially
heard, at a number of parties in London society,
where tongues wagged with an ungaugeable
velocity, without at least some stories getting
abroad about him in one way or another. They
would probably be more or less false, exag-
gerated or unbelievable, but, all the same,
somebody must have launched a few on
the ever-restless waters of social gossip; any
contrary notion was inconceivable. Besides, this
lady of such large dimensions had used the phrase

" I happen to know " when questioned respecting
his age, and this might be significant. Although
I had only seen this man for at most twenty
minutes, and heard him taking large portions of
gilt off the gingerbread of some of our most
precious prejudices in addition (a procedure at that
time of my life which struck me as almost laugh·
able), yet there was a magnetism, a gentleness, and
at once also a strength about his entire personality,
which drew me towards him in a manner I could
not get away from. He made one feel, in spite of
one's utter disagreement with the things he said, as
if he were profoundly wise, and yet, through the
very saying of them at a supper party, and before
two entire strangers at that, as if he were also most
strangely innocent. It even struck me, as it
afterwards struck me for a moment at our next
meeting, that he might be a little mad, and was
endowed with that very sincerity which is a sign of
madness. It is, in fact, only mad people who can
make the most unheard-of statements with absolute
sincerity, they alone being convinced that what
they are saying is absolutely true.

These reflections had, of course, been occupying
my mind while still confronting the stout lady,
who in the meantime made conversation of a nature
I found no necessity of paying much heed to. I
was really waiting (while she deplored she could

not just *fly* to parties and " at homes " or press buttons and be in one place or another—anything to prevent this awful standing about for one's carriage) for the end of this " talk at all costs " kind of remarks, to extract from her some burst of confidence respecting this strange being she " happened to know was well over fifty-five."

" But to revert to this man," I said; " *how* do you know he's as old as *that*? "

" He's got a married daughter who looks thirty-eight, if she looks a day," was her answer.

" Was she here to-night? "

" She went back to Rome about a fortnight ago."

" But are you certain she was his daughter? " I queried.

" He introduced her as such—but, of course, one can never be certain of anything," she added uncharitably, " at least, of relationships."

"Mrs. Jameson's carriage," shouted a voice from outside; and that ended my interrogation, and also the episode of my first meeting with the man I have paradoxically called " The Wise Innocent," for at that meeting (and the subsequent one) he struck me as an embodiment of this pair of opposites.

CHAPTER III

THE SECOND MEETING

I CONFESS that for some days after this first encounter I found myself thinking of that supper party and its central figure with a persistence and frequency which seldom occurred in my world of thought. Apart from the unsolved question as to who he was (for his name conveyed very little to me), a series of further questions kept forming in my mind, which the science of deduction failed in any satisfactory manner to answer. Nor did the few acquaintances I approached respecting him aid me any more than the stout lady I had questioned that evening in the vestibule : for the answers they gave were as uncommunicative as hers. I wish to obtrude myself in these impressions of a strange and noble being as little as possible, but there are certain matters in which I would be liable to misrepresent him if I kept a complete silence respecting one or two of my own reflections. The way, for instance, he had juggled with the word " childishness " caused me at first to wonder whether he was troubled by an overwhelming conceit; but when I reflected he had referred to it with as much absence of the personal as one might refer to a cloud or a cloudless day, the idea of conceit all but vanished from my speculations.

And then one day we met by accident in Kensington Gardens, from which meeting a friendship ensued which has set that and most other questionings at rest.

I was seated dreamily contemplating that part of the Serpentine which looks like a countrified river flowing between peaceful green swards, when to my surprise he came upon me all of a sudden and sat down beside me.

" We are destined to be friends," he said, laying his hand for a moment on my arm, " and, that being so, the sooner we begin our friendship the better."

I murmured something about being honoured and pleased : for the remark gave me pleasure, although I thought it a trifle peculiar.

" We do not waste our breath on preliminary trivialities," he continued, " but go straight to the point, as you observe. Talking for the sake of talking is seldom advisable."

I agreed that people as a rule *did* talk too much, but I wondered in my own mind what the " we " meant—it seemed to have no application to myself.

" I remember," he went on, " when I said good-bye to you in Egypt under rather tragic circumstances some two thousand years ago, I tried to comfort you by the assurance that we should meet

under far happier conditions; you were a woman
in those days."

" Oh, indeed! " I said with a presence of mind
I had hardly thought myself endowed with, considering it flashed through my brain that I might
be in the company of a lunatic. After all, some
lunatics can be charming. He looked at me for a
moment with a friendly twinkle in his eye.

" Do you remember an aunt of yours, called
Aunt Jane, by surname Mrs. Wibley? " he asked.

I admitted I did—she used to be regarded as
the family crank.

" I know her," he said.

" Know her? " I repeated; " Why, she has been
dead these twenty years."

" That is no obstacle to our acquaintanceship,"
came the ready reply.

" Look here," I said, laughing, but inwardly a
little nettled; " are you joking? "

" I forgive you for casting such an aspersion on
me," he said, laughing also; " but wait and see.
Do you remember," he continued, " your Aunt
was the subject of a certain amount of moderately
friendly derision on account of her spiritistic
tendencies? "

I did remember.

" Do you further remember she vowed, after a
certain family discussion, she would convince her

opponents one day by sending a message from the other side? "

I remembered perfectly.

" Very well, then, she has sent that message."

" What is it? " I asked with scanty credulity.

He told me—and I am bound to confess it was very convincing, for it made allusion to a matter which concerned nobody but myself.

" However did you get it? " I asked.

He told me at some length. " I suppose you are a spiritist yourself? " I said after his explanation.

" Hardly in the sense you mean it," was his reply. " I am everything and, if you like, nothing. To be born in a certain belief is good—to die in it is unfortunate. Beliefs are the crutches by which some people hobble towards Truth—when one arrives there, one throws the crutches away. Many devout religionists believe, but to believe is not of necessity to *know;* only the practical occultist *knows.*"

" You are an occultist, then? "

" Yes, I think I may be called by that name," he said modestly.

" Tell me," I asked with a burst of curiosity, " how is it that a man like you can find the least pleasure in doing the tedious round of London society? "

He laughed. "A thing is tedious or pleasant according to what you yourself bring to it," he said. "If you really wish to know, I am on the search for spiritual adventures."

I failed to understand exactly his meaning, and told him so.

"I admit the phrase is ambiguous," he said, "but it is hard to express it otherwise in one short sentence."

"I am really genuinely interested, and would honestly like to know," I urged.

"Well, it is this way: I have a hobby: it may seem to you a strange one, but I endeavour to alter people's point of view in order to adjust their difficulties. If you want to call me by a pleasant name, you would call me a certain sort of philanthropist: a dispenser of moral charity."

A little understanding began to dawn upon me.

"I take no credit to myself," he continued; "it is a pastime like others, but it has one great advantage—it does somebody else some good. The sportsman *gives* other living things pain in order to get pleasure himself—the ideal sport is to derive pleasure oneself from *relieving* other people's pain."

"Yours, then, is the doctrine of giving?" I inferred.

" Yes," he said, " but there are two kinds of giving—one sort of gift is fleeting, the other is enduring."

I did not quite follow him.

" If you give a hungry and lazy tramp sixpence," he said, " in an hour or so, having spent his sixpence, he is hungry again; but if you present him, so to speak, with a point of view that renders him, genuinely desirous of working, you have given him something of priceless value."

I told him his philosophy struck me as replete with practical wisdom.

" Now," he continued, " there are plenty of people who selflessly go into the slums and dispense monetary charity; but *who* goes into the slums, as it were, of society and dispenses comfort to deserted wives and love-sick girls and jilted lovers, and bereaved husbands, and the multitude of unhappy mortals with whom society abounds ? "

" Evidently *you* do," said I.

" At any rate, I *try* to," he said smiling.

I took out my cigarette case and offered him a cigarette, which he accepted. But then I found I had forgotten my matchbox. He produced a little gold box from his pocket. A strong spring-time breeze was blowing, and every match he lighted annoyingly went out. I watched him with some amusement, for he showed a complete absence of all impatience, which struck me as quite phenomenal.

"Do you never get impatient?" I asked at last.

He looked at me laughingly askance.

"Impatient?" he said; "why should I? I have Eternity in front of me."

And then he lighted my cigarette with the last match in the box.

"And so *now* (to return to your question) you know why I do the rounds of London society," he said.

"And society will be the better for it," said I.

He waved the compliment aside, as he invariably did.

"But there is one thing you do not know," he added.

I asked him what it was.

"You don't know that I dislike talking about myself." After which remark he rose to go.

I laughed. "By the way," said I, rising to shake hands, "I don't think you know my name; we have never been formally introduced."

"You forget your aunt," he said, with a twinkle.

I laughed again; it certainly was a novelty in introductions.

"We meet at Mrs Darnley's on Wednesday," he added as he moved away.

" But I have not been invited," said I; " besides, I have another engagement that evening."

" We meet there, all the same." And he walked towards the path.

" I love that man," I thought to myself, as I watched him out of sight. And strangely enough, when I got home, I found a postponement of my Wednesday engagement, while the next delivery brought me an invitation from Mrs Darnley.

CHAPTER IV

THE CONVENTIONS OF MRS DARNLEY

I soon discovered it was a certain harmless idiosyncracy on the part of J.M.H. to shock people as it were at his own expense. The greater portion of mankind are chary of giving expression to the unexpected, and, when compelled to do so, prelude their assertions with such a liberal abundance of excuses, that the unexpected becomes transformed into the merely expected at the end of it all. Now, my friend had a twofold purpose in casting conversational bombs into the arid chatter of conventional society—it obviously amused him on the one hand, and it made people *think* on the other. " There are two ways " (he said to me one day) " of being emphatic—one is to shout, which is often objectionable; the other is to state a usually unknown truth as if you were saying the most obvious thing on earth." And certainly this method bore its results, for I may say I remembered every word of his conversation to me in Kensington Gardens that day, as well as most other of his (shall I say?) discourses. But there was one thing he never indulged in : he never said anything startling merely to make effect : everything he did say he believed to be true, and he said it with a convinced simplicity that implied he knew his listeners believed it to be true also. The further result of this was to tincture his personality with an innocence and childlike naiveté which could not fail to captivate and convince those who came into contact with him. People, in fact, when they were shocked, were pleasantly shocked, and, therefore, never in a manner which awakened in them the faintest suspicion of resentment. Nor could it be otherwise, for he never attacked their sacred beliefs with the weapon of ridicule: his method of exposing error lay seldom in pointing out that they were wrong, but in pointing out that something else was right. There was an exception, however, to this rule he adopted, and this exception was related to what he called the modern Pharisees. " Here," said he, " I must reluctantly use the hammer and break up false idols."

Mrs Darnley was an old acquaintance of mine whose hospitality expressed itself most frequently in the shape of very diminutive dinner parties. Indeed, on arriving there that particular evening I was not surprised (but, on the other hand, pleased) to find no other guests than Moreward Haig and myself. Thus our little party consisted of Mrs Darnley, her youngish and attractive daughter Sylvia, and our two selves. Nor did it remain at that, for, dinner being over, Sylvia, with some apologies, took her departure in order to put in an appearance at a series of "At Homes" which threatened to detain her long after we had betaken ourselves to rest.

Mrs Darnley kissed her daughter "Good night" with an affection which unblushingly savoured more of convention than love, and watched her departure with a reflective gaze that betokened thoughts very soon to find expression for our benefit in words.

"That girl worries me," she observed meditatively; "I don't always like the look of things."

We both expressed our sympathy and inquired as to the nature of the trouble.

"A poet is the trouble at present," came the reply.

We laughed. "A friendship with a poet?" observed Haig.

"*You* call it a friendship!" she said; "but I don't believe in friendships between young men and women."

We moderated another slight outbreak of laughter to suit the occasion.

"Oh, come," said I; "friendship is the only word to apply, when a woman is not a man's wife or his fiancée or his——"

"Now don't say that word," she interrupted hastily, "or you will shock me dreadfully; *of course*, she is none of those things."

" Friendship," said Moreward smiling upon her, " is a beautiful word, and a still more beautiful thing; then why wish to deny its existence? "

" I don't deny its existence in the right place and between the right people; but Sylvia is so sentimental," she said, a little peevishly, " not to say sloppy."

" Is sloppiness, then, a synonym for love in your vocabulary? " I asked.

" You know perfectly well what I mean."

" Yes, but are you sure that *you* know what you mean? " I persisted.

" How rude you are," she said; "really, I *ought* to know."

"But surely, sentiment added to friendship," said Moreward after this little passage of words, " is a most fortunate element: it makes the friendship more complete. Are you not glad that your daughter should feel something that will add to her happiness? "

" I don't think it *will* add to her happiness," she replied; " besides, I don't think it quite proper."

" Then you don't think it proper for your daughter ever to be fond of anybody but you— and herself? " said I mischievously.

" Don't be ridiculous, Broadbent! " she said, laughing in spite of herself.

" Well, that's what it amounts to," said I

" Is it your opinion, then," asked Moreward,
but without the least touch of sarcasm, " that a
person should love *only* his enemies? "

" Well, of course not."

" I have heard of a precept which runs, ' Love
your neighbour,' " I remarked with a twinkle;
" I am sure *you* live up to it."

" I try to," she said with momentary piety.

" But you don't think your daughter ought to
love *her* neighbour, especially if he be a man, and
more especially a poet? " I continued, with the
same twinkle.

" You know perfectly well," she said, getting
the worst of it, " it doesn't mean that sort of love."

" Ah, isn't that just where you make the mistake? " said Moreward with a certain gentle
earnestness. " In reality there is only *one* sort of
love, and the difference you make, and other
people, too, who perhaps have never deeply
thought about it, is a difference of degree and not
of kind."

She cast a look at me as much as to say " I can
listen to *this* man, because at any rate he doesn't
make fun of me."

" You say you can't believe in platonic love,"
he continued; " at least, so I inferred; but if you
could believe in it, you would agree as to its value."

" Perhaps I would," she acquiesced reflectively.

" Very well, but what, after all, *is* platonic love?
It is simply a combination of mental sympathy and
physical antipathy."

" The best definition I have ever heard," I
interposed.

" I am afraid I am not clever enough to grasp
it," said Mrs Darnley with a modesty not quite
genuine.

" Well, it means this," I explained, " that a man
enjoys (as long as he can sit at the opposite end of
the sofa) a woman's conversation, because he likes
her mind, but would hate to get any nearer to her,
because he *dislikes* her body. Isn't that it? " I
asked Moreward.

" Somewhat crudely put—it is," he agreed,
laughing.

" I don't think it sounds very nice," remarked
Mrs Darnley.

" It is a trifle dull," I observed mischievously.

" And yet," pursued Moreward after this interruption, " Plato never meant it in that sense at all;
he merely meant a species of self-control; a love
which refrains from giving vent to the complete
expression of physical passion."

" Oh, indeed! " said Mrs Darnley, not knowing whether she ought to be shocked or not. " I
have never heard that before."

" Like so many things," I interposed, " the

Pharisees have adjusted its original meaning to suit their petty conventions."

"Pharisees!" she repeated. "Why, surely they do not exist nowadays?"

It was on the tip of my tongue to tell her I thought *she* was a Pharisee, but I refrained.

"Don't you think it is just the modern Pharisees, perhaps," said Moreward, "that hypnotised you into believing that it is improper (which means in other words slightly wrong) for your daughter to be fond of this man? Looked at from a spiritual point of view, the wrong would exist if she were *not* fond of him."

"Really, Mr Haig," she said, "you do turn things round so."

"Surely it is the Pharisee who turns things round," said I; "he says 'Thou shalt *not* love thy neighbour."

She laughed impotently.

"Would you have your daughter possess an unloving heart?" said Moreward with calm simplicity.

"I should like her to love somebody one day— the *right* person, of course," came the answer.

"Right from a pecuniary point of view?" I inferred.

"Right from *every* point of view," she corrected.

"*Your* meat might be *her* poison," I remarked.

She feigned not to understand, but really she understood perfectly.

" Has it ever struck you, Mrs Darnley," said Moreward with deference, " why there are so many unhappy marriages? "

" Well, I have never thought very much about it," she said.

" Don't you think it may be because too many mothers look at all friendships from the matrimonial point of view? "

" Perhaps—but that is just what I am *not* doing——"

" Pardon me," he said with courtly gentleness and a motion of the hand, " but that is just what you *are* doing. You are, as it were, swinging between the two horns of the matrimonial dilemma."

She looked genuinely puzzled, and told him so.

" I mean," he explained, " that you are afraid your daughter may want to marry this man, and you are also afraid she may *not* want to marry him. In short, your attitude towards love is marriage or nothing. That attitude, dear friend, is the cause of most conjugal unhappiness. Young people marry unsuitable acquaintances instead of real friends."

" It is all very well for you to talk," she said unconvincedly, " but really I cannot allow my daughter to have a series of 'affairs.' Whatever would people think? "

"To think of other people's aspersions is vanity," he said gently; "to think of one's daughter's happiness is *love*. I am sure you will choose the latter," he added, laying his hand upon her arm.

"Well—well," she remarked, pleased with the compliment, but doubtful whether she would live up to it. "Well—well, we shall see."

And that put an end to the discussion, for Miss Sylvia herself entered the room, to our surprise.

"I really couldn't stand another of them," she said, "the first was so unspeakably boring—so I came home."

Soon after that we *went* home.

CHAPTER V

THE GARDEN PARTY

Some ten days later we found ourselves together again at Lady Appleyard's garden party. I had seen J.M.H. a few times at his own house and elsewhere betweenwhiles and he had told me that, if possible, he intended to render Miss Sylvia some slight service.

"Her aura exhibits fine qualities," he said, "and if she is only permitted to love and to live a little she will make great progress in this incarnation."

And I may say, in passing, that this occult observation and others of a like nature struck me no longer as startling or especially cryptic, since a good deal of discussion on occult philosophy had in the meantime led me to a relatively serviceable understanding of that absorbing subject.

We had led the not unwilling Mrs Darnley to a shady spot in a corner of Lady Appleyard's tasteful and extensive garden. Conventional as she was, she obviously admired and liked my wise friend a good deal more than she liked most people. As for me—well, I may say I amused her, if I did nothing else.

"And your daughter's poetic friendship," he said, "I trust you are not putting obstacles in its way?"

"What obstacles *can* I put in its way?" she said.

" Lack of sympathy " said Moreward.

" I can hardly be expected to sympathise with a thing I don't approve of."

" The truest sympathy is that which sympathises with things one does not agree with," he said gently, but earnestly; " sympathy for sympathy's sake—sympathy for love's sake."

" Perhaps you don't love your daughter," I said with the imp of mischief in me.

" How *can* you! " she ejaculated.

" You have had some correspondence with this poet, I think? " he said, after a glance at me which conveyed the impression that we must be serious for the present. Mrs Darnley looked genuinely surprised.

" How can you possibly know that? " she said. " Even Sylvia doesn't know it."

" There are many ways of knowing things without being told," he answered smiling. " You have, I think, one of his letters in your bag? "

She was still more surprised.

" Might I have that letter just to hold in my hand? I will not read it, of course."

She opened her bag with a puzzled expression and handed him the letter.

" Thank you. And now," he continued, " supposing I were to describe this man and his character to you, and supposing we found the character to be a good one, would you alter your attitude? "

" I don't know," she said doubtfully.

" Well, let us see," he continued, gently feeling the letter between his thumb and finger. " He is a tall dark man, clean shaven, with an ascetic but healthy face, high forehead, hair brushed straight back, penetrating eyes, greyish green in colour. That is correct, I think? "

" Absolutely; but however——"

He ignored her astonishment.

" His character coincides with his face. He has a fine type of mind and an unselfish temperament and an altogether sympathetic and elevating atmosphere. I congratulate you, Mrs Darnley, on this friendship for your daughter."

He again ignored her increased astonishment.

" And now let us see what the future has in store." He pondered for a moment. " Your daughter will not marry this man," he said slowly. " Thwart them, however, in their friendship, and they will fall violently in love with one another, and there will be trouble in store for all three of you. Allow them to see as much of one another as you can, and everything will adjust itself to your satisfaction."

Mrs Darnley's astonishment and conventional

vanity indulged in a tug-of-war, and vanity got the upper hand.

"But if I take your advice," she said at length, "how can I prevent people talking?"

"To be upset by the jabbering of a few parrots," he said, but without intolerance, "is a form of childishness which I hardly think *you* will be guilty of."

There was a pause, in which Mrs Darnley, I am sure, was realising she *would* be guilty of it, though she would not call it childish, of course.

"Are you fond of poetry?" he asked by way of slightly changing the subject, at the same time handing back the letter.

"Devotedly," she said with enthusiasm.

"But not of poets?" said I. "A poet is not without honour save in a family of beautiful daughters."

"Can't you teach him to be serious?" she said appealingly to Moreward.

"That is his way," he answered with generosity. "He serves you a profound truth in a dainty manner."

"There is one thing about men," she observed, laughing; "they do stick up for one another—very different from women."

"Therefore, I may be pardoned for sticking up

for a poet at the present moment," said Moreward
suavely.

"You will take my advice?" he asked after a
pause, in which Mrs Darnley looked as if she
wished the creation of poetry could be achieved by
a sort of parthenogenesis, namely, without a poet.

"It is all very well for you to talk," she replied;
"you haven't a daughter: if you had, you would
think differently."

"Pardon me," he said smiling; "but I have a
daughter."

Mrs Darnley showed surprise.   "But, at any
rate she is not grown up," she said.

"But she *is* grown up."

"And you never told me," reproached Mrs
Darnley with increased astonishment.   "How
very unkind of you not to have brought her to see
me. Dear me!" she added, "at whatever age
could you have married?"

"Not so very young," he replied, amused at her
astonishment.   "After all, a youthful appearance
is merely a matter of a calm soul, combined with
purity of nourishment. I think some old moralist
said: 'A loving heart makes a youthful body.'"

"Well, really!" ejaculated Mrs Darnley. "Wonders never cease!"

"Wonders never cease because they never exist,"
he corrected, smiling. "What to one person

seems a wonder, to another may be an everyday occurrence. I astonished you a moment ago by a slight display of psychometry because you have never heard of it, and yet nothing could be more natural to those who cultivate the faculty."

" The only real sin in life," said I, with mock severity, " is ignorance."

" That is indeed true," agreed Moreward, readily.

" Oh dear, oh dear! I wish I were clever," sighed Mrs Darnley as she got up from her chair and told us that she must be going.

We arose to bid her goodbye.

" You will not forget my advice? " persisted Moreward, patting her hand.

" We shall see," she replied with feminine obstinacy.

He bowed courteously, and watched her out of sight.

" Pshooh! " he sighed good-humouredly when she was no longer to be seen. I confess the atmosphere of a Pharisee is particularly stifling— her departure is like the lifting of a heavy thundercloud."

I laughed.

" Truly," he added, " the Pharisees are far from the Kingdom of Heaven—to see impropriety in all

harmless and beautiful things is to live in a sort
of earth-made hell."

"I suppose Sylvia and her poet are really in
love now," I observed, "though you didn't give
them away?"

"Yes," he said, "and an excellent thing, too.
He needs her to stimulate his creative faculties,
and she needs him to draw out her latent qualities.
The sentimental side will die out sooner or later,
but the friendship will remain."

"You think the mother will prove tiresome"
I asked.

"For a time, yes. Conventionality, my friend,
is one of the worst forms of vanity because so
insidious.   Mrs Darnley, poor creature, is a
coward by reason of her vanity; her one fear in life
is what others will think. She does not live in the
great world of love, but in a prison. By the way,"
he added, "you see Miss Sylvia oftener than I do;
if she gets into difficulties, you will let me know?"

"I will," said I.

CHAPTER VI

THE FIGURE IN THE ROOM

FROM the foregoing chapter, it will be realised that Justin Moreward Haig possessed certain powers, which are, at any rate, not to be found in the majority of people, although one is apt to meet them more frequently nowadays than at the time of which I write. That they should have astonished me was, of course, to be expected, and also, as a result, that I should have endeavoured to probe Haig on the subject was equally to be expected; but that I should induce him to display them to me or others, merely to *prove* their exist-ence, this was quite another matter. Indeed, he even begged me to refrain from spreading abroad in any form whatever my knowledge that he had the power to exercise any faculties outside the ordinary; telling me that when he felt called upon to use one or other of his powers in order to help a fellow creature, the gossip that ensued was far from his liking, and therefore he felt especially desirous it should not be unnecessarily increased.

"The greatest men on this planet," he would say when discussing the subject, " would not make use of their powers even in the harmless way I have done on occasion, though, respecting psychometry, it is as comparatively commonplace as playing the piano with adequate dexterity or making a fine speech. As a matter of fact, these powers, and far greater ones in addition, are merely stepping stones whereby the disciple of occult wisdom learns to acquire faith : and I refer to that most valuable species of faith which gives him the encouragement to pursue his way along the very difficult pathway to final emancipation. An adept in occult science will for this reason teach his students some of these so-called miraculous powers, but as to demonstrating them to humanity at large, he would never dream of doing such a thing—it would be neither ethical, wise nor safe, for humanity is not ready for them as yet."

One day, when we were—together with a few other interested students—encouraging Moreward to expound the mysteries of his occult science, the question arose as to the possibility of reading other people's thoughts, and also the *permissibility* of so doing, when the faculty has been developed. And in answer to this question, Moreward told us a story which, had it come from the lips of anyone else, were hardly believable in the extreme luridness of its villany.

" I must, of course, adopt fictitious names," he began, " as one or other persons connected with the matter are probably still alive, and certainly the chief figure in the story—a student of mine—is not only so, but even living in London at the present moment. Well, it all happened when this student was undergoing the process known as ' waking up,' that is to say, his latent psychic faculties were beginning to come into manifestation, but he had so far not learnt how to exercise proper control over them. We will call him Sinclair for our present purpose, and I must tell you he was a man of very powerful physique, and some 38 years of age. The other persons connected with this little drama were three in number, namely, two brothers whom we will call respectively Henry and Charles Thompson, and a woman we will call Ethel Thompson, in that she was Henry's wife.

"Now, this man Henry was by no means happily married, and the world, as it is called, was perfectly aware of the fact, for neither he nor Ethel possessed the faculty of dissembling beyond a display of the most frigid politeness in front of other people : a politeness more significant in fact than occasional open discord. Moreover, it was known that Henry took drugs—driven to them, gossip declared, by his wife's ill temper and general unpleasantness, though I think, if truth be told, it was more owing to his own neurotic temperament than any doing of her's.

" Well, Henry was the elder brother, and through his father's will possessed of a considerable

property, embracing a beautiful country estate, a
large house in town, and plenty of spare cash in
addition; all of which, according to the will, would
pass on to the younger brother in the event of his
death.   Why his wife under these circumstances
did not urge a separation is, of course, easy to
divine, for, as it was said by her so-called friends,
she had married him for his money, and it was
hardly likely she would break with him and thus
lose a large part of the object of her marriage.
There was also another reason why she avoided a
separation, for this man with all his wealth was
deplorably mean, and she knew full well that to
live apart from him was to live apart from his
riches and be reduced to an allowance which would
be anything but bountiful.   Indeed, he in his
parsimony was, on his side, quite averse to making
her any separation allowance at all, and preferred to
put up with her and her tantrums rather than
permit her to make use of money for the main-
tenance of any household in which he did not par-
ticipate.   Such, indeed, is the nature of meanness:
it would rather buy misery with its money than
nothing at all.

" As to Charles Thompson, he felt that species
of contempt for his brother which the man of a
certain kind of strong physique, combined with
strong physical desires and appetites, feels toward

the weak.   He regarded his neurotic brother as a disgrace to the family tree, and, being at the same time envious of his inheritance, although for many reasons he found it convenient to keep in with him, yet in his heart he hated and despised him.

" Nor were these reasons far to seek, for by keeping up friendly relations with his brother, Charles was enabled from time to time to enjoy the luxuries and also the amusements (shooting, hunting, etc.) afforded by wealth and a large estate.

" As to Sinclair, his interest in this family was purely altruistic, based upon an old association with Henry; for they had been school-fellows together to begin with, and then Oxford undergraduates later.   Henry, in fact, liked Sinclair as much as it were possible for a man of so mean a nature to like anybody, and Sinclair, hoping to achieve some little widow's mite of good for him, fostered the friendship, instead of permitting it to die what would otherwise have been a natural death.

" The utterly villainous incident I am going to relate occurred at the Thompson's country estate while Sinclair and Charles Thompson were guests together in the house.   They were, in fact, the only guests at the time, for the effects of Henry's drug-taking were becoming more and more apparent, and his wife was chary of inviting others to witness so degrading a spectacle.   Charles

Thompson and Sinclair were thus left a good deal
together; they walked, they rode out, or sat reading
over the fire; and at all other times when Ethel
Thompson was too busy with her own affairs to be
present with them, and Henry himself too restless
in mind and body to attach himself to the company of others.

" And then it was that Sinclair found himself
confronted with a rather strange feeling of mind:
for whenever he was left alone with Charles, and
they were not actually conversing, a certain picture
began to present itself to his imagination; and a
very horrible picture it was. True, the first time
he became conscious of it, there was a vagueness of
outline and detail which caused him to dismiss the
whole thing from his mind as one of those foolish
imaginative day-dreams which are liable to intrude
themselves into our more negatively meditative
states of consciousness; but when, as the time went
on, it persisted, growing more definite and detailed,
he became forcibly alive to the fact that it must bear
some strange, if not evil, significance. For he
noticed another thing which might be connected
with it, namely, that whenever he himself was particularly conscious of its intrusion, Charles, his
companion, was especially *distrait*, or staring into
space with an especially concentrated expression of
face. Moreover, another factor gradually became

sensible to his imaginative senses: a feeling of intense hatred and cunning, which, try as he would, he was unable to banish from his consciousness.

"But the picture," we asked, interrupting the story, "what was it?"

"It was the picture of Charles Thompson standing by Ethel's bedside, smothering her with a pillow, and then pouring the contents of a little blue bottle down her throat."

We all gave way to some ejaculations.

"That was *part* of the picture," he continued; "the rest of it you will see later, for to tell you now would spoil the story.

"Well, three days went by, and this murderous picture obtruded itself more and more on Sinclair's consciousness, until it seemed almost an obsession, bringing him finally to the conviction that he was confronted, not with a mere thought, but actually with a most diabolical *intention*. And yet, how to act? That was the problem which faced his tortured mind; for to accuse this man of *intending* to murder his sister-in-law was hardly feasible, not to say highly inadvisable into the bargain. Indeed, as you will be asking yourselves, what possible object could this man have in getting rid of Ethel? For I must further tell you that the bulk of the money did not fall to her at his brother's death, but to Charles himself. Moreover, nobody could have

the slightest reason to suppose that Charles and
Ethel were not on friendly terms; rather had it
been rumoured by some that Charles was of late
inclined to pay her a little more attention than was
altogether conventional for a brother-in-law.

" There was one course, however, he felt he
might try, and that was to warn Ethel he had a
dreadful presentiment concerning her, and beg her
to be specially on her guard, or, better still, to
make some excuse and return to London, immediately. But, unfortunately, here he was confronted not only with a very matter-of-fact woman
who looked upon all occult feelings with that
indulgent contempt born of complete ignorance of
the subject, but also a woman of intense obstinacy.
The moment he threw out even a hint in that direction, it was treated with good-natured scorn, and
he himself accused of indulging in old-maidish
superstitions and long-exploded fancies; while as
to her taking the advice he had intended to offer,
of this he saw so little chance that he gave up at
once the intention and let the matter rest.

"All the same, one thing he did attain by broach-
ing the subject to her, and that was a deeper conviction of the nefarious intentions of Charles
Thompson; for Ethel, by way of chaffing Sinclair,
introduced the matter into the dinner-table conversation, and he was thus in a position to perceive

what effect was by that means brought about, the
effect being exactly as he had expected.   True it
was that the unsuspecting eyes of Ethel and Henry
detected nothing, for the simple reason they were
looking for nothing; but to the alert eyes of Sinclair himself, Charles's discomfort was convincingly
manifest.

" I have already told you that Ethel and Henry
were not on good terms, and therefore you will
not be surprised to learn they occupied separate
rooms, and rooms, moreover, that were not adjoining, but almost at opposite extremes of the house.
As it happened, on this particular occasion, Sinclair's room was next to Mrs Thompson's, and
Charles's midway between hers and that of her
husband, all the rooms being on the same floor and
leading out of one long corridor.   That Sinclair,
in his ever growing conviction of impending
murder, could induce Mrs Thompson to lock her
door at night was, of course, out of the question,
seeing the manner in which she had already greeted
his presentiments, so along the line of even that
slight precaution he knew any argument were useless.   But in place of it, he did what will seem to
you at this stage of our story a very strange and
irrelevant thing : he began to wrack his brains for
some means to induce Henry Thompson to leave
the house, and leave it for several days on end.

" But Henry Thompson's life was not threatened," we interrupted variously.

" That is just the strange part of the story, but wait and see," was his patient but puzzling answer.

" Well, the first idea that suggested itself was to arrange with some friend in London to send Henry a bogus telegram demanding his presence on some pretext or other, and one which would detain him for some considerable time ; but, naturally, such a pretext was very difficult to find, so much so that Sinclair was soon compelled on reflection to give up the idea altogether. As to falling back on the unfertile procedure of imploring Henry to leave the house, merely because the presentiment of danger for him was in his own mind, this he knew would be as useless in the case of Henry as it had been in the case of his wife. There was in the end, in fact, only one thing that he *could* do, and that was simply to wait and to watch, passing, of course, utterly sleepless nights at his unlatched door listening for Charles's footsteps creeping stealthily towards Ethel's bedroom.

" And yet, even in doing this, he still saw danger to Ethel's life; for, should he prevent Charles from entering that room—which, of course, would not be a difficult matter—yet he would have no plausible evidence for accusing him of his murderous intentions As to letting him actually

enter, and, by following, catch him in the very act
of smothering her, there was always the possibility
he might lock the door, and, on a disturbance being
created, hide behind the lesser evil of pretended
adultery.

"Well, for three nights Sinclair spent the long
hours in what seemed an endless vigil, and yet
nothing whatever happened. He had taken his
armchair and placed it by the door, which he closed
to the extent of making its appearance from the
outside such as to lead anyone to suppose it were
latched. Having arranged this, he then sat in such
a position that his ear was against the crack, and he
was enabled to hear the least sound in the
passage.

"It was upon the fourth night, and, utterly
worn out with sleeplessness, he must (as he puts it)
have fallen into a sort of doze, when he became
aware of what seemed like a voice, speaking within
his own head, yet in some strange way exterior to
himself. It said in a tone of command: 'Wake
up and act!' Opening his eyes, with a start of
horror lest his lapse should have cost Ethel her very
life, he looked up and saw standing in front of him
a figure, and it was the figure of a man he knew.
'You must save the three,' it seemed to command.
'Creep into her room and lie down out of sight
behind the further side of the bed—then wait!

Close your door and her door!   Be quick, but silent! '

" It was the work of a minute to carry out this behest, and when he entered Ethel's room, he could hear by her breathing she was unsuspectingly in the deepest sleep of the night.   Fortunately, there was a full moon, and he could discern all the objects in the bedroom, and so was in no danger of bumping against some chair or table and thus waking her up. And so very stealthily he crept towards the far side of the bed as he had been directed, and lay down on the floor to wait.

" Five minutes or ten minutes it may have been that he lay listening to what cheap novelists would call the throbbing of his own heart against his breast; and then at length he heard the door open very quietly and close again, footsteps approached the other side of the bed, and then the dull thud of a down pillow clapped over somebody's face.

" A few seconds, and he had rushed round, flung himself on Charles from behind, knocked the little blue bottle on to the floor, while Ethel herself whipped the pillow from her face, suddenly sitting up in bed with the intensity of the shock and the force of her utter bewilderment.   What precisely happened immediately afterwards Sinclair finds it difficult to remember, for he was engaged in both a struggle with bodies and a struggle with words.

his first endeavour being to prevent Charles from
rushing out of the room before Ethel could dis
cover who he was. What he did remember, however, was a confused medley of three voices, all
asking the same question at once, and Ethel jumping out of bed and switching on the light. Then
he found himself disengaged from Charles and
standing with his back guarding the door, imploring them both to abate their voices so as not to
wake the servants and cause a scandal.

"Well, you can imagine what followed.
Charles, finding himself cornered, tried to bluff,
and did it exceedingly badly. On Ethel indig-
nantly demanding what it all meant—the pillow
with which someone had tried to smother her, and
the bottle of laudanum on the floor—he immediately turned on Sinclair and accused him of
attempted murder: he had heard a slight noise,
and, thinking there must be burglars in the house,
had come out into the passage, just in time to see
Sinclair going into Ethel's room, and so he had
followed; this was the lie which he attempted to
thrust upon her. But Sinclair was equal to the
occasion. He rushed for the pillow which had
fallen on the floor, and held it with arms like a
vice. 'It won't work,' he said; 'this pillow is out
of the red room—that room is Charles's—and Red
Room is marked on it; that bottle is out of Henry's
room, which is next to yours, and you stole it from

his bedside; deny it if you can.   Henry can easily
be called to prove it.'

"Then Charles tried to bluff again.   'Good
God, man,' he cried, ' what possible object could I
have for murdering my sister-in-law.   Do you
suppose that any jury is going to believe that
damned nonsense? '

" ' You accused *me* a moment ago of attempting
to murder her, yet *I* could have no possible object
whatever : the family money would certainly not
pass to *me* at her death,' was Sinclair's calm
rejoinder.

" ' And do you suppose it would pass to me, you
fool ? ' he snarled.   ' Why, if I was going to
murder anybody for money, it would have been
my brother.'

" 'It *was* your brother,' said Sinclair very slowly.
' You were going to murder your sister-in-law, so
that your brother should be hanged for it.'

" Then Charles collapsed."

And here Moreward paused for a moment as if
to recollect the remainder of the story, if any
remainder there was.

"But I don't quite understand," said one of
us, " I don't quite see the connection between the
pillow and the laudanum."

" You will understand when I have explained
what happened afterwards," he replied, smiling.
" Ethel was not an emotional woman; emotional

women are not given to marrying men for their
money; on the contrary, she was a cold and hard
specimen of her sex; and so she neither had
hysterics nor showed any special signs of fear. She
was merely furious, with the fury born of so-called
righteous indignation. She wanted justice, but
she did not want to take revenge, because she was
very loth to have it known that she possessed any
relationship whatever with a murderer. It was
very evident to her at once that Charles was guilty
of, at any rate, something particularly dastardly,
because the contrast between the manner of the two
men was all too evident; but until Sinclair explained
to her the whole train of sinister circumstances
which led him to act as he did in the effort of
saving her, she was not convinced of the utter
villainy of her brother-in-law.

" The picture which Sinclair had seen in its
entirety (for you will remember I only represented
it to you in part) was the image of Charles, stealing
into Henry's room while he was in one of those
sound sleeps which only drugs can produce, remov ·
ing his bottle of laudanum, then smothering Ethel
with a pillow, and finally pouring the poison down
her throat. That was the first part of the picture,
but the second was a scene in the law courts with
Henry in the dock, being committed for the
murder of his wife, and eventually hanged.
Whether this would really have been the final

result, and an innocent man condemned in place of
the guilty one, is hard to say—certainly Henry and
Ethel were known to live together in almost open
discord. Charles had paid marked attentions to her
of late, in order to give further apparent reasons
for Henry to murder her—namely, out of jealousy
—and thus if Sinclair had not intervened, it is more
than probable that one of the most horrible
tragedies of modern times would have ensued.

" What did occur, however, was fortunately of
an entirely different nature; for Sinclair subse-
quently convinced both Ethel and Henry of
Charles's guilt, and he was finally persuaded to leave
the country in exchange for a promise that no proceedings would be taken against him whatsoever.
And that ends my story of the attempted murder of
two innocent people for the love of possession,
which is the mother of many tragedies."

" And yet not quite the end," said one of us,
" for you have not told us who was the figure in
the room."

"The figure in the room," said Moreward reflectively, " that, I think, is of little consequence."

" Why, bless my soul, surely that is half the
story."

" Can I rely on your discretion? " he asked
earnestly.

We gave our assurances.

" Well, then, *I* was the figure in the room."

CHAPTER VII

DAISY TEMPLEMORE'S REBUFF-

I HAD known Daisy Templemore since she was nine years old, and even at that early age I (and others also) had predicted she would grow up into a most audacious flirt—and she did. From about her seventeenth year till the time of this episode— ten years later—she indulged in a series of so-called "violent flirtations," which her engagement with an Anglo-Indian officer (when she was twenty-six) by no means put an end to.

He came over from India, won her hand (as old novelists describe it) and a very minute portion of her heart, and then returned from whence he came, leaving her unencumbered by his presence, to pursue the even tenor of her flirtatious existence.

Although I was some twelve years older than Daisy, this frivolity of heart on her side did not militate against our being what is colloquially called "pals" : and, I may add, I was one of the very few men to whom she paid what, under the circumstances, I considered a real compliment, in that she confided in me very extensively, and did me the very great honour *not* to flirt with me.

Being very much in request (for nobody could deny either her prettiness or wittiness) in a certain

section of London society, it stood to reason that
she should strike up an acquaintance with my large-
hearted friend as soon as occasion offered itself.
Nor was I at all surprised to hear she had started
her flirtatious machinations in connection with that
greatly-desired but equally elusive personage.

And I must here say a word respecting his attitude towards women. If one could imagine that
a beautiful landscape were endowed with a human
faculty of talking and enjoying and suffering, as well
as merely being beautiful; and if one could further
imagine its beholder admiring, sympathising, but,
of course, never feeling any desire for ownership :
in other words, asking nothing whatever from that
landscape but that it should merely be itself; one
might get an inkling of this highly evolved man's
attitude towards the opposite sex—indeed, I might
add, towards everybody and everything. His
feeling towards mankind was one of intense kindliness, which can only be described by the word love.
And from those people he came into contact with,
he asked nothing but that they should *be themselves*; except in cases where the relationship was
one, as it were, of pupil and teacher—for in such
instances he demanded (but with phenomenal
patience and tolerance) certain qualities, not to
benefit himself, but to benefit their own characters.

And here it was that Daisy Templemore tried to

take, much to my disgust, a mean advantage of
him. Finding her flirtatious attacks were returned
with merely that loving friendliness he showed
towards all the other members of her sex, and not
being satisfied with this indistinctive attitude, she
adopted the dubious method of enrolling herself
as his pupil, and asked him to teach her occult
wisdom. Her utter failure, I confess, gave me
the greatest satisfaction.

Moreward was not one of those proudly English
natures who fear to show their affectional feelings.
If a human soul could be benefited by the outward
expression of love, he had no hesitation whatever
in embracing man, woman or child. The effect on
the more Pharisaical members of society was to
make them misrepresent him, but their slanderous
babblings had as little effect upon his quiet mind as
the bleatings of a few sheep. " The beautiful and
peaceful sensation of human affection," he said to
me one day, " is robbed of some of its value unless
we can convey it to others. The touch of a com·
passionate hand or the embrace of loving arms may
often convey more comfort to the suffering than a
thousand words, and the withholdment of these
outward signs, all too frequently arises from vanity,
namely, the supposition that to love is in some
mysterious way to debase oneself."

Whether Daisy was really taking him in, is a

matter I speculated upon to a considerable extent, and I even went so far as to warn him of her designing nature. However, he merely laughed, and said his eyes were not easily blinded by feminine attractiveness; and there the matter ended for the time being.

Then one day I ran across a certain Miss Dickenson, who professed herself about the only female friend Daisy possessed, and who told me a few things which caused my speculations to be renewed.

"Your ascetic friend does not seem quite so invulnerable as some people supposed," she began.

"Oh indeed!" said I. "What is happening now?"

"Haven't you heard about Daisy and him?"

"Not anything particular," I said.

"Then you are behind the times."

"Perhaps," I said affecting scant interest.

"Haven't you heard he is in love with her, and that she at any rate pretends to be greatly perturbed on account of her fiancé?"

I felt an inward rage. "Who told you this?" I demanded somewhat hotly.

"Bless me, it's common talk," she answered.

"It's common balderdash!" said I.

"Well, you needn't get annoyed," said she.

"Daisy is always up to this silly game, and really I am no longer amused at it," I returned with unabated annoyance. " It is all very well to flirt, but when she pretends, first that a man is in love with her, and then that she is upset about it—well, it's worse than ridiculous. I suppose she told you this herself? " I added more quietly.

Miss Dickenson hesitated.

" She obviously did," I inferred. " Well, I bet you anything you like Moreward is not in love with her for an instant."

" Don't you be too certain," she said.

And then I changed the subject.

But the next time I saw Moreward I told him of this conversation, and also of my extreme annoyance.

Again he only laughed with a quiet sort of amusement—as if he were quite blind to anything but the humorous side of the matter.

" Your indignation," he said at length, "was generous, my friend, but wasted. Why trouble to be annoyed for *my* sake, when the thing holds no annoyance for me whatever? "

" But I thought it *would*," I said; "such ingratitude on Daisy's part deserves to be reprimanded."

" The law of cause and effect punishes people by reason of its own nature," he said quietly; " therefore, nobody need trouble to punish another by exhibiting anger, or by any other method."

" But I really don't think one can allow people to take advantage of one's friends," I persisted.

" It is advisable sometimes to interfere, but why be annoyed about it? If a cat meows in a room, take the cat out of the room, but don't curse the cat—it is the nature of cats to meow; it is the nature of some human beings to be ungrateful."

" I wish I had as much philosophy as you " I said with admiration.

He smiled in acknowledgement, but otherwise ignored the compliment.

" Nothing is annoying *in itself*," he pursued reflectively; " a grown-up person is not upset by the things that upset a child : because a man is a little nearer to unconditional happiness than a child. Let a person but identify his mind with the happiness that is *within*, and nothing on earth can either annoy or cause him sorrow."

" It is difficult to attain," I said doubtfully.

" Time and inclination," he answered, " achieve everything. As to Miss Daisy, she will need more your sympathy than your anger."

" How so? " I asked with a little astonishment.

" She will suffer from her own anger, and the smarting of her wounded vanity. Her own actions will bring her own punishment," he answered.

And so it turned out, as I was very soon to learn.

I had not seen Daisy Templemore for some time, so one afternoon I presented myself at her house, and was shown up into her boudoir, where to my satisfaction I found her without any other visitor. She was in a very bad humour, and took no pains to hide it. I asked her what was the matter, but with feminine perversity she denied that anything at all was the matter, so I changed the subject, and this simple piece of strategy had the desired effect. After putting a full stop, by means of monosyllabic rejoinders to every topic I ventured forth upon, she finally blurted out the secret of her annoyance.

"A *nice* friend you have got," she exclaimed. "I have never been so disgracefully treated in all my life before."

I informed her quietly that I possessed many friends, and that it would be wise to specify the particular one.

"Oh! I mean your sage, or mystic, or philosopher, or whatever you like to call him," she answered rudely.

"Look at this," she said, fumbling in her bag and producing a letter.

I took the proffered piece of paper and recognised the writing.

The letter ran as follows:—

"My friend,—I fear we shall be at cross purposes in our relationship, unless we are both a little more explicit as to our separate intentions. I have given you within the last few weeks several hints which I earnestly hoped you would take without further ado, in order to spare you the humility and annoyance likely to follow as the result of this laying bare of undeniable facts. My hopes, however, have not been realised, and I am thus compelled to write this letter (asking you to forgive me at the same time) in order to tell you that any further tutelage respecting occult wisdom and higher truths must come 'o an end, for you yourself have closed with your own hands the very first gate on the Pathway to Knowledge.   Indeed, to be quite frank, your intentions from the beginning were not to open this gate at all, but merely to endeavour to obtain a closer and more distinctive intimacy with me, using the pursuit of Divine Wisdom as an excuse to carry out your design.   This might have been (although dishonest) to some extent excusable (I speak, of course, relatively, for all human weaknesses are excusable to the really tolerant-minded)   had   you   been   actuated   by motives of love, rather than absolute and undeniable vanity.   The latter being the case, however, I cannot in any sense whatever encourage a quality in you which must inevitably sooner or later result in your downfall : and I am con-

strained to apprise you of the fact in a manner
admitting of no further ambiguity whatever.
Three times you have written letters full of
reproach for the infrequency of my visits, and
also of my invitations, pointing out, on the one
hand, that I am an *un*enthusiastic teacher where
you are concerned, but, on the other, an
enthusiastic one where Mrs H. is—she, as you
ungenerously imply, being a less worthy pupil
than yourself on account of what you and others
term ' her past.'   My friend, let me point out
to you that there are ' pasts ' and ' pasts,' and
that much shall be forgiven those who have loved
much : for I may add, a truly loving heart is the
best of all requisite qualities for the way to
Knowledge.   Your own countless affairs (if I
may be pardoned for alluding to them) are not
' affairs of love '; they are solely ' affairs of
vanity,' and therein lies the regrettable distinction.
You have indulged in the pain-bearing action
of ' arousing men's love-passions without any
intention of gratifying them,' and you attempted
the same pursuit with myself, but without success : in that passions drop away from those who
find interest in more absorbing things.   The
very ' past,' then, you so thoughtlessly throw in
the face of another human being, is the very
thing that you are not strong enough and selfless

enough to have obtained for yourself. Your
vanity pulls you in two directions at once, so to
speak, for you crave that an incessant deluge of
love shall be poured into your ears, to gratify
one aspect of your vanity, and give nothing
whatever in return, in order to retain an unsullied
reputation, and pose as an inaccessible queen, by
this means gratifying another aspect of it.

"All this being so, can I, as however modest
a member of a Brotherhood which has at
heart the spiritual advancement of Humanity
and nothing else, employ my time in teaching
you the wisdom you have no desire to learn?
Had you sincerely that desire, even your vanity
would not stand in the light of my attempted
tuition, for sooner or later it would fall away
from you of its own accord. Not having that
desire, however, I reluctantly remain in future,
no longer your instructor, but merely, yet truly,
                    "Your friend,
                        J. M. H."

"A remarkable letter," I said drily, when I had
finished reading it—"so remarkable that I should
like to keep it. But I am surprised you showed
it to me, since it casts such an aspersion on you
and not on him."

And Daisy Templemore at this observation was
so absorbed by her extreme annoyance that she

forgot to demand the letter from me, the result
being that it has lain in my desk to this day.

Since then a little coolness has existed between
us—the result, perhaps of her one and only rebuff.

As to Moreward, the next time I saw him, I, of
course, mentioned the fact that I had seen his letter,
and made a few comments on the thoroughly
deserved reproofs it contained. But his attitude
towards it, and to Daisy herself, showed me that if
the rebuke was in his pen, so to put it, it was not in
his heart, for, after speaking of her with an extreme
gentleness, he told me a little Indian story.

" There was once a large snake," he said, " who
lived in a tree by the roadside, and amused itself by
attacking and killing every passer-by. One day a
great sage came along, and asked it why it took
delight in such evil deeds, pointing out that suffering to itself could only accrue sooner or later as the
result : so that the snake promised to refrain from
attacking people in future, and the sage went on
his way. In a few weeks' time, however, the sage
came back again, and, finding the snake in a sorry
plight, asked it what was the matter. Then the
snake said, ' O, sage! I took your advice, and see
the result—when I ceased to attack the passers-by,
they attacked me instead, and reduced me to this.
' Ah! ' answered the sage, with a smile of compassion, ' I told you, merely not to molest them;

I did not tell you not to frighten them, if they tried to take a mean advantage of you.' "

" And so your letter was merely to frighten her? " I asked, laughing. " But surely you must have guessed her real nature from the beginning? "

" Both deduction and psychic prognostication are never infallible," he said quietly. " You may take a very bellicose dog out for a walk, and, seeing another dog in the distance, you presage with a certain amount of assurance that a fight will ensue; and yet, after all, nothing happens; ten things may intervene to prevent it."

I laughed at the simile.

"And so," he continued, "we never turn anyone from the door—we give our forecasts the chance of being wrong. All the same, I hazard the further prophecy that Miss Daisy will be encumbered by a ' past ' before very long. She will marry her officer and be divorced within three years."

And so it turned out.

CHAPTER VIII

ARCHDEACON WILTON was the typical archdeacon one might expect to find in any six-shilling
novel; he dined well every evening, enjoyed one or
two glasses of the best claret, was portly in consequence, and carried on a number of spiritual
flirtations with the passably good-looking members
of his congregation. Nor must we forget to add,
he spoke in an emphatically ecclesiastical manner,
or, to alter the phrase into one of glamourless
candour, he put on a great deal of side.

The Archdeacon was not a believer in celibacy,
for he had married young, taking unto himself a
wife at the early age of twenty-one. At the time
of my acquaintanceship with him, however, he was
a quite consolable widower, and possessed of an
only daughter, whom his parishoners regarded " as
the apple of his eye," though, as Moreward
remarked drily, but with no diminution of his
accustomed tolerance, the apple was more like the
apple of Eve, in that it acted as a temptation to call
forth an amount of selfishness on the Archdeacon's
part, quite inconsistent with Christian piety. His
devotion to her, in fact, consisted of an uninterrupted attempt to imprison her in the four walls of

his own very narrow ideas : in religion and politics, literature, art or what not; while, at the same time, anything less abstract in the shape of an intimate friend (not to talk of a member of the opposite sex) was subtly, but absolutely, eschewed. In short, to quote another remark of Moreward's, " he did not love his daughter, but loved himself *through* her."

Now, the result of all this was that, although he demanded a great devotion and the frequent expression thereof from his daughter, all he got was an insincere attempt at the latter, and a very lukewarm feeling which had to do poor service for the former. Miss Wilton found her father, to put it in perfectly plain speech, an unutterable nuisance; for all the harmless enjoyment she derived from life was bought at the expense of underhand contrivance, or else at the expense of paternal displeasure, called in colloquial parlance " a horrid row."

At the end of each day (unless some kind fortune in the shape of a sick parishioner intervened) the Archdeacon, under the guise of affectionate interestedness, demanded from his daughter a recital of her entire actions : which recital (as may easily be imagined) was tinctured, when necessity demanded, with a liberal abundance of prevarications, not to say untruths. All this seemed obvious to everybody (including the servants, who, doting on Miss

Wilton, assisted her with all their power) except to
the father himself, who appeared to live securely in
the bliss of his own unruffled ignorance.

And now to come to an important factor (at any
rate, for me) in this narrative : I was rather in love
with Miss Wilton, and, finding things very difficult
to manipulate under the circumstances, I drew the
ever sympathetic and helpful Moreward into the
field of action. Indeed, that inestimable friend
subjected himself to the frequent tedious and Pharisaical discourses of the Archdeacon, in a manner
which called forth my grateful admiration to its
very fullest degree. Time after time he engaged
the attention of his Reverence in the dining-room,
in order to provide me with a tête-à-tête with Miss
Wilton ; but what they talked about, was a matter
he did not always relate to me in detail ; I only
know the Archdeacon usually emerged from those
discussions with a very red face.

As already said, I wish to obtrude myself as little
as possible in the written impressions of my friend;
and that being so, those who look for the story of
my amour with Miss Wilton are liable to disappointment— this story mostly concerns the conversion of the Archdeacon as achieved by Moreward, and the manner he set about it, as far as I
can gather the details from his own lips.

It was our custom after dinner in Ashbroke

Gardens, where Miss Wilton lived, to walk home
across the park together: and the conversation
which took place on those many occasions I relate
as the subject of this particular episode. I remember after our first dinner there à trois, Moreward
gave audible vent to certain of his reflections. " It
is a strange trait in certain religious temperaments,"
he said, " that if you prove a man's religion to him
on a rational basis, he is undeniably shocked."

I felt great interest, and encouraged him to be
communicative.

" Well, I spent a large part of an hour trying to
prove to the Archdeacon what he believes; and
instead of being glad that it *is* susceptible of proof,
he merely considered me very wicked."

I laughed.

" He is convinced there *is* an after-life," he continued; " but an inquiry into the where, when, and
how, he regards as iniquitous. Nor did my
quotation from St. Paul, 'that faith, alone, is good,
but far better when coupled with understanding,'
cause him to alter his opinion. He is, as one
might expect, utterly ignorant of the true meaning
of his Bible."

" Do go on," I urged; " what else did you say?"

" Then there is the question of love. Now,
Christianity is essentially the religion of love; but
not only has he no real love in his heart (I can see

that from his aura), but he even thinks it—well, certainly ' not quite the thing ' to care for anybody except, perhaps, one's own wife or children."

" What about God? " I asked.

" Ah there is the point; he maintains one must only love God."

" And does he? "

" How can he? If you have no love in your nature, how can you love? "

" That is obvious," I agreed.

" So again I met him on his own ground, and pointed out that God *is* Love, in the words of his own religion : and therefore, the more of love you admit (by a process of cultivation, as it were) into your own soul, the more of God are you manifesting—the more at one are you with God."

" And could he see it? " I asked.

" Oh, dear, no," he replied, smiling. " In vain I tried to show him that to love God is to be one with an unconditional love which must perforce embrace humanity as well, because humanity itself is a part of God. But even the quotation which runs, ' By this shall all men know that ye are My disciples, if ye have love for one another,' failed to convince him."

" And his daughter? " I asked.

" He imagines he loves her, but his love is really only selfishness. He never thinks of her happiness—he is in a continual state of trepidation lest she should marry and leave him to loneliness. He fears even her female friendships. I feel great compassion for him; he is an unhappy man, and I am grateful to you for having given me the opportunity of trying to alter his so saddening point of view."

The next time Moreward and I crossed the park on our way home from the Archdeacon's, I gathered from his remarks that the conversation on that occasion had turned upon charity.

" Charity, my friend," he said meditatively, " is little understood except where giving money is concerned. The Biblical phrase ought to have been rendered, ' The greatest of all is *tolerance*,' for tolerance is the most valuable of all qualities."

I encouraged him to continue.

" There is a great deal talked about forgiveness in the pulpit; but if more were preached about tolerance, forgiveness would not be necessary; the perfectly tolerant man never needs to forgive, in the sense that the preachers understand the action, for his whole attitude towards humanity is one of uninterrupted forgiveness; he forgives his neighbour his sins, so to speak, before they have been committed."

He pondered for a moment, and then continued in the same strain:

" Perfect love and perfect tolerance are insepar-
able. Nobody can truly love a man and feel a
sense of condemnation towards him at the same
time : such a thing is a contradiction. For a feeling of condemnation is nothing else than a feeling,
however slight or momentary, of hatred. Well
does the Bible say that he who uses harsh language
towards his brother is in danger of being eventually
burnt as a criminal : hatred is often the mother of
murder."

" Then what is your attitude towards sin ? " I
asked.

" Sin is a form of childishness," he answered
quietly; " it is the roundabout way to spiritual
happiness instead of the direct way. But would
anybody condemn a child for being a child ? "

I begged him to be a little more explicit.

" An ignorant child puts its finger in the fire,
and the fire burns it. The child committed a mistake, and learns its lesson through suffering. Why
did it put its finger in the fire ? Because it was
searching for pleasure, but it searched in the wrong
way. An adult is just a little wiser : he does not
put his finger in the fire, but he commits a forgery.
He, too, is searching for pleasure, but likewise in
the wrong way; and, being found out, he, too,
suffers. All sins, therefore, are nothing but a
searching for happiness in the wrong direction; and

all sinners are but children who will eventually grow up. Tolerance is the recognition of this fact."

" And what about punishment? " I asked.

" Punishment is nothing more than a species of revenge. Therefore for one man to punish his neighbour is merely to add one wrong to another. As to legal punishment: criminals ought to be restricted and reformed with kindness and good example, but never punished."

" Is this what you have been telling the Archdeacon this evening? " I asked with some amusement.

" Pretty much," he answered quietly. And I heard that on the following Sunday the Archdeacon's sermon was the best he had ever preached. The fact is, Moreward had been converting the Archdeacon, and when I next saw Miss Wilton, she told me with genuine joy that a change had come over her father: " He is becoming more human," she said.

And then, one evening, an accident of the most awkward nature occurred. Truth to tell, I was so intent on Miss Wilton that the Archdeacon and Moreward entered unperceived by either of us at a moment when we were sitting in somewhat compromising proximity. The Archdeacon looked both infuriated and thunderstruck. He sent his daughter off to bed on some quite unreasonable pretext, which I have forgotten, and then permitted his internal fury to boil over with as much dignity as he could command—and that was very little.

"Am I to understand, sir," he stammered, "you have been abusing my hospitality in order to pay your attentions to my daughter, without consulting my wishes on the subject?"

I felt, and I am sure, looked, extremely and undignifiedly sheepish—so much so, that Moreward, with a glance that said "Better leave it all to me," stepped into the breach and conducted my case.

"Come, come," he said, soothingly, putting his hand on the Archdeacon's arm, "a little affection is not a crime; rather must it be considered a virtue."

And this observation took the wind out of the Archdeacon's sails; he was at a loss how to meet it for the moment, and spluttered some incoherency. Then of a sudden he thought of another factor.

"The deception, sir; the deception!" he exclaimed. "Do you realise that my daughter and this man have perhaps been deceiving me for weeks?"

But Moreward had a ready answer, which he delivered with the quintessence of soothing tranquility.

"Deception," he said, "my dear Archdeacon, is merely a weapon which some people are compelled to use in self-defence, when too much is exacted from them."

The Archdeacon made a click of impatience with his false teeth, for again he could find no immediate rejoinder.

" Have you not exacted from your daughter," Haig continued in the same soothing manner, " a little too much self-abnegation? Have you not asked her perhaps to refrain from things which in *her* opinion are perfectly harmless? That being so, I think you will hardly blame her for your own inability to convince her of their harmfulness? You, with your insight into human nature, I am sure, can realise her point of view. Isn't it likely she has thought on many occasions, 'I really can see no reason why I should not do this or that, but as father and I can't agree on the subject, the best thing is for me to say nothing about it, so as not to annoy him'?"

The Archdeacon was beginning to get a little calmer, for nobody could be really angry in Moreward's presence for long.

" Am I to take it," he said, sadly reproachful, "that *you* have been an accomplice in this matter?"

" I have been endeavouring," he answered, smiling, " to kill, as it were, three birds with one stone. Yes," he added with adopted humility, " I must own to be also a culprit."

The Archdeacon did not understand the simile.

"Well, my dear Archdeacon," he explained, "will you pardon me if I say I was very sorry for your daughter, and that my observations have shown me she is not happy—she is a prisoner?"

"Not happy—a prisoner?" the Archdeacon repeated with some astonishment.

"Now, although I am sure you are the kindest of men," he pursued with the same tone of voice, "yet your idea of happiness *for* her, and her *own*, differ materially."

"I have been a loving, dutiful father, and have given her an extra large allowance," the Archdeacon interposed; "what more can be expected of me?"

"To allow her a few things that you yourself can *not* give," he said very persuasively.

"I fail to understand," returned the Archdeacon.

"You can allow her the affection of others; you can allow her freedom of thought, and you can allow her more freedom of action. In short, you can allow her to obtain her own happiness in her own way."

"But supposing I consider her way the wrong way?"

"Then you can lovingly advise her to consider *your* way; but if she does not take your advice, do nothing further."

The Archdeacon did not know what to answer for the moment.

"And now as to my own guilt in this matter," Moreward went on. "I have tried to alter your point of view concerning certain things, because I know that altered view-point brings peace. I have tried to show my friendship for Charles, here, by seeking your pleasant society, so that he might enjoy the society of your daughter; and I have tried to make your daughter happy, by contriving that she should enjoy the affectionate friendship of a fine-charactered man. All this very trifling service I have called killing three birds with one stone. Will you forgive me?" he added, smiling, "and, above all, forgive *him* and *her*. I think there is no doubt you will, for the first thing a really devout Christian does is to forgive."

And what else could the Archdeacon do but forgive? Or, at any rate, pretend to outwardly, since Moreward had so contrived the argument that to continue his resentment would be at once to show himself other than a true Christian.

As for me, I sat silent and wondering during this process of soothing, continually blessing the luck which gave me an unruffled champion to take up the cudgels I should have wielded so badly myself. And the end of it was, I was dismissed for the time being with some reproaches, and the intimation that nothing further would and should be done in the matter for the present.

Needless to say, as Moreward and I walked home across the park that evening, I was full of expressions of gratitude. And that gratitude was to be augmented before long in consequence of further assistance on the part of Moreward.

He had observed to me some few days later, " You are not especially anxious to marry Miss Wilton, I take it, or she you? "

I told him he had inferred correctly.

" In other words, the friendship on both sides is one of sentimental affection, and not passion? " he asked.

I assented.

" Well, the only thing to be done is for me to interview the father and see what comes of it," he said.

And what did come of it, and the unexpected event which occurred some weeks later, forms the matter for our next chapter.

CHAPTER IX

THE PHILOSOPHY OF DEATH

It was arranged after several interviews between Moreward and the Archdeacon—in which the former assured the latter that I had no intentions of robbing Miss Wilton's father (matrimonially) of her presence—that no obstacle should be placed between our friendship, provided in future "I behaved myself," as the Archdeacon put it. And certainly no *gross* obstacle *was* put, but a good many subtle ones, the most obvious being that I was no longer invited to dine. She was not forbidden to see me if I called, nor to answer my letters, nor, of course, to speak to me if we met at other people's houses; but she was expected to inform her father if any of these occurrences took place. Moreover, to safeguard himself against a wilful lapse of memory on her part, the Archdeacon asked her every day had she seen me, had she heard from me, and so on and so forth, while, if the answer was "Yes," he manifested ill-humour for the rest of the evening, while if the answer was "No," nothing further was said. In short, the Archdeacon behaved like a child—or shall we say as an extremely foolish woman suffering from married jealousy. This went on for some time until a slight incident caused matters to take

another turn.   Miss Wilton had bought me a
birthday present, and wilfully omitted to mention
the fact to her father.   It just happened, however,
that he knew my birthday owing to a remark I had
made one evening identifying the day of my birth
with a certain historical event which chanced to
interest him considerably.

"Did you give Broadbent a birthday present?"
was the question he put casually to his daughter as
the result of this inconvenient piece of memory on
his part.   And she felt compelled to answer in the
affirmative, upon which a deluge of reproaches was
showered upon her, causing her to make a stand
against him and tell him exactly her views on the
subject.

The next time Moreward called upon him, the
Archdeacon was full of complaints against his
daughter and her unjustifiable secretiveness.   Moreward (as he afterwards told me) listened with great
sympathy, and then endeavoured to enter upon a
further stage of the Archdeacon's education.

"I have not interfered with this friendship," the
Archdeacon had said bitterly, "and this is all the
thanks I get.   I am being estranged from my
daughter."

"Interference," said Moreward sympathetically,
smiling, "is of two natures—gross and subtle;
your interference perhaps is of the latter kind?"

" How so? " said the Archdeacon, pretending
not to understand.

" Do you not, perhaps, make your daughter pay
for her confidences by the price of your—shall we
say—lack of sympathy? "

The Archdeacon kept a guilty silence.

" You see, first of all, she has to pay for this
friendship with the discomfort of your continual
displeasure, dear friend; and then she has to pay
the further price of your *increased* displeasure when
she confides in you—a confidence you yourself
enforce by your repeated questions. In other
words, she is ' had ' (to use a piece of slang) in all
directions.

" Humph! " murmured the Archdeacon.

" All this being so, I am sure you will forgive
me if I point out that it is *your* attitude which is
responsible for the estrangement between you and
her, and Charles is really a negligible quantity in
the matter."

And, this argument being unanswerable, combined with the gently persuasive and conciliating
way it was put forward, the Archdeacon had very
little to say; in fact, he gazed into the fire with a
meditative expression and kept silence.

" Come," pursued Moreward with brisker persuasiveness, " is not this really a piece of good
fortune put in your way to draw you and your
daughter closer together? Allow her the enjoy-

ment of this friendship ungrudgingly, and you gain everything : her increased love, her gratitude, and her admiration : forbid it, however, and you lose everything : for nobody can really love a being who acts as a jailer, even if that being be a father."

And the outcome of this interview (which, of course, not being present, I have reconstructed from all Moreward narrated) was that after a little debating the Archdeacon saw the wisdom of it all, and made up his mind to try and follow it. Whether he would have succeeded nobody can tell, for a sudden and a sad event happened—a week later he had a stroke of apoplexy, and died within two days.

Moreward himself brought me the news. He prepared me solicitously for what he knew would be a shock, and then handed me Miss Wilton's letter. It ran :—

"Dear kind friend,—A dreadful piece of news I have to give you. Father has had a stroke, and the doctors say he cannot possibly get over it, and may not last more than a day or two. Please come to us; father asks for *you*. Break it to Charlie. I am just longing to see him, but feel I can't ask him to come now, because I know it would hurt father. Please tell him to write and comfort me. I can't say more now, I am too upset.   Yours always,

"GERTRUDE WILTON."

I was filled with pity for Gertrude and a kind of remorse for the pain I had caused her father. And Moreward divined my feelings.

"Don't mind, dear fellow," he said, putting his hand on my shoulder; "indirectly you have done this man a great good."

And then he departed, and I sat down at once and wrote pages to Gertrude.

And so it was, the dignitary of the Church of England, instead of sending for his colleague to comfort his dying moments, sent for a man who professed no religion, though he believed in all. For Moreward understood the real philosophy of death, and hence of comfort. He believed in the after-life state of consciousness because he *knew* it, and could function on that plane while his body remained on this one. And it very soon dawned on me why I had been the indirect cause of doing the Archdeacon a genuine good. It was I who had brought Moreward into his life, though Moreward himself had been too modest to do more than merely hint at this fact for my own comfort. What he did say afterwards, though, was that I had acted as a stimulus to enlarge the Archdeacon's mind to see life from a less circumscribed point of view—and hence a less selfish one, and one that would stand him in good stead on the next plane of consciousness.

I cannot describe that death-bed scene, for I was not there; but at any rate towards the end, Moreward told me the patient lost all fear of death. Gertrude's father was glad to know the how, when, and where of the post-mortem state when it came to facing that state; and the mere speculations (resting solely on hearsay) of the clergy paled before the knowledge of an occultist.

" We die, as it were, every night in our sleep," said Moreward, talking to me about it afterwards, " and come back to life again in the morning. The ordinary man does not remember where he has been, but the trained occultist does; he alone, through establishing the connection by reason of his training between his physical brain and astral body, can remember everything."

I asked him what sort of an existence Gertrude's father had in front of him.

" Relatively speaking," he answered, " rather monotonous. Without being uncharitable, we must face facts. The Archdeacon's pleasures in this life were mostly material—the few pleasures he had were either born of the senses or of vanity. There is no eating and drinking, of course, when the gross body has been shaken off (and there are no titles evoking adulation on the next plane); the only thing that counts is love. To live on the earth and to be devoid of love is therefore a misfortune which pursues a man after his death. The creed of lovelessness, my friend, is the worst of all creeds, and to be without love in the post-mortem existence is, as it were, to be without breath in this —to half-exist merely—that is why the harlot is nearer the Kingdom of Heaven than the (loveless) Pharisees. Death does not change a person's character."

"Tell me more," I said.

"The physical body is like a grand overcoat which somebody gives to a shabby beggar; when the overcoat is discarded, all the shabbiness shows underneath—it was but an illusory covering. And so the inner man may be clothed with a grand physical body, but when the body is discarded, all his poverty of character is laid bare. For, as I said, only those who are rich in love are not beggared after death. That is why I encourage all people to love, as in the case of you and Miss Wilton; and, of course, the ignorant Pharisee would say I was encouraging a flirtation—let him call it what he likes: names of condemnation grow thick as blackberries where ignorance abounds."

As to the funeral, of course, it was conducted with "great pomp and circumstance," and Moreward told me, with an amused expression, he could see the astral body of the Archdeacon looking on with great satisfaction.

" As a matter of logic," he said to me when it was all over, " this display of gloom is ridiculous from a Christian point of view. It is as if people dressed up in black and wept copious tears when a man went away for his holiday. Here are all these parishioners thinking the Archdeacon has gone to indescribable bliss, weeping for something about which they ought to be rejoicing. And not only that, but they lay flowers on his body as if it were himself, in spite of the fact that all their lives they have been hearing that the body is only a garment of flesh and the real man is the soul. I confess the inconsistency of mankind baffles me."

What a depth of comfort Moreward was to Gertrude for the following weeks only an occultist can effectually imagine. He communicated with her father, and brought news, which very soon dispelled all ideas of separation. " How different it all is from what I expected," he told Moreward one day; " but, dear me, to be rid of that cumbersome body is a delight in itself. All the same, I wish I had made more friends while I was on earth; these people here shine with a sort of love radiance which makes me feel almost poverty-stricken. It is all very remarkable. For a long time I could not realise I was dead, but then I remembered all you told me. Tell Broadbent, although he made me suffer, I am glad now—he brought *you* to me.

After all, he was quite right to be fond of Gertrude. My mother and dear wife are here, and very good to me, and then *you* come to me often, which seems the strangest of all things, because you are still what people erroneously call 'alive.' Bless my soul, it is we who are really alive."

And here my story of the death of the Archdeason ends. As to his daughter and myself, we are true comrades, the sentimental side of our affection having worn away. The truth is, although for a long time I was blind to the fact, she developed an attachment for Moreward, and not even her recent marriage with a barrister prevents her from confiding to me that she still loves " the wisest and noblest man she has ever met."

CHAPTER X

IT occurred to me that if there was one person alive who could help with comfort and advice my old friend Wilfred Buckingham over his domestic upheaval, that man was Moreward; and accordingly I broached the subject of his intervention to both these men, and after a little hesitation on Buckingham's part, brought them into closer friendship.

The trouble was as follows : —

Buckingham had married somewhat early in life a woman of his own age, with whom he had lived for some sixteen years in tolerable domestic happiness. In fact, everything had gone smoothly without either of the matrimonially united parties even " looking " at a third person, as the phrase goes, until at the dangerous age of forty Mrs Buckingham had all of a sudden developed " a grand passion " for an intimate friend of her husband, the complications ensuing being easy of imagination. The two lovers had carried on their amours for some months without being discovered, but, things eventually proving too complex for them, Mrs Buckingham confessed the whole matter to her husband, left his house, and took a little flat of her own (as she was not without means), so as to live an untramelled existence, and be free to see her lover whenever she desired. As may be supposed, Buckingham himself was left to suffer a conglomeration of distressing emotions: jealousy, anger, wounded vanity, sorrow and other less defined feelings, pulling his not over-highly evolved soul in all directions at once. Like those who see others dying around them, yet forget they must die one day likewise, he had seen other people's domestic tragedies take place, but never for a moment imagined that tragedies of a like nature could ever happen in connection with himself. And that being so, he had never given an instant of thought as to how he should act under similar circumstances, so that when the blow fell he was like a child thrown into troublous waters and quite unable to swim. Moreward it was, then, whom I brought to the rescue; and the first step he took in that direction was to encourage the Major to come to his house whenever he desired, and let off the steam of his pent-up emotions by an unreserved pouring out of all his woes into Moreward's sympathetic ear—and also, when I was present, into mine. And it was to these meetings I owe my acquaintance with Moreward's remarkable and, to my mind, selflessly exalted views on marriage and all pertaining thereunto. It is true, I should be very blind if I did not realise that his views may be shocking to the orthodox · for an unusual virtue

(as he himself said in other words) shocks a certain
type of conventional mind far more than a usual
vice.   But as a faithful chronicler, I cannot tone
my impressions down to mere platitudes in order
to please the taste of the Majority; my first duty is
to be true to him, and my second is to be true to
myself.

We used to sit, of an evening, at his little house,
which had something of the peaceful atmosphere
of a monk's cell, minus its lack of comfort, and
gaze into the fire (it was autumn at the time) until
late into the night, the Major from time to time
walking up and down when overtaken with especial
eloquence during the recital of his many woes.
Moreward would sit in his rather upright armchair,
the tips of his long elegant fingers placed one
against the other, looking, as he so often did, the
very incarnation of lovingness and soul tranquility.
It seemed to me often as if the Major was a child
of six (though in reality he looked older than
Moreward) and Moreward himself a man of sixty,
contemplating with loving indulgence the recital
of some infantile sorrow.

And I must confess, after one of these outbreaks
on the part of the Major, I could not help smiling.
Such a point of view (as his outbreaks denoted)
was beginning to strike me, after some months of
association with my unperturbed philosophical

friend, as something essentially primitive—feelings that the race ought long ago to have outgrown; a childish sense of possession inconsistent with human evolution. But how was this man to be converted? That was the difficulty. And then one day Moreward embarked on the hazardous mission.

The Major had talked himself out. He had reiterated for the hundredth time his intentions, and had ended up by saying, " Well, it is damned hard on you fellows to have to listen to this, but I tell you it does me a world of good to heave it off my chest, and I'm jolly grateful to have somebody to talk to about it. All the same, I'm going to chuck it. It's no use, one gets no further. So if you chaps have got anything to suggest, I'm quite game to think over what you have to say."

"Ah! that is better," said Moreward soothingly; " our thoughts and emotions are like monkeys ; let them jump about by all means for a time, and when they begin to get tired of the jumping, then is the time to take our opportunity."

The Major smiled rather bitterly.

"You know full well you have all our deepest sympathy," Moreward continued; " but sympathy is not everything, and is almost useless if it cannot bring any help along with it. So let us see if we can't assist you somehow."

" But *how*, in heaven's name? " the Major asked rather peevishly.

" Well, has it ever struck you that a point of view is a preventive against most troubles? "

" I can't say it has," said the Major.

" Well, it is; and what we want to try to do, is just to alter your point of view."

" You'll find it deuced hard," the Major observed.

" But it is well worth the effort," returned Moreward with earnestness. " You are a brave man, my dear Major; you acted like a hero in the Boer War, where physical courage was concerned, and I think you will act like a hero in this domestic war, where moral courage is concerned."

" I don't quite follow you," said the Major.

" Let us go slowly, then. . . . Has it ever occurred to you to wonder whether your wife still loves you? "

" What's the use of wondering—how can she if she goes and falls in love with another man? "

" That answer implies," said Moreward very kindly, " that you think if Broadbent, here, fell in love with some woman, he would lose all affection, let us say, for *me*? "

" Bah! " said the Major curtly; " that is quite different."

" Which is exactly the reply I expected,"

returned Moreward, conciliatingly. "And so, will you forgive me if I put it rather crudely; but *you*, like many others, are hypnotised by the catch-phrases of people who have not thought about the real truth of things; the difference is by no means as great as you suppose."

The Major looked puzzled. "How so?" he said.

"If you and your wife have lived together for twenty years, there must surely have developed an element of friendship between you?"

"Oh, well, I daresay."

"When you first fell in love with your wife, do you happen to remember whom it was you first told about the circumstance?"

"I went along to old Wilkins—poor old chap—he was shot near Ladysmith."

Moreward smiled. "Then you went to your best friend and confided in him at once. And far from losing any affection for him by falling in love, you felt you had never liked him so much in your life before?"

"Well, now you draw my attention to it, I realise it was so."

"But supposing that friend of yours," pursued Moreward, "instead of meeting your confidences with sympathy and understanding, had met them with anger—what then?"

" What then?   I should have sent him to the devil," came the ready answer.

" Which is exactly what you have done to your best friend—your wife," said Moreward with a conciliating smile.   " Major," he continued more briskly, " you have let slip one of the greatest opportunities of your married life; but it is not too late to retrieve it."

The rather slow-witted Major looked astonished, having failed to understand.

" You threw away the golden opportunity of sympathising with your wife," he explained with quiet eloquence.

" Sympathising! " shouted the Major.   " Well, I'm damned! "

We both laughed.   " The idea is perhaps a little startling to you," said Moreward soothingly, " but believe me, I earnestly mean what I say.   To sympathise with your wife would be to act like the moral hero we spoke of.   What is more, I can assure you it would repay you."

" You mean," cried the Major excitedly, " to allow my wife to have a lover, and not to turn a hair?   Thank you.   And a nice ass I should look. And pray, what sort of morality would that be, I should like to know? "

" There is a great distinction between a man allowing his wife to have a lover," said Moreward gently, " and condoning it when she has got one, because he knows that her passion is stronger than herself. Why, dear friend, do you condemn her for her weakness in not being able to renounce this man, yet omit to condemn your own weakness in not being able to forgive? "

The Major had no ready argument for this unanswerable question, so kept a confused silence.

" As to looking an ass, as you put it," Moreward went on, in the same quiet tone, " I fear, in the eyes of the world there is often only a hair's breadth between a fool and a hero; but in the eyes of truth, a true hero never minds being considered a fool. You see the fool, because of his vanity, does not mind being thought a hero; but the hero, because of his *lack* of vanity, does not mind being thought a fool."

Moreward, in fact, with this last daintily-put truism, had placed the Major in a dilemma from which with merit he could not easily emerge. So, with considerable dexterity, my tactful friend invented a most plausible pretext for abruptly changing the subject. " But, my dear fellow," he said, " you have come to the end of your cigar; do let me go and get you another. I am really most remiss, allowing you to smoke that nasty stump."

And he went to his cupboard and fetched the cigar-boxes.

After the Major had left that evening, Moreward remarked to me :

" The ' finesse ' of virtue must always be
administered in small doses; give a man too much
all at once, and he cannot assimilate it. However,
we have at any rate managed to put in the thin end
of the wedge."

The next day, I was sent on a mission to Mrs
Buckingham. I knew her pretty well, so I did not
embark upon the undertaking with any great feeling of nervousness. She was not at all the sort of
woman who could resent my talking quite openly
on the subject with her; indeed, she was likely to
welcome the opportunity of unburdening her mind
if I had read her character aright; and, as it happened, I did read it aright.

She received me very cordially, started the subject of her own accord, and gave me an insight into
the whole matter, for which I was extremely grateful, being genuinely anxious to assist Moreward
with the adjustment of so distressing an affair.

As he had inferred the previous evening, Mrs
Buckingham was still attached to her husband as far
as affection went, but for the time being she was
swept off her feet by the intensity of her feelings
for this other man. I say " for the time being "
from my own surmises on the subject, for she herself never suggested a time limit to her passion.

What she did say, was that her love for both men was deep and lasting, but of an entirely different character. The friendship, resulting from twenty years' conjugal companionship (she told me), cannot die in a day, and if her husband had only made the smallest endeavour to understand her in her present condition, things could have been very different between them.   As it was, he had merely made himself an unbearable creature to live with.   I even gathered that her affection for her husband was of a far higher order all along than his for her —it was both less selfish and less sensual—so that when this other passion on her part had come into existence, an entire obliteration of her affection was far from being the result. She was quite undecided as to what course to pursue, but she told me that, at any rate, there was one thing she would not do, and that was to live openly with her lover under the same roof.   After all, the Major for the most part lived in the country, and it was by no means thought so very strange for his wife to have a flat in town.   As to telling her to give up this other man, and make some attempt to return to her husband, well, I knew it would be useless, and so I never suggested it.   And she thanked me in so many words for my perspicacity in refraining.   " It is all very well," she said, " for him to curse me and treat me as he is doing.   I simply couldn't help it. I never wanted to fall in love with Basil, but the thing was *plus fort que moi,* and there's the end of it." She also went on to say that she hated being regarded as an enemy, and was really " longing to be friends " with her husband once more.

This, then, was the content of my interview with Mrs Buckingham; and on my informing Moreward of the fact, he telephoned to the Major and invited him to dine a few evenings later. After the Major had been apprised by me (for I was invited also) of all that had taken place between his wife and myself, and after he had been afforded an opportunity, as usual, of giving vent to his conflicting emotions, Moreward embarked upon a further stage of his education in super-morality.

" You see, my dear Major," he said, " your wife still loves you, as I predicted, and her affection must be really deep and true if she can fall in love with another and still love *you.* As I said the other night, if you remember perhaps, you have been led by a process of hypnosis, so to speak, to believe that one love kills another. That it untrue; the criterion of real love is that it lasts beyond the birth of a new passion."

The Major thought this all very clever, but found it difficult to be convinced of its truth.

" You have your wife's own remarks to bear it out," insisted Moreward, quietly.

"How do I know she isn't lying?" suggested the Major shortly.

"First of all," I interposed, "it is pretty easy to detect when people aren't telling the truth, and, secondly, I fail to see what object she would have."

The Major shrugged his shoulders. "You may be right," he said doubtfully.

"Come, my friend," began Moreward afresh and in a very persuasive tone, "let us try and look at this thing from both a heroic and a practical point of view. To begin with, your deep distress over the matter implies that you certainly do not wish to lose your wife. Further, you wish to avoid a scandal: you have told us also that this man has had many affairs before, and that sooner or later he is likely to leave her in the lurch. Thus, in addition to these other things, you wish to save her."

"I don't think she deserves it," muttered the Major bad-humouredly.

Moreward smilingly ignored the remark and proceeded :

"Above all, you wish to recover her love. Well, there is only one thing to do, and that is to take her back, show her sympathy, affection and understanding, and then bide your time."

"You surely can't expect me to do that?" exclaimed the Major.

" In your case, my friend, I should certainly feel inclined to. There is really nothing else to be done unless you wish to lose your wife for ever; to lose her love likewise, to create a scandal, and to ruin her (since you refuse to divorce her, you say)."

The Major gazed moodily into the fire.

" I suppose you really *did* love your wife? " asked Moreward quietly, after a pause.

The Major assented.

" Has it ever struck you that true love always thinks of the happiness of the beloved? And if that happiness comes even through another man's arms, true love doesn't mind."

" I'm not a saint," said the Major shortly.

" But why not *be* one? "

" It's too infernally difficult."

" Not if you can find the right point of view."

The Major was silent. His brain utterly failed to take in such heights of morality; he could rather see it as immorality; extremes are often so alike in appearance that he could only just perceive the faintest glimmer of a difference.

And so Moreward left it at that for the time being, and renewed the subject on the next occasion we were all three together. But on that occasion he let his persuasive eloquence have full sway, and finally he gained his goal.

" What, after all, is marriage," he began with,

after a few preliminaries, "and what does it
become? The ordinary man starts matrimony
with a mixture of romantic sentiment and physical
passion; the sentiment by degrees dies away, the
passion dies away also (dwindling into an occasional gratification of the senses), and in the place
of these two things comes either friendship or utter
indifference. If the latter, then, for a man to be
upset when his wife falls in love with somebody
else seems unreasonable; if the former, then, for
him to be upset seems equally unreasonable, true
friendship being greatly enhanced when it can act
as the receiver of confidences. You yourself
admitted you were never so fond of your friend
(I mean the one who died near Ladysmith) as when
you were able to confide in him your own romantic
passion. And what does that mean? Why, that
if you had sympathised with your wife over this
new love of hers, and let her fearlessly confide in
you, she on her side would never have felt so fond
of you as during that exchange of confidence and
sympathy."

I thought for the first time that Buckingham
was beginning to see a small glimmer of light,
although he said but little.

"And it *would* be so," Moreward continued
eloquently, "because she, all the time, would sense
the nobility of your unexpressed forgiveness, and
therefore not only be grateful, but full of admira-

tion as well. Indeed, nothing augments affection so much as gratitude and admiration combined. And, therefore, I cannot think I was wrong when the other night I told you you had let slip the great opportunity of your married life."

The Major drummed his fingers meditatively, and kept a partially consenting silence, as he gazed into space.

" For," continued Moreward again, " where there is true affection, no opportunity is so golden as the one which affords us something to forgive, since to forgive is at the same time to manifest nobility of character, and thus to show ourselves noble before the object of our love. Yet, as one form of forgiveness may need to express itself in words, the greatest of any is that which is so self-evident it requires no words to express it at all, its presence being rendered all the more conspicuous by its very absence. Nay, real love forgives its object always—even before there would seem something to forgive—and all true friends love each other the better, the one for having some fault to pardon, and the other for being pardoned respecting that fault."

Once more the Major was silent.

" And so, my friend, is it not obvious what is the most heroic and practical thing for you to do? Take your wife back again, and bide your time, and show her, by pointing out that hitherto you have not acted as nobly as you might have done, that she, too, on her part has something to forgive; for she will think you far the nobler (as you will be) for confessing to being at fault as well, and the result will be that both of you can enjoy the felicity of forgiving the other."

The Major looked doubtful.

"You are not altogether convinced?" Moreward queried, smiling. "Yet surely, although not to forgive is a form of childishness, there can be little doubt that *to* forgive is not only the best policy, but also a true joy."

"You are asking me to do a great deal more than to merely forgive," said the Major at last. "To take her back, knowing all the time she is carrying on with another man—hang it all, that is a bit more than I can stand."

"But why?" asked Moreward quietly.

"Why? Because—well, doesn't she belong to me?" exclaimed the Major.

And then once again Moreward let the flow of his eloquence have full sway. "My friend," he said, "the seat of nearly all trouble is the sense of possession or the feeling of mine and me. And in your own case this undoubtedly applies, as it applies in too many other cases as well: for in your heart you say to yourself, 'She is my wife,' yet fail to make the wisdom-fraught distinction that, although she be your wife, she herself, soul and

body, is not completely and undeniably *yours*.
And therefore, to desire that she should be so—
since a person's soul belongs to himself or herself
only, and to nobody besides—is in reality as futile
as the desire to exercise ownership over the sun or
the moon; while to grieve because this may not be
so, is to waste one's grief on the ' desert air,' and
one's activity of mind and emotion as well. And
even if you think to discard the soul, and care only
for ownership over the body, your predicament is
scarcely the less, for since you cannot enclose your
wife in a prison, spying on her and her actions
from morning till night, she is at liberty to do with
her body whatever she likes : and should you exact
from her more than she can fulfil, she will only
deceive you in consequence, and more wrong will
be added to the sum of her actions. Besides, after
all, for what is your grief, when you trouble to
try and regard its real cause? For, truly, is the
exchange of a kiss here and there worthy of so
much distress, and is the merely physical, which
has gained so much importance in the eyes of the
world, really not infinitely less than the love of the
soul, and the affection which hardly cares for the
physical at all? Surely the eyes of the world are
blinded when they would repay one fault by a fault
far greater, and make one sin an excuse for a far
greater sin in return? And just because you have
the world to encourage you in a lapse of nobility,

permitting you to cast your wife away on account of a little passion which sooner or later by reason of the transience of all passion must fade of its own accord, are you really going to succumb, and thus lose the great because of the little? Truly the action were not the action of a hero, and, that being so, you will take the nobler course instead."

And here Moreward paused, whilst the Major looked at him with a certain sort of wonder and admiration.

" May I ask one thing? " he said. " Did you carry out all these amazing ideas on your own wife? "

" Well, yes, I did," replied Moreward, with modesty.

" Do you mean to say that the same sort of thing happened to you? " asked the Major excitedly.

" Pretty much the same," Moreward assented.

" And you never told us about it? "

" I never regard my own affairs as especially interesting to others."

But we both declared we could not let him off, and so we sat far into the night listening to the one episode I have ever been able to extract from Moreward vitally concerning himself. My only regret is that I cannot reproduce his inimitable style, which had, as he himself, a touch of poetry and a melodiousness of language fascinating to any listener.

CHAPTER XI

THE TRIUMPH OF NOBILITY

" I SHALL really have to try and collect the scattered threads of memory," he began; " it seems so far back in my life that a great many of the details I have naturally forgotten; besides, some of them are of no interest."

He got up from his chair and began to walk up and down the room in a state of meditation. " Ah, yes," he remembered, " it was when we had a villa near Florence—about ten years after my marriage—and the man's name was—well, I must be discreet, so we will call him Henshaw for our present purpose; after all, he is a most respectable married man with a large family now, so it would not do to give him away. Yes, now I am beginning to remember a little."

And then he started without any further preamble, as he sat down in his big chair by the fire.

" Henshaw had been my guest for about a month, for, as may readily be imagined, I did not care to invite any friend to make that long journey from England for the space of a few days; besides, I had a great affection for him, and was glad that he should remain. And then he proved also an agreeable companion for my wife in times when I was compelled to be away from her for many hours of the day, leaving her to what would otherwise have been loneliness, for she had not many friends and was not over-fond of mere acquaintances. And thus it was to be expected that a close friendship should spring up between my wife and this man; and the wonder was I never divined, before the end of his visit, how close it had become, and how that friendship had finally expanded into love. Yes, indeed, there came a day, the very day of his departure, when I discovered their hitherto well-guarded secret, for, returning at a far earlier time than I had previously intended, I took them quite unawares in the very last hour they had imagined themselves free to take an amorous farewell. And so I saw; and saw what they would have given many a long heartache that I should never have seen; for my wife's face blanched with fear and embarrassment; and as for Henshaw, he looked the embodiment of guilt and self-reproach and sorrow and pity, all blended into one.

" There was nothing to be done but to retire, so with my sweetest smile, and without the least touch of sarcasm, I told them, in so many words, I was extremely sorry to have come upon them so unexpectedly; after which I very hastily withdrew in my confusion. They started to say something, but I did not wait to listen,but, making my way downstairs, fetched myself a cigar, and passed out into the garden. Then I sat down and began to reproach myself. . . .

" Why had I not done something, at least, to herald my ill-timed approach? The idea of coming upon them like a thief in the night tormented me exceedingly. For she had looked so frightened, and that caused me heart-pangs. But, then, of course I had not known; what with the door being slightly ajar, and the complete silence within the room. ' If only she had told me,' I reflected, though upon this thought immediately followed the counterthought of ' how difficult she had probably found it to do so.' She had evidently imagined I should be angry, and in self-defence she had deceived me, and so the whole thing was more or less my fault. Indeed, I ought to have foreseen it all, and, when Henshaw became such a constant guest in the house, have realised that they would fall in love, and have warned her that I should not mind, since, after all, what could be more natural? Was he not a lovable being? And as to her, well, to my mind she was certainly of the most fascinating type. It was self-evident that I had given her a wrong impression of how I *might* behave under certain circumstances, and so she had been obliged to hide everything from me. . . . And yet this deception did not weigh in the least on my

mind, for I knew full well she need not have
deceived me, and I would take great delight in
showing her so.   For it is the blow we receive to
our vanities which causes us to be so apprehensive
and hurt at being deceived ; it is the most humi-
liating reflection that, after all, we really *are*
jealous, although we may pretend not to be, and
that the ' deceiver ' knows this to be a fact, and
hence is, as it were, compelled to dissemble.   But
with me this was not so, because whatever many
vices I can lay at my door, jealousy is not one of
them, and hence the thought of others, that I *was*,
or that I *might* be, did not upset my mental
equilibrium.   One is seldom hurt at being thought
to be a thing one is *not*, because it is so easy to
clear up the mistake; but to be thought to be a
thing one really *is*, that is what rankles in our mind.
She had apparently thought me in this case to be
the old-fashioned sort of husband, for ever lurking
round the corner with a pistol ready to shoot any
intruder upon his rights—the constant pryer into
his wife's secrets and affairs—indeed, a dreadful
nightmare of a husband; and had I really been that,
had I really ' tiptoed ' along the passage on purpose, such a conception of me would have been
very rancorous.   But I had *not* done such a mean
thing, the meanest of all things—for I loved her.
And so the whole point was to relieve them of

their anxiety.   For, it certainly occurred to me,
they must at the moment be feeling extremely
uncomfortable.   What was to be done?   Should
I go back and tell them all was well, or should I
send him a note—for somehow I found it rather
awkward to meet him, not knowing what I was
going to say.   And then all of a sudden I remembered he was leaving that very afternoon, and I
wondered whether I might ' disappear ' till he had
gone, and afterwards write to him, when I had
made it all right with *her*.   She could, in fact,
enlighten him first, so that a letter from me might
not prove too great a shock after what I had led him
to believe.   In one sense, I was glad the thing had
happened; and glad, because I wou'd be able to
sympathise with her, if she would let me, and make
it all so much easier for them.   The constant
apprehension of my finding out must have been a
considerable blot on their happiness, and I wished
to remove it. . . .

"And here my reflections came to an end, for I
saw my wife coming towards me across the lawn,
with a look on her face portraying an admixture of
determination, apprehension and distress.   I had
seated myself in an arbour at the far end of the
garden, so when I saw her approach I went to meet
her, and led her back with me to where I had been
sitting, showing her an affection she had been far

from expecting.   So great seemed her astonishment, in fact, that she burst into tears and left me
to comfort her as best I could, while (I remember)
she made several efforts to say something, which,
on account of her sobbing, I was unable to comprehend.   And then finally she became articulate,
and told me that, although she had struggled
against falling in love with this man, she couldn't
resist it, and so at last had given way, and had
deceived me, because she was afraid to cause me
unhappiness.   'You see, I simply couldn't help
it,' she repeated again and again.   And my answer
to that was, 'I don't think *anybody* can help it, so
you are wasting all these self reproaches on the
desert air.'   And then I remember, as with all
women, a certain doubt came into her mind, for
she said all of a sudden, 'I can't believe in this
kindness; somehow I think you must be torturing
me to punish me all the more afterwards.'

   " 'Have I ever tortured you yet?' I asked
mildly.

   " 'No,' came her answer, 'but then I have
always been a good wife to you before.'

   " 'And that is all the more reason why I should
not torture you now,' I smiled, 'out of gratitude.'

   " 'But the deception,' she doubted; 'do you
realise how I have deceived you?'

   " 'That is perhaps something of a misfortune:

you might have spared yourself the trouble,' I said without sarcasm; 'but then I suppose you were frightened to do otherwise.'

" ' I can't believe it all,' she reiterated; and then musingly she questioned, ' I wonder if you can *really* love me? Do you mean to say you don't mind . . . *truly* don't mind?'

" ' Not in the least,' was my perfectly sincere answer.

" ' Then you *can't* love me,' she exclaimed.

" ' If your idea of love is to act in a way calculated to make the object of one's love intensely and cruelly unhappy—then no; but if your idea of it is to have a person continually in one's thoughts, and to place her happiness before anything else—then, yes.'

" ' After all, it is very simple,' I urged. ' Can you see a loved one suffer, when just a little self-schooling could avert that suffering? Besides, supposing I were to " cut up rough," or strike you, or do something equally revengeful, undignified or childish, what then—you would merely hate me? And if I advise you to give up Henshaw, I should only be like a doctor advising the most impecunious of his patients to take a trip round the world; and thus be merely advising something—quite sound in the abstract, no doubt—but almost impossible to carry out.'

" And then she poured into my ears a deluge of
admiration, affection and love which I would
refrain from mentioning, were I not trying to show
you, dear friend, that to be sympathetic even about
your wife's love affairs (if she has any) repays you
a thousandfold. I remember she told me how
other men would have talked about their wounded
honour, and other rather childish things; while I,
in return, told her that I considered honour only a
polite name for vanity, and there were certain countries where a man would foolishly choose rather to
have a bullet in his stomach than a wound in his
vanity. And also I went on to tell her that, when
she promised to love, honour and obey me, she
might as well have added a promise to live till
eighty years of age, with as much certainty of
being able to fulfil such a condition. How long
that joyful interview would have lasted I cannot
guess, for we were both so happy that I think it
might have gone on for hours, had not the more
plebeian affairs of everyday domestic life put an
untimely end to it. But, I will tell you, that
moment, I blest in my heart the man whom the
majority of people would say had done me an
injury ; for in reality he was the cause of a far
greater unity of soul springing up between my wife
and myself, so that each of us knew that, owing to
him, our own love had gone through the great

fiery ordeal and stood the great test, which perhaps
no other combination of circumstances could ever
have achieved."

He paused for a moment, and then continued in
a slightly altered tone:

"And, my friend what was the result of it all,
and how did it finally pan out? As may be supposed, I let those two see of each other as much as
they desired, making no conditions and asking no
questions, treating that man as my friend, and
asking him to be my guest whenever he so felt
inclined. And for some months, things continued
like that, until circumstances took him away to
India, and finally put an end to my wife's amour, in
that it died of its own accord as the result of separation. But needless to say, it fell to me to comfort
her through the distress of that farewell; and,
although I felt a real sorrow for her, yet I felt a
great joy in that comforting, which seemed to draw
our souls nearer even than they had been before.
And as to what happened after that, it seems hardly
necessary to relate, as, in my mind, there is only
one thing that could possibly happen with a nature
as true and noble as that of my wife. As the intensity of her sentiment for this other man was really
only to a large part the physical in disguise, when
he was no longer there to serve as a magnet to
draw forth her love, she began to lose interest in

him, and, judging from the growing infrequency of his letters, he also in her; and the whole thing dwindled away as if it had never been, yet as already said, leaving our own love the richer, through the very thing that might have torn us irrevocably apart. For in having given my wife no cause for resentment against me, or no reason to feel she was a prisoner in any sense of the word, nothing could act as a factor to stifle her love for myself, but rather augment it to its fullest extent. And seeing also I put no obstacle in her way, not only did I bring no scandal on her, for which she was truly grateful, but I brought no scandal to bear on the matter at all, and the people, who might have been all too ready to pronounce me a cuckold, were disarmed from the very first.

" And so, my friend, I think you will be ready to admit that the course I have tried to advise you to pursue, at any rate, was a success in my own case; and I think it must be likewise a success in yours. For remember, the husband who acts up always to the best and truest in him towards his wife must always gain the day, in that lovers are unstable things, coming and going according to varying circumstances; but true conjugal friendship, based on long association, sympathy, and understanding, lasts for ever."

And here Moreward ceased, and the Major, looking at him with an admiration and respect he had not shown to so great an extent hitherto, put a question: "Do you hold, then," he asked, "that every husband should allow his wife to have a lover whenever she wants one?"

And Moreward smiled as he answered his question: "To that I must reply both 'yes' and 'no'; for what you ask depends entirely on the circumstances of the case, and on the wives and husbands concerned, and therefore can never be regulated according to rule. And just as it is one thing for you to allow your wife lovers, as you allow her jewels and fine dresses, it is quite another to forgive her and condone her actions when she is already in love. For if you command her to renounce the object of her affections, she will either leave you, as in your own case, or else deceive you, to guard herself against the effects of your anger—in that you are exacting something from human nature which it can rarely be expected to fulfil. Moreover, there is nothing which makes a person desire a thing so much as an obstacle put in the way of its gratification, just as there is also nothing that kills affection so soon as the feeling of imprisonment; so that to thwart your wife, is to impel her all the more quickly into the arms of the other man, by reason of the resentment you awaken in her heart towards yourself; and thus by trying, as it were, to obtain her love by force, you only succeed in losing it altogether."

And here Moreward ceased again.

" Well, all I can say is," exclaimed the Major, " you are a most amazing fellow, and, what is more, you have done me no end of good."

And that ended the matter; and it ended well, for in the course of a few weeks we heard that Mrs Buckingham and her husband were once more living together, and, as far as one could judge, in evident happiness.

As for Moreward, he said to me, when the Major had left : " It is a strange thing what a lot of talking it requires to convince a person of one of the most obvious things in the world. Here am I, having had, as it were, to place an absurd halo of nobility around myself, in order to hold out an inducement for this good man to go and follow my example."

" Nobility is always relative," I said, " and what to your evolved nature is obvious, is to the Major's heroically noble.

And as I said good-night to him, I wondered, was it modesty that made such a very wise man seem at times so remarkably innocent?

CHAPTER XII

THE STRANGE ALTERATION IN JUSTIN
MOREWARD HAIG

THE utter unconventionality of Justin Moreward Haig's spiritually educational methods never
struck me very forcibly, until an acquaintanceship
was contracted which demonstrated to what lengths
this remarkable man would go contrary to his own
refined personality, in order to bring about certain
results in students of a particular temperament.

There was, in fact, one disciple I met at his
house (for disciple I may rightly call him) who can
best be described by that slangy but expressive
substantive " a Sissy," and who, although I afterwards learned possessed some high qualities of
heart, yet on the surface appeared, as the nursery
phrase has it, quite unable even to say boo to a
goose. He seemed to be one of those ultra-
feminine souls who have had the misfortune to be
born in a man's body, with the necessity for
wearing much abominated trousers, when he would
greatly have preferred to wear skirts instead. Also
there was an air about him which suggested the
probability that he was, if not " too pure to live "
at all, at any rate, too pure to live long. Nor, as I
came to know, was his femininity confined solely

to his outward general mien, but showed itself also
in the fact, for instance, that he not only sewed on
his own buttons, but also those of a young man
with whom he shared rooms. In a word, if, as
Moreward correctly said, he possessed " qualities
of heart," they were those of an unusually kind
old maid, who performed " such things as she
could " for those she cared about, fussing around
them, warming their slippers, and doing a thousand
trifling services of a similar nature, called in one
encompassing term, motherliness. For, be it
remembered, old maids often possess more of this
element than many a mother in the most accurate
sense of the word.

Toni Bland (both the nickname and surname
were particularly suitable) was, quite consistent
with old-maidishness, small of body and small of
bone: also somewhat dried up for his thirty-five
years. Neatness, precision and softness of speech,
as may readily be imagined, were furthermore the
concomitants of his already mentioned characteristics. As to his admiration for Moreward, I must
confess that, just in this one instance, it struck me
as difficult to account for, since the latter was an
utterly changed being when in his company.
Indeed it was only necessary for Bland to put in
an appearance, and all the more obvious signs of
spirituality, gentleness, and suavity immediately

disappeared for something of an entirely contrary nature. His manner of speaking became hard and shrill, his laugh unpleasantly loud, and even vulgar, his conversation interspersed with swear-words and bold expressions, and his manners, usually so courteous and picturesquely ceremonious, almost boorish in their nonchalance. That the little old-maidlike frame of Toni Bland spent most of its time wincing, as its susceptibilities got repeatedly trodden upon, I had no difficulty in perceiving; but I also perceived as time went on, that attempts were made to render it less obvious. Toni Bland began to be a little ashamed of his sensitiveness, and took some steps to hide it. As for myself, the first time I encountered this startling alteration in Moreward Haig, I was, of course, taken very considerably aback, though my surprise was later on to be transformed into heightened admiration, the policy thereof being explained to my entire satisfaction.

It was as the result of my many chance calls on Moreward that I met Toni Bland. He was primly seated, with hands folded, on the edge of a chair, while his companion stood with his back to the fire, his thumbs inserted in the armholes of his waistcoat, and, quite contrary to his usual custom, smoking a very large cigar, from which the room was rendered unpleasantly thick with fumes. Without deigning to move, he nodded to me as I entered, and in a rather loud and " bounderish " manner introduced us.

" Hello," I said, " since when have you taken to smoking cigars ? "

He laughed loudly. " Smoking, my dear fellow, is a vice of mine which I need to use on some of my hyper-sensitive students as a medicine for their spiritual welfare." After which cryptic remark he added " Bland has some views on the subject, haven't you, Antonia ? "

But in answer to this, as might be expected, Bland only smiled, looked embarrassed, and gently rubbed his hands.

" Well, aren't you going to expound them ? " urged Moreward.

" Oh—eh—I only think perhaps it is a pity to— eh—well—it strikes me as rather an unpleasant habit—especially when indulged in to excess. You see," he pursued hesitatingly, and turning to me, " Justin smokes all day long, and that really can't be good."

This was news to me, and I probably showed it, but Moreward offered no explanation. " Come, come," he said, "you're hedging; you're not truthful enough to say that you think all people who smoke like chimneys are *beasts*—especially cigar smokers; you need not be afraid to speak out. Broadbent, *have* a cigar! "

I cast a glance at Bland, hesitating whether to accept under the circumstances; but Moreward gave me a look which undoubtedly showed he did not wish me to refuse, so I took one.

" That's it. Now then, Antonia, what were we talking about? " he said.

" The various forms of Yoga," said Bland in a contrastingly mild tone of voice.

" Yog," shouted Moreward good-humouredly. Didn't I tell you the ' a ' was silent and the word pronounced like y-o-g-u-e? "

" But it sounds so much prettier with the ' a," lisped Toni.

" Prettier be damned," said Moreward. " Cholmondeley sounds prettier, as you call it, than Chumley, but all the same the latter is correct. However, have it as you wish; in northern India it is called Yog, and in southern Yoga; call it by the latter, and, for reasons I needn't go into, certain people will consider you an ignoramus."

" Haven't I seen the name paraded by sandwichmen up and down Regent Street? " I asked.

" Very likely," returned Moreward; " professional palmists, clairvoyants and people of that ilk, are fond of defiling the sublimest science in the

Note.—Yoga is the Science; Yogi, the practitioner.

world by associating it with their low-down vocations."

"But what about those in India who smear themselves with ashes and do all sorts of queer tricks?" queried Bland tentatively.

" No *great* Yogi ever parades his attainments before the world," said Moreward. " On the contrary, the greater the man, the more ordinary does he try to appear to the uninitiated. It is only people of very moderate sanctity, like some of your parsons, who affect an unctuous voice and wear mourning, as if to say, ' I'd have you know I am a good man,' and that in spite of the Biblical injunctions against any outward show of piety. There are, in fact, two forms of hypocrisy, if we can use the word at all—the hypocrisy of the great man who pretends he is ordinary, and the hypocrisy of the ordinary man who pretends he is great. They are both deceivers, if you like, but one is the deception of modesty and high ethics, and the other of vanity. So the Yogis you refer to, my Antonia. are not worthy examples of Yog any more than the pale young curate is a worthy example of true Christian spirituality "

" All the same, I've known some delightful curates," mused Bland almost inaudibly.

Moreward burst into laughter, and asked how many slippers he had embroidered for them.

As for me, I felt more and more that if Toni was a milksop addicted to utterly obvious and old-maidish remarks, Moreward spared no pains to make him appear ridiculous: a procedure quite contrary to any I had ever witnessed on his part hitherto. And yet, the reason for it all never dawned on me at the time, though I dimly sensed there must be one; and what is more, that very reason and a discourse on Yoga are my excuse for writing about Toni Bland at all, since he offers no " episode " of special interest, but was merely a type, calling for treatment, as already said, of a very unusual nature.

He had merely responded to Moreward's last bit of chaff by a slightly embarrassed and non-committal giggle. And personally I opined he was quite capable of spending a large part of his time in embroidering slippers for curates, although no doubt I did him an injustice. In fact, he offended me, this mincing little man, and I felt disposed to give him a rousing smack on the back and shake him into some semblance of masculinity. Moreward, however, made a remark which rendered me painfully aware that my reflections and inclinations were not exactly of the most charitable order. "Run a man down," he said, " and Antonia will stick up for him. Outward appearances, my dear Broadbent, *are* deceptive, though the statement is

damned trite. Do *you* take that in?" he added,
turning to Bland. "No you don't, and there's
the trouble."

He began to stride about the room, his left
thumb still inserted in the armhole of his waistcoat.

"Yes," he repeated, "that's just the trouble,
this silly notion that spirituality and formality and
milk-soppishness can ever be coincident. Don't
you realise that the goal of mankind is God-consciousness, cosmic consciousness, and yet can anyone suppose for a moment that the consciousness
of a pale young curate or an old maid can in any
way resemble the consciousness of Deity? Guts,
my dear fellow are the first thing necessary to
arrive at God-consciousness."

Toni blinked, smiled genteelly and re-folded his
hands. "I can't quite see how—what is it—
reversing the peristaltic action of the digestion, as
the Yogis do, can tend to union with God?" he
mused audibly.

"Can't you? Well, I'll tell you this much,"
said Moreward with a certain good-humoured
aggressiveness, "that anything remarkable that
anybody can do, is a step Godward and a step
towards freedom. Impotence is the strongest of
all fetters. Talk about being like God, Who pro-
jected this Universe from Himself, and yet be
incapable of doing anything but twirl the thumbs!

Bless my soul! what a conception! Besides, I'll
tell you another thing : it is mighty difficult to have
God-consciousness if you've got a rotten body.
Perfect health is not only essential to this highest
state of Bliss, but it is also an attribute of God.
Just imagine God ill! God miserable! God in
tears! " He laughed. " And as to these Yogis,
whom you disapprove of because you know nothing
about them, I tell you their science in itself is the
highest thing on earth. There is hardly a miracle,
so-called, that these Yogis cannot learn to perform;
but just because they won't come to London and
give a show in St. James's Hall, people won't
believe it, although they are quite ready to believe
that the great Yogi of Nazareth performed miracles
some two thousand years ago. Oh, I grant you
that some of these lower-grade Yogis perform hair-
raising feats out there in India before a wondering
public; but the type who uses his powers either to
gratify his vanity or to obtain money, never gets
any further : acquisitiveness and vanity very soon
block the way to further consciousness."

He sat down in his armchair and put his feet on
the mantlepiece, after throwing away his cigar and
lighting another.

" But I'll tell you a deuced valuable asset that
Yog possesses," he continued; " its states of consciousness are arrived at through physiological

methods, and not through hypnotic ones nor
through the agency of drugs. And what does that
imply? Why, that nobody can pretend with the
assurance of ignorance that imagination plays any
part in the matter. In order to hypnotise yourself you have to dwell on some idea or image until
you imagine you actually see the thing you are
thinking about, but Yog is quite different from
this. Inside the body are certain latent forces:
wake these up through purely physiological pro-
cesses known to Yogis, and you alter your entire
consciousness; begin to see things, hear things, and
perceive things that are around you, but of which
you were hitherto quite unaware."

"And can anybody practice Yog?" I asked.

"If you can find a teacher, which I admit is not
easy," he answered.

"I suppose it means going to India?" I inferred.

He laughed. "Yog is to be found in all countries if you know where to look," was his reply;
"it has been in England for over three hundred
years, and there are Adepts in London now."

"It is all very interesting," observed Toni, as
he got up from his chair, "but I am afraid I must
be going."

"Time to be off, eh?" said Moreward without
rising. "Well, so long, Antonia; let me know
when you're coming again." He shook hands,

from his seat by the fire, and then chucked away his
cigar.

Toni bade me good-bye with the remark that he
hoped he would meet me again soon, and took a
prim departure.

" What does all this mean? " I said, when I
knew by the closing of the front door that Bland
was out of hearing.

Moreward took down his feet from the mantlepiece and indulged in one of his ordinary genial
peals of laughter. " First of all," he said, getting
up and going to open the window, " we'll let some
of this smoke out; I fear it has rather inconveni-
enced you. And now I'll tell you exactly what it
does mean, although I would have thought you'd
have guessed already." He was utterly himself
again; his voice had resumed its normal tone, his
manner once again taken on that picturesque slight
ceremoniousness which was one of his so pleasant
characteristics. " You didn't know I was something of an actor? " he questioned.

I admitted that the thought had not struck me.

" And yet there are some people," he went on,
" towards whom it is essential to adopt a certain
manner which shall counteract their misconceptions
on the one hand, and brace them up on the other.
Toni, as you observed, is too lady-like; he lacks
power, that is already a stumbling block in his

path of itself, but a worse one is the supposition
that the pre-requisite to spirituality is this primness
and this quintessence of propriety.   In other
words, the least thing shocks him. Well, the only
way to counteract this is to harden him : to make
a man of him by offending his sensibilities to such
an extent that they eventually become annihilated.
You've heard of the hardening system in therapeutics; well, some people need the hardening
system in spiritual therapeutics.   There is no
other way."

Certainly the wisdom of this struck me as undeniable; all the same, I wondered whether in this
case any good would accrue. Toni Bland, as I saw
him, seemed to me a person one can alone describe
as " hopeless."   In fact, I couldn't resist expressing my views to Moreward. " There is one thing
puzzles me about you sometimes," I said, " and
that is the amazing amount of trouble you take
with—I don't want to be intolerant—but I call
them utterly stupid people."

" You do Toni an injustice," was his reply. " He
is deplorably shy before strangers, but he is far
from stupid fundamentally. He has plenty to say
when nobody else is present. Let him once get to
know you, and he will not favour you with any
more trite remarks.   I grant you he is a very
feminine soul and has much to contend against,

but if you had had four or five previous incarnations as a woman, as he has had, you'd be pretty much the same as he is. His destiny is a difficult one."

"But there are others," I reminded him, "as ordinary as he and more hopeless, and yet you have taken what would seem to me endless trouble over them."

"You have not yet accustomed yourself to think in eternities," he replied smiling. "I have known each of those people in the past, and each of them has done me some service. Well, ingratitude ought hardly to be one of our vices, and so I can but desire to repay them. Do you think Toni, for instance, would put up with my boorish ways if there had been no previous association to draw us together? Time after time Toni comes here for what he honours me by calling my wisdom and knowledge of occult subjects, and puts up with the slang and the swear-words because, in spite of them —well, he believes in me, and is subconsciously aware we have been together before. So you see, my friend, an enlarged memory alters the perspective of things, and the apparently meaningless becomes full of meaning. Toni has fine qualities of soul perceptible to those who know him, but, even if he had not, I would still make the attempt to further his spiritual happiness, as a grateful repayment of that old service rendered; and if he were not ripe for the Path in this incarnation, I would try again in his next; for affection will always draw us together again, life after life."

*　　*　　*　　*　　*

I never saw Toni Bland again, but that one meeting with him showed me indirectly more and more the grandeur of a life which dealt with thousands of years instead of the short span of three score years and ten. Certainly there was in Moreward's remarkable philosophy no waste, no meaninglessness of the smallest emotion or action apparently. Through his example and tuition, life became something infinitely grand; all sense of futility vanished for ever; and even such a thing as the use of a swear-word in his philosophy, had, in its ridiculousness, a flavour of the sublime.

CHAPTER XIII

Pembley Manor, Warwickshire,
Tuesday.

My dear Charlie,

You don't deserve to get a letter from me at all, because it never seems to occur to you to send even a few lines to ask how we are, which I think extremely remiss. However, I know it is no use scolding: you are just incorrigible where letter-writing is concerned, and I hope you realise I am returning good for evil in not remaining utterly silent—that is to say, as silent as you. [The fact is, my sister, as a rule, writes such very arid letters that I do not wish to encourage her by answering them, apart from which I candidly dislike writing letters myself.] All the same, if you don't answer this letter, you will be in my very worst of all books for a long time to come, so I tell you this at once. The fact is, you old miscreant, I have met the extraordinary man you have been so full of for the last six months (at least, you were the one time I saw you, and everybody tells me you always are). Well, he has been down here for the week-end, and I don't wonder now that you are so taken up with him: he is quite the most remarkable

creature I have ever met. Everyone down here
is fascinated with him. For one thing, he is not a
bit like anyone else in the world (at all events, not
anyone I have ever seen), and you know how
refreshing it is to come across somebody who is
different from the usual lot of dull people one
meets at house parties. Of course I am dying to
ask you loads of questions about him, but I sup
pose if I don't tell you a lot of news first, you
simply won't answer them; besides, I believe for
once you will be really interested in my letter.
[" Perhaps for once I shall be," I thought.] Well,
I came down here on Friday, and he arrived the
next day. Until his arrival I thought I was in for
a deadly week-end. There were the Julian Smiths
(whom I never could like) and that boring Miss
Clifford (how ugly and tedious she is!), and then
old Mr Sandlands (I am sure he is dotty),
[" Charity is certainly not one of your virtues," I
thought], and finally Lady Eddisfield. It was
she who brought him—though, how he can be such
a friend of hers, or, I mean really, she such a friend
of his, I can't say. At least I couldn't say then,
but after seeing him for two days I have discovered
that he makes everyone his friend : I have never
seen anything like it. I wonder what it feels like
to be fond of everyone you meet, sort of thing.
[" Why don't you try and see? " I thought.]

Well, he arrived just in time for tea with his companion, Lady E., and what a couple they were—she always on the go in a perfect whirlpool of excitement and fidgets, shouting at the top of her voice; and he, calm as a mill-pond. Somehow he seemed as if he were a spectator at the Zoo, looking at a lot of monkeys jumping about inside the cage—he had such a sense of aloofness about him : I don't mean superiority or conceit, of course, [" No, I should think not," I thought], but of being a sort of onlooker. And then, when he began to talk, first of all he has such a soothing voice, and secondly, everything he says seems so extraordinary, and he never uses slang; it was too funny; I noticed after a little that everybody began to drop their slangy way of talking as if they were ashamed to go on like that in front of him. And then another thing, he never would join in when the others began to run down people; he simply kept silent and looked at them all, like one looks at a lot of children when they babble nonsense or try to show off. It wasn't exactly a bored expression, but a sort of indulgent one. It was too amusing to see them all drop running down people after a bit, like they did with the slang. [" It is a pity *you* have not dropped it permanently, too," I thought, " since it is such a futile occupation."] After tea we took a stroll in the garden, and on

into the woods, and then I told him I was your
sister, and he said heaps of most awfully nice things
about *you*, which I am sure you don't deserve in
the least. ["Thank you," I thought; "perhaps
he knows me a good deal better than you do if the
truth be told."]   And then he seemed to take an
enormous interest in me: I was really quite
flattered; besides, he looked at me in such an affec-
itonate sort of way, I thought he must be a bit of a
flirt at first, but when I found he looked at everybody like that—well, never mind what I thought.
["You were a bit sold," I opined.]   I wondered if
he were an artist or poet, or something of that kind,
because as we walked about he showed me all sorts
of beautiful glimpses and things I had never
noticed before; but when I asked Lady E. what he
was, she said he was nothing, or perhaps, she said,
merely a gentleman of means, or at large, or something like that (I really can't remember what she
said, and it doesn't matter).   At dinner he told us
the most extraordinary things.   He is really the
most brilliant conversationalist I ever met, and
never once does he talk of himself—I think even
the butler got so interested he forgot to wait
properly, and I saw Lady Drummond frown at him
(the butler, I mean) once or twice very severely.
He took me in to dinner, so I was sitting next to
him, and I noticed he let all the meat courses pass,

and only took vegetables and sweets, so I asked
him why he didn't eat meat, and he just smiled and
said it was a pity to kill unoffending animals.
Wasn't it extraordinary? You never told me he
was a vegetarian. After dinner we all sat in the
big hall over a fire (it was a bit chilly, so they had
lighted it), and then he told us all sorts of wonderful things about ghosts and Mahatmas and Fakirs
he had seen on his travels in India—really interesting. I had never believed in that sort of thing
before, but somehow, when he talks about it, it is
all quite different, and one thinks it must be true.
We sat up listening to him all hours of the night,
and when we went to bed Henry called him " the
charming lunatic." I thought of what you had
called him, " the wise imbecile or infant or innocent," wasn't it? All the same, Henry was awfully
impressed, although he pretended not to be.

On Sunday a rather funny thing happened. He
came down to breakfast, and then, when it was
over, he disappeared for the rest of the morning.
I was walking in a part of the garden nobody goes
to as a rule, and fancy, all of a sudden I came upon
him. He was sitting cross-legged like a tailor,
but bolt upright, with his eyes shut, and not lean-
ing against anything, but as still as if he were
asleep. Well, somehow, I didn't like to say anything, so I moved off. However, I was so

curious, I went back there again in about half an hour, and, lo and behold, he was in exactly the same position as when I had left him, and I am sure he had never moved.   Do tell me, whatever was he doing?   I think it most extraordinary, and I was dying to ask him afterwards, but somehow I didn't like to.   [" And if he had told you, you wouldn't understand," I thought.]   Well, this epistle is getting very long, so I shall stop now; but I want to know all about him.   Whatever is he, and what does he do?   And how old can he be?   And tell me, is he very rich?   And who and what are his people.   I can't get anything out of Lady E.; she puts on a silly air of mystery when I ask her, but I don't believe she knows anything, and wants to cover up the fact.

Well, now, goodbye, and remember, if you don't answer me I shall never forgive you.

Much love from

Your affectionate sister,

ETHEL.

P.S.—Why don't you come and spend a week-end with us—It is ages since you've been.

CHAPTER XIV

As already implied, the letter comprising our last chapter was from my married sister. But I possessed another and younger one, who was of so different a temperament that the theory of heredity, in face of that fact, always struck me as only partially true, and not wholly so. Indeed, as Moreward explained when discussing the subject with me, heredity is only the effect, and not the cause. A man, for instance, who drinks, will in his next incarnation be drawn into a family where he will be able to gratify his desire. Heredity would then imply that he drank because his father drank; in other words, he inherits a body troubled by the tendency to drink. And that is true as far as it goes, but the reason of his inheriting it is left out, and the theory of heredity is regarded as the first *cause*, instead of only the effect; the cause lying much further back. Or take another example: A man who was a musician in his last incarnation will require, in his present one, a body and brain of a certain sensitiveness; he needs, therefore, to incarnate in a family where, let us say, his mother is musical, so that he can inherit her particular type of body, or, missing a generation, his grandmother's for the matter of that; it makes little difference. Now, most people would say at once, "That man gets his music from his mother," but in point of fact, the statement is only very partially correct; he had his music long before he met his mother, so to speak, his mother merely being the means of helping him to bring his musical faculties into manifestation on the physical plane in his present incarnation, and nothing further. Of course, the theory of heredity will satisfy most people, because they have not as yet acquired the faculty of remembering their past incarnations; but to those who *can* remember, heredity must inevitably be regarded as effect, and not cause, and therein lies the enormous difference.

It will be remembered, from the conversation I had with Moreward in Kensington Gardens, that day on which he startled me by a reference to our past lives, that he believed in re-incarnation, and not only as a theory, but as an undeniable fact. And yet it surprised me why so little was known on the subject in the Western world, at any rate, until quite recently. But here again Moreward had a ready explanation. "You see," he said, "people deny re-incarnation because they cannot recollect their past lives—absence of memory to them is a sufficient proof of non-existence. And yet, if I asked you exactly what you were doing on

a certain day, say, fifteen years ago, your memory
fails you, though you are quite convinced you were
alive at that time. Now the point is this, that
with each incarnation the ego obtains a new body,
and hence a new brain, and it is solely the brain
which remembers; that being so, the brain cannot
register anything which took place before it was
formed; indeed, it cannot even recall a great many
things that took place *after* it was formed. For
were I to ask you, as another instance, what you
were thinking of ten minutes ago, you will find
you have entirely forgotten. All the same, within
everyone of us are certain rudimentary organs
which, by a process known to occultists, we can
cause to function ; let these organs once function,
and a memory which is not dependent on the
physical brain is the result. That is why, and how,
the initiate remembers his past lives."

I have related Moreward's views on the subject,
partly because of their interest, and partly because
of their bearing on the following episode.

We were both of us invited to a certain house
party for a few days, at which my younger sister
(Gladys by name) was present, and also a young
man for whom she had, at any rate, a weakness,
while he on his side was unquestionably in love.
But it was fairly evident that, whatever their sentiments were for one another, there was something

distinctly inharmonious between them; for Gordon
Mellor (that was his name) could hardly disguise
an utter dejection of manner, which the quick eye
and intuition of my wise friend were at no pains
to detect. Nor was it long before he was drawn
into the matter, for my sister took at once a fancy
to him (though of no amatory nature), which very
shortly showed itself in a desire to speak quite
frankly in his presence, after an invitation on his
part that she should do so.

Personally, I knew what the trouble was, namely,
a false pride and vanity on her side; but as all my
attempts to set it right were met with the remark
that I was a man, and could therefore never understand a woman's point of view—besides which, " I
had very peculiar ideas "—I gave all such attempts
up as quite useless. Moreover, a prophet having
no honour in his own family, made my endeavours
even more impotent than otherwise they might
have been. And so the trouble had gone on for
some weeks, or even months, for all I knew, without any satisfactory solution.

From the first day of our arrival, Moreward
talked in such a way concerning matters spiritual
and otherwise that he very soon awakened my
sister's admiration, and, seeing that to be the case,
I took the first opportunity of telling him my
sister was in the midst of a difficulty, which, to my

mind, demanded his sympathetic interference. Of course, as was ever the case, he showed himself only too ready to assist in any way he could, so that I contrived that we three should be left to our own devices, in order to discuss the matter without fear of interruption; a thing, under the circumstances, quite easy of accomplishment.

I began the subject myself, as we were enjoying an afternoon ramble together à trois across the country fields. " Your friend Gordon," said I " does not exactly seem to thrive under your friendship, my dear Gladys."

She blushed, and tried to parry the remark, but succeeded very badly.

" By the way," said Moreward kindly, " you and he, Miss Broadbent, interest me greatly. I have reasons to believe that you are both very, very old friends; your friendship dates back through many incarnations, if I am not mistaken."

My sister looked pleased, and much interested all of a sudden. She was by no means averse to occult subjects, and was much inclined to believe in them. " Fancy your being able to tell that," she said with enthusiasm; " but how on earth do you do it? "

" That is fairly simple," he answered, smiling; " if you look at two people in the ordinary way, you can generally see if they are in harmony. The relationship of mother and son, for instance, is usually discernible from similarities in the physical body; for relationship of a subtler kind, one must look at people's mental bodies; in that way one can perceive whether they are soul affinities or not."

"And you think Gordon and I are soul-affinities?" she asked.

"I most certainly do," he answered.

"Hah! Hah!" I exclaimed with triumph. "Perhaps now that you know this, you will treat him better."

"I have never treated him badly," she declared somewhat hotly.

"I call it badly," said I, "and you know my views on the subject, and I bet you if we told Moreward he would share them."

"What is the trouble?" asked Moreward sympathetically. "Could I be of the least assistance?"

She looked at him gratefully as she said: "Well, there are difficulties, you see."

"That is more or less nonsense; the difficulties are at any rate adjustable. But the fact is, you are a prig," I said, laughing to temper my uncomplimentary remark a little.

"Dear me!" said Moreward soothingly. "These brothers are not flattering, are they?"

"Oh, he is very rude," she observed coldly.

" The trouble is this," I said, taking the matter into my own hands. " Gladys dislikes marriage, and can't make up her mind to marry, but loves this man and wants him to be in love with her. As they are not engaged, however, she thinks they ought to be—well, *absolutely* platonic; in fact, she won't even own up she loves the man, because she thinks even that is improper."

Moreward laughed with noticeable tolerance.

" Well, don't you think I **am** right," she asked, appealing to him.

" Hardly *quite* right," he said, smiling very kindly.

" There, what did I tell you? " I exclaimed triumphantly.

" But really Mr Haig," she said persuasively, " it isn't done—not in the society I go about in, at any rate. We're not Bohemians, you know, and we can't do that sort of thing."

" But where does the unfortunate man come in?' he asked, looking at her paternally. " Isn't it rather hard on him? "

" Sheer cruelty," I exclaimed.

My sister pondered.

" Why, she won't send the man away," I said, turning to Moreward, " and she won't show him an atom of love. I call that flirting—yes, flirting; and of the very worst type."

" I have never flirted in my life," she declared,
warmly.

" But isn't there perhaps a form of flirting,"
observed Moreward gently, " that is so insidious
it hardly seems like flirting at all? "

" And therefore is all the more reprehensible,"
I added.

My sister looked puzzled. " I don't quite
understand," she said.

" Well," he explained, but in a tone of great
kindliness, " if you crave for the certainty that a
man loves you, tantalising him with your personal
presence, and, knowing that he suffers, yet give
him nothing whatever in return—is that not what
we might call a very insidious form of flirting? "

My sister kept an embarrassed silence.

" I know," he continued, " flirting is an
ambiguous term, and much is called flirting which,
to my mind, is not flirting at all. For instance,
two persons may be genuinely fond of one another
and demonstrate the fact, though they may have
no intention of marrying; that, however, is strictly
speaking not flirting, for it is not insincere merely
because unmatrimonial, if I may so express myself.
On the other hand, if two people contrive to arouse
sentiments in each other merely to gratify vanity,
and not because they feel any love, that we may
certainly call flirting, for it is insidiously asking

for something and intending to give nothing in return."

" But surely that doesn't apply to me," she protested.

" Well, let us look at the situation a little critically," he said. " In permitting this man a liberal amount of your society, you lead him to suppose you are fond of him, don't you? And that gives him certain hopes which you have no intention of allowing him to realise, either in the way of marriage *or in any way whatever*. The result is, I fear, that he suffers. In other words, dear friend, are you not buying your pleasure with the price of his suffering, and thus asking from him very much and giving nothing in return? "

" But in the opinion of the world," she began to object.

" The opinions of the world," he interrupted gently, " are based upon selfishness and vanity, and not on altruism and love."

" My dear Gladys," I said, " it's no use; your behaviour is that of both a prig and a flirt; and the sooner you realise it the better."

" Wouldn't it perhaps be better to be quite honest with this man," pursued Moreward, " and tell him that you love him, but that your views on marriage are such that you do not want to enter into it? This course would have, not only the advantage of being honest and straightforward, but also of giving him the choice of either leaving you or being content with your love."

"But that would never do," she objected; "he would—well—immediately want to kiss me."

"You are the most amazing prig I have ever struck," I said warmly; "your vanity is simply phenomenal, and you are niggardly into the bargain. Here you keep this unfortunate man hanging about and dangling for ever between hope and despair, in order to gratify your insane vanity, and you are too niggardly, either to own up you love him, or to give him a kiss which would just raise him into the seventh heaven."

Moreward cast me a glance which was very like approval; as to my sister, she merely cast one of anger.

"Let us sit down," he said, "and admire the view." We threw ourselves upon the grass, and then I noticed Moreward gazing at my sister with a certain contemplativeness.

"You see," he mused after a moment or so, "there are two kinds of virtues in the world : true virtues and false virtues. The false ones are those based upon vanity, the true ones are those based upon unselfishness; yet as far as outside appearance goes, they are not always easy to detect, because they look much alike to the unreflecting. Well,

dear Miss Gladys, I hope you will forgive me for
using a crude word, but the attitude you adopt
towards this man, however correct and laudable it
may seem from the worldly point of view, is, when
looked at from a more spiritual one—well, merely
selfishness. In regarding your aura, instead of
finding it large and expansive, I find it cramped and
circumscribed. And then I see indications that
you have gone through this little drama, with this
very same man, in many lives before, and each time
it has brought suffering; and yet, instead of the
lesson being learned by that suffering, it has each
time remained unlearned, so that in your present
life you are going through it all again. For love is a
tie which links us together incarnation after incarnation; but only as that love is unselfish and noble
can we reap happiness from it, and should it be
otherwise, the link is rather a misfortune than a
joy, as in *your* case it proves to be because of the
attitude you seem so loth to alter. And what has
happened before, I fear, must happen again, for in
these past lives this man has left you each time
and given the whole thing up in despair, because in
his love for you he has looked for breadth and
unselfishness, and has been disillusioned in the end
instead."

He had glided into that rather melodious flow of

utterance which was so characteristic of him whenever he discoursed on subjects of this sort, though alas, my attempts to reproduce it are deplorably inadequate.

"You see," he continued, eloquent though at the same time gentle, "you have followed the strict conventions of the world in this matter, without ever questioning whether they be right or wrong, or based on the selfish or the noble. For in this case, as with many others, you have regarded a precept right by reason of the world proclaiming it so, but have omitted to reflect as to whether it be right in itself. For the world's laws and conventions are based upon rules, making no allowance whatever for exceptions and the individual circumstances of the case. And just as a thing is sometimes right, and yet at others that selfsame thing may be utterly wrong, so a strict adherence to the conventions of the world may at times be utterly reprehensible in the eyes of the Divine. Moreover, to conform to a convention we know in our souls to be wrong is never a virtue, but only vanity and cowardice in disguise, and therefore unworthy of admittance into so selfless a quality as real and untainted love. And if that conformity be not only prompted by vanity, but at the same time bring suffering to a being who is innocent, and whose intentions are upright and honourable, then it is doubly to be eschewed; for love which takes no account of the welfare of its object is not love at all, but another emotion masquerading under that name instead."

He paused for a moment, and looked at my sister with a benign persuasiveness, putting his hand on her arm.

"And now," he said, "it is, as in most things, a question of choice, and which of the two is the sweeter, pride or love; and is it worth while to let the childish and fleeting stand in the way of that which endures, and the lesser illusion cover the greater reality? For truly is pride but an illusion, in that those who are proud attach it invariably to things it but seldom fits, leaving it altogether aside when it might be best employed. For you, like many another, are proud to conceal instead of to avow, and proud to be cold of heart instead of warm; and yet, not one of these things is worthy of pride, but rather the reverse, in that they are but errors clothed in the semblance of virtues, but nevertheless errors in spite of whatever the world may say. For niggardliness is the same, be it attached to money or love, and deception is also the same, and coldness of heart; and to be proud of any of these is to be proud of that which is weak and childish, instead of wise and consequently strong."

And here Moreward ceased speaking, and looked at her with a gentle appeal. " A man's happiness at stake is my plea for a little preaching, "he said apologetically, " and your own happiness as well, but, although your love may not be very intense, you love that man as much as you are capable of loving anybody at present, and you will suffer if you lose him, which I fear will be the case very soon. And now, enough moral philosophy for one day; we are missing the sunset over the hills there, which has a philosophy of its own."

And yet, however convincing Moreward's eloquence seemed, at any rate to me, on this occasion, as on most others, his intervention in the matter either came too late, or else my sister's vanity still retained the upper hand, and she was incapable of changing her attitude, however guilty she may have felt in her own soul. Indeed, we had almost forgotten the incident altogether, when a month or so later Moreward handed me a letter in Gladys's handwriting. It ran:—

" Dear Mr Haig,—I am very unhappy, and, as you tried to help me once, though I was foolish enough not to take your advice, I feel sure you will help me again in spite of what may seem my ingratitude. Gordon has left me, as you predicted. He said, quite simply, that he could not stand it any longer, and that he prefers not to see me again. I have written to him several times, but he does not answer, and so I am afraid there is little hope of things ever coming right. It would be a great comfort to me if I could have a talk with you, and I am sure you will forgive me for bothering you, but I know you are always ready to help anybody in trouble.

　" With kindest regards,

　　" Very sincerely yours,

　　　" Gladys Broadbent."

" Of course, I will do what I can," he said, when I finished reading the note, " but I think you had better interview the man and see what his attitude is regarding the whole affair."

" It strikes me you wasted your philosophy on Gladys," I said, " and cast pearls before—well, the word is not a pretty one."

" A little philosophy even to the unreceptive is never entirely wasted," he answered, smiling, " for, although your sister may be doomed to suffer, in that she exacted everything and gave nothing, thinking that vanity was virtue and weakness was love, yet at the same time she has now got an inkling *why* she must suffer, and will learn her lesson all the more easily in consequence.　For now, at any rate, she will not add to the sum of her errors by blaming *him* instead of herself; and during the remainder of her present incarnation may learn that the essence of real love is to give, and not to withhold, thinking all the time of self, instead of the object of her affection. So, when they meet in a future incarnation, as they undoubtedly will, each falling in love with the other again, her little addition of knowledge will stand her in good part, and what was this time tainted by suffering will be imbued with understanding and happiness instead."

CHAPTER XV

I HAD come to regard Justin Moreward Haig (as well I might) a doctor of souls, and when any of my acquaintances seemed in need of mental medicine, and not utterly past redemption, I unhesitatingly asked him to come with me and visit them, as one would take a doctor to a patient—except, of course, that no fee was attached to the matter. There was a middle-aged lady I had known for some time, by name Mrs Burton, who struck me as particularly in need of a change of outlook upon life, for she was one of those persons who might be said to possess the possibility of having everything, yet enjoying absolutely nothing. She had, in fact, built a sort of wall around her personality, and lived in a state of shut-in-ness, which caused her a great deal of distress without her being able to divine in any sense the reason. As I was personally not clever enough to deal with her case with any degree of success, I once again brought Moreward to the rescue, as I had done in the instance of Major Buckingham; and although Mrs. Burton offers no story of adventure, she affords a further exposition of my wise friend's philosophy of peace.

I remember the first time we visited her together

at her spacious flat in Belgravia.   It was a bright
London day, but with a slight haze, and as we got
into the neighbourhood of Belgrave Square, Moreward remarked with good-humoured disgust that
we had come into contact with almost the worst
aura in London.   " One could well-nigh cut the
mental atmosphere here with a knife," he said, " it
is so stiflingly thick."   And I laughed : for to my
insensitive mentality I could perceive no difference
between one place and another, except where ugli-
ness and beauty were concerned.   On arriving I
must confess (for I like my afternoon tea better
than any other meal) that Mrs Burton provided us
with the daintiest and most *recherché* of little
meals, and I " tucked in " in a manner which
caused me an inner blush, and, what is more, pro-
voked the remark (to somebody else, repeated to
me some days later) that I was very greedy.   Criticism, in fact, was Mrs Burton's sole occupation in
life : she looked through a peep-hole in her self-
made prison, and criticised everything and everybody, her idea being that to do this was to look at
life as it *really* is, and therefore to be truly practical.

Moreward's first step was to "draw her out " and
let her talk. I am fully aware that he only had to
look at her aura in order to know her character
very thoroughly, but, as he said to me, " that
method for the present would hardly do; she must

be permitted to talk, so that she may realise I have gauged her personality by perfectly straightforward and practical means, and by no other."

" Yes," she said, after a few other remarks, " I do not make many friends."

" That is a pity, isn't it? " said Moreward very sympathetically. " Life is apt to become so lonely."

" It is indeed," she replied with a touch of sadness, " but then, so few people make suitable friends; I have had many disappointments in life."

" You have found people untrustworthy perhaps? " he said.

" Oh, very untrustworthy," she assented, " and then it is so difficult to find people who really understand one."

" Oh, of course, if one really wishes to be understood, it is, as you say, difficult."

He glanced at me for the fraction of a second, with a twinkle which said, as it were, " What nonsense we are talking! "

" I suppose you find no difficulty yourself in understanding others? " he added deferentially.

" Well, I cannot exactly say I do," she assented, pleased with the compliment; " but, of course, one never knows."

" I should have thought you would have so many friends," I said, with hidden insincerity.

" Not *real* friends," she corrected.

" But, at any rate, people who are fond of *you*."

" Exactly," echoed Moreward.

She forced a laugh of mock modesty.

" But if one can't be fond of them in return, it is so—eh—unsatisfactory," she said.

" Nothing that pleases one's vanity is entirely unsatisfactory," I remarked.

" Yet, that sort of satisfaction *would* hardly please Mrs Burton," corrected Moreward flatteringly.

" Well, to be quite honest," returned Mrs Burton, smiling with more modesty, " it really doesn't."

" I suppose a woman of your temperament would naturally expect a great deal from your friends? " inferred Moreward sympathetically.

" Well, yes, one does," agreed Mrs Burton; " at least, I don't know about a great deal, but one does, of course expect a *little*."

" It might be a good plan to expect nothing," said Moreward, as if the idea had struck him for the first time.

" That *would* be funny," she said; " but I don't quite see how one could."

" Simply by cultivating an attitude of tolerance towards them," he answered.

" But that would be so bad for them."

" I wonder," mused Moreward.

" It's a very pleasant sensation," I observed ; " he taught me how to cultivate it."

" Oh, indeed," she said; " what a funny thing to teach you. I hardly thought one could learn such things as that."

" But one can," I insisted.

" Well, well," she observed with the wisdom of ignorance. " I'm afraid I couldn't. I fear I'm too critical and too practical."

" I wonder if to be critical is really to be practical," mused Moreward, again as if the idea had just struck him.

" One can't be a dreamer," said Mrs Burton; " one really must see life as it is."

" But somehow I doubt whether anybody really sees life as it is," he said; "it is always the question of ' a pair of spectacles '—put on a blue pair, and everything seems blue."

" Better to look blue than unreal," persisted Mrs Burton.

" But to look blue *is* to look unreal," he corrected.

" Do you think so ? "

" Well the landscape hardly looks blue unless you look at it through blue glass, does it ? "

" But life isn't a landscape," she said.

" I'm not so sure of that."

Mrs Burton smiled, but didn't answer.

" I see what it is," added Moreward. " You are one of those clever people who find it difficult to be happy."

Mrs Burton put up a hand in pleasurable protest.

" I am not so *very* unhappy," she remarked simply.

" But indifferent? " he queried.

" Perhaps."

" Lady Morton," said the maid, as she ushered this somewhat august personage into the room. And shortly afterwards we took our leave, with the request on the part of Mrs Burton that we should both come again soon.

" I fear your friend will prove a very difficult case," Moreward said, as we walked away. " She has surrounded herself with a mental shell, which even the most loving thoughts will not be able to penetrate, so that her whole emotional and mental being is utterly starved. The cause of her trouble is fear and vanity combined—she is afraid to feel, afraid of the slightest rebuff, afraid of life altogether, and I see little hope of her emerging from her prison house in this incarnation, unless something very unexpected happens."

" What, for instance? " I asked.

" Well, a very deep and passionate love affair," he said.

" Good Heavens! " I laughed.

" That is the only thing," he insisted. " Her aura is a mass of grey—depression that means—and it will need a very strong wave of emotion to dispel it. I think you said she was a widow, and I take it she is about forty-five? She is therefore between the dangerous age and the very dangerous age." I laughed.

" As a matter of fact," I said, " I don't think she *is* a widow; she is either separated or has divorced her husband (I am rather vague about her history); so if you go and recommend her a love affair, you may be letting her in for no end of trouble—that is, if she is only separated."

He laughed with that gentle laugh of his.

" My friend," he said, " you have often done me the honour to call me a doctor of souls. A doctor administers medicines—some of those medicines taste sweet and some bitter, some are poison and some are innocuous—but their object is always to effect a cure."

" Well? " I queried.

" Well, when it is a matter of curing souls," he explained with earnestness, " one is often constrained to advise, so to speak, a thing which tastes nasty, to the outside world; the world, in fact, is like a child let loose in a herbalist's shop—tasting with its undiscerning mind each herb, and pro-

nouncing it good or bad according to its sweetness
or bitterness. And yet are not bitter things often
more curative than sweet, for nothing is good or
bad in itself? "

" Go on," I said.

" Supposing, then, that Mrs Burton is merely
separated; even so, a love affair, which the world
will regard as improper, is under the circumstances
the only thing that can save her soul. 'He that
would save his life must lose it ' means a great deal
more than it says, for it often means ' She that
would save her *virtue* must lose it.' "

" The uninitiated would say ' dangerous doctrines,' " I replied.

" Bella donna is a dangerous poison, but the
homœopathist finds it invaluable in many cases."
He paused for a moment, and then he said : "There
was once a molly-coddle who went to an Indian
sage and asked how he might attain to liberation;
and the sage, seeing he was a very weak specimen
of a creature, asked him : ' Have you ever told a
lie ? ' And that young man was shocked and
horrified as he answered in the negative. Then
said the sage : ' Learn to tell a lie and to do it well;
that is the first step.' And on my part I should
say to Mrs Burton : ' Learn to love and to do it
well, in order to develop your love-nature; and
learn not to mind what the world says as the conse-

quence, in order to kill out your vanity and develop your moral courage.' Strange doctrines from the mundane point of view, if you like; but from the healing point of view, invaluable."

But, in spite of what Moreward regarded as the fatal gravity of the case, with his untiring patience and good nature he was prepared to visit Mrs Burton again, and make another effort in the direction of her emancipation. And so some ten days later we presented ourselves once more at her door.

"Mrs Burton is out, sir," replied the maid to my inquiry; "but she is expected back soon, and Miss Mabel and Miss Iris are at home."

We accordingly entered, and were received by the two vivacious twins, with whom I was really more closely acquainted than with their mother. They were, in fact, as easy to "know well" as their parent was hard to know, for they represented a certain type of modern young lady almost devoid of reticence. Among their many traits, such a thing as parental respect did not exist, except as a convenience put on when the parent was present, and then removed immediately she was out of sight. They frankly informed their friends "that mother was a great nuisance," and, if the truth be told, I think they regarded her as an unpleasant joke rather than anything else.

After a warm and vivacious welcome, in which they both talked at once, Miss Mabel (I think it was Mabel, they are both so much alike) informed us that " Mother was paying calls. She hates paying calls, and loves doing things she hates; that is mother all over—funny taste isn't it? I wish *we* liked doing things we hated, then we shouldn't have to hear from morning till night how selfish we were."

Moreward laughed. " Unselfishness," he said affably, " by no means goes hand in hand with martyrdom, though it is difficult to make people realise the fact."

" Hurray," said Miss Iris, clapping her hands; " we've found another kindred soul."

" What an adorable person," whispered Miss Mabel to me.

" Some people have got into their heads that blessed is the uncheerful giver," added Moreward, smiling.

" That's it," said Miss Iris; " pull the long face, and do everything as if it hurt, and everybody thinks one a saint. Give *me* a saint with a round face like a cherry."

" How *is* your mother, by the way? " I remarked. " Somebody told me she had a bad cold."

" Oh, yes," they replied simultaneously, Miss Iris leaving the rest of the sentence to her sister.

" Mother thought she was very seedy for a day or two—just to get a bit of sympathy, you know; however, she's all right again now, and very busy with uncheerful giving " (they both laughed), " bazaars, and all that sort of thing."

" I've heard wonderful things about *you*," said Miss Iris, turning to Moreward. " People say you turn the world upside down."

He bowed, laughing. " It is easy to turn the world upside down in theory," he said, " because when a thing's round, nobody can tell which side up it is, can they? "

Miss Iris jumped up and poked the fire, by way of giving vent to her latent vivacity. Moreward looked so contrastingly calm, that I remembered my sister's remark about monkeys and the Zoo.

" I see you take life happily," he said; " a happy person shows much wisdom."

" Well, somebody has to be happy," she replied. " Mother takes life gloomily, so *we* have to make up for *her*. Mother seems to think everything is wrong; we think everything is right—it makes existence so much more fun."

" There was a very wise man," he observed, " who said life is too serious to take seriously. Perhaps you realise the profundity of that axiom, so live up to it."

"Perhaps we do," she said. "I suppose he meant life is so dull, one has to stick the fun into it oneself."

"I see you are very perspicacious," he replied; "that is pretty much what it *does* mean."

"One good mark for Iris," she exclaimed gleefully.

"Have some more tea," said Miss Mabel to me, "and lots more to eat; we believe in nursery teas here, not in the strawberry to a cow sort of thing you get when paying a call."

But, as I had been steadily indulging all the time (Mrs Burton being out and hence her critical eye not upon me), I refrained from any further consumption of her dainties. And then all at once she entered the room, and I must add that the vivacity of the twins all of a sudden subsided like a pricked balloon. What is more, after they had sat glum for a little time, they both, more or less surreptitiously, retired from the room.

Mrs Burton entertained us, or rather did *not* entertain us, with a few conventional remarks of no interest to anybody, and then Moreward contrived to draw the conversation into more useful topics.

"Your daughters," he said with appreciation, "have been making things very pleasant for us in your absence; they are both witty and amusing."

" I fear you flatter them," she replied. " Personally, I feel it would be a great advantage if they could develop a little more seriousness."

"That will come of itself as they grow older," he said; " at present they have so much love in their nature that they are happy without being serious, as you put it. Love replaces the seriousness."

" Love? " questioned Mrs Burton.

" Like most twins," he explained, " there is great unity between them; and, strange as it may sound, their love for one another, which has existed for many lives, is the cause of their being twins in this incarnation." (He cast a look at me, with that twinkle in his eyes I knew so well. It said, " Now we'll shock her.")

" What a funny idea," remarked Mrs Burton, with disapproving incredulity.

" Does it strike you as funny?" he asked sympathetically. And yet is it so strange, when we reflect that love is simply the principle of attraction and that the whole universe hangs together through love? That is why love is the most important thing in the world."

Mrs Burton made no attempt to follow this idea, which she obviously regarded as " sloppy." " I fear I *can't* see much love about them," she observed regretfully; " they seem to me sometimes deplorably selfish, and I am often obliged to tell them so; they have not learnt that sense of duty which makes it desirable to do good works."

Moreward obviously suppressed a chuckle.

" Do you think good works are good?" he asked soothingly, " if performed merely as a duty? "

" I do not see much merit in doing a thing one likes," she answered reprovingly.

" Blessed is the cheerful giver," I said, with mischief in me.

" Which means," he explained, before Mrs Burton had time to answer, " that good works done without love are of meagre value, whereas the very feeling of love towards others is a good work in itself, being as food to a hungry soul."

Mrs Burton looked as if she thought the world an ungrateful place. Here was a man telling her, as it were, that all the good works she had done were of meagre value, whereas, in *her* estimation, the very fact of her feeling tedium in the doing of them was an added merit.

" You both certainly have very strange ideas," she said impotently.

" You see," explained Moreward conciliatingly, " things are not quite as they look. A human being is not merely his physical body: he has an emotional body, a mental body, and a spiritual body as well; all of these interpenetrating his physical one. In throwing out a feeling of love, to a person, you are actually enriching those subtler bodies; in merely doing good works, so-called, you are only assisting the transient part of him, for those subtle bodies are more or less eternal, while the gross body dies in but a few years. To feed the starving material man, I grant you, is practical; but to feed the inner eternal man is still more practical, for the more lasting the effect of a thing the more practical it is. And, although to give money is to give a portion of one's belongings, and is not without merit, yet to love is to give a portion of one's self. That is why he who can love truly is never really selfish."

Mrs Burton could find no rejoinder to this, so looked at the speaker wonderingly and kept silence.

" Selfishness and unselfishness are words bandied about by people." he pursued, " with very hazy ideas as to their meanings. Selfishness is the centring of one's mind on oneself; to love is not only to centre the mind on someone other than self, but at the same time to give a portion of that self to the being to whom one directs that love. The most practical of all good deeds, therefore, is to give our labour and money and ourselves combined. And what is more, in doing this we reap happiness, for to love is to feel the most pleasant of all sensations."

Mrs Burton took refuge in that pseudo good-natured sort of laughter which some people resort to when they do not agree with a thing, yet have no ready argument to refute it. In other words, she laughed because she was somewhat embarrassed for a lack of words to uphold her own convictions, if convictions they could be called.

"I see you think me and my ideas a little mad," he said with perfect good humour, "and yet I assure you they are older than Christianity itself and commonplacely sane. To be quite frank with you, Mrs Burton," he pursued more briskly, "I gathered from our conversation the other day that you are not inherently happy. Now *I* am, and the first thing a truly happy person desires is that others should be happy as well; it is quite a commonplace wish—as commonplace as recommending a sick man a certain doctor because one has been cured by him oneself."

Mrs Burton laughed a little, as she remarked, "You are very kind." But his intentions and manner seemed so solicitous and sincere that she genuinely felt a touch of gratitude, and could not help showing it.

"And what is your prescription?" she asked.

"More fresh air," he said simply. "Around us all are wonderful planes of happiness, perceptible to those who open the windows of the mind, and shut

out to those who keep them closed." He paused
for a moment, and pondered, " The shut mind is
bound to feel unhappy, for in a small area a number
of human sorrows may be herded together ; but
go out into the infinite and eternal, and how far
apart are all human sorrows then? It is like getting out of a slum into the vastness of the sky and
ocean : once out there, the divine indifference
comes into the soul, and then all criticism, all
regarding everything as wrong, falls away, because
the feeling is cramped and childish : to criticise
seems not worth the doing. Your trouble, dear
friend," he added, laying his hand on her hand for
a moment, " is that you regard everything as
wrong (even your daughters' lightheartedness).
Reverse the process, and regard everything as right,
and await the result. I assure you, you will never
regret it."

He got up to go, shaking her warmly by the
hand, and, although she said very little, I felt he
had made a certain impression, and that perhaps
one day she would tire of her self-made prison, and
come to regard him as right.

CHAPTER XVI

THE CONVERSION OF FLOSSY MACDONALD

I CALLED late one evening at my friend's house, and found him at home, but in the company of a woman who obviously belonged to that class whose virtue is said to be easy. And for the moment I confess I was taken aback, especially when I reflected on a certain indecisive manner on the part of Moreward's factotum as I asked was his master at home. Indeed, had not the prompt words, "This is Miss Macdonald; do sit down, dear friend, I am so glad to see you," called me to my senses, I think I should have stared at them both in some embarrassment.

"Flossy," he said to her, "you have often heard me speak of Mr Broadbent; well, here he is."

She smiled at me a little shyly, then turned an obviously loving gaze on Moreward.

We talked a few pleasantries for the space of about ten minutes, and then Flossy got up to go, Moreward accompanying her to the front door, where they lingered in murmured conversation for a few moments. He looked at me when he returned with an amused smile. "The obvious is not always the correct," was his remark. "As to Flossy, she is a psychological study of the most interesting nature : I would not have missed meeting her for a great deal."

" The obvious is so far correct that she is in love with you," I said tentatively.

" Well—yes," he answered with modesty, " perhaps she does do me that honour. And after all, love is a useful factor when it is a question of leading someone along the path of soul-evolution."

I was not quite clear as to his meaning.

" If a girl is in love with a man," he explained, " she will do more for that man than if she were not. Let his influence be a good one, and he will exalt her all the more easily. To have a woman in love with one, my friend, affords a golden opportunity for doing good—even if one cannot return that love in exactly the same way."

" Are you, then, endeavouring to lead Miss Flossy back into the path of virtue ? " I asked. " Can you persuade her to give up her present sort of life ? "

" She will need no persuasion when the time is ripe," he said; " she will give it up of her own accord."

" That seems rather curious," I reflected; " that sort of women don't as a rule."

" That is owing to two causes," was his reply, " the most serious being the intolerance of society. Society does not permit these women to give up their sad vocations; once a girl goes wrong, by regarding her as a pariah, it puts the most effective

stop to her ever coming right again. Apart from
being childish in itself, lack of forgiveness is often
the worst policy. To cure an evil, one must forgive it; in that society fails to forgive a so-called
' fallen woman,' it leaves her no choice between
starvation and the streets."

" And the other cause? " I asked.

" The other cause is much rarer, though more
obvious—namely, disinclination for chastity."

" And Flossy? " I asked.

" Flossy comes into the latter category," he said,
smiling indulgently, " and yet, all the same, she has
a fine soul—and she has loved much."

I became keenly interested, and asked him to tell
me about her, and in what way he was setting about
her conversion.

And it turned out that Flossy's nature was such
that she kept a widowed aunt and some young
cousins on her earnings; she also tried to exercise a
good influence on her clients—strange though it
may sound—persuading them with a certain gentle
womanly oratory to give up excessive drinking in
some cases, and to be less brutal in others, and so
on and so forth; in short, realising her vocation was
relatively speaking an evil one, she endeavoured to
put as much good into it as she was able, and,
according to Moreward, she succeeded.

" Flossy," he remarked after relating the foregoing to me, " is a splendid example of that rare
principle of utilising one's vices in order to acquire
virtues. If more people realised the excellence of
that principle, they would not waste so much useless
energy in remorse over weaknesses they find difficulty in being rid of; on the contrary, they would
bring so many virtues into the area of their particular vice that finally the vice would be ousted
altogether. That is why I said Flossy would nee 1
no persuasion to give up her unpleasant vocation."

" You are the most practical moralist I have ever
met," I exclaimed with admiration.

" And yet the world would call me an immoral-
ist," he said smiling. " You see, the trouble is,
that although virtue is said to be its own reward,
few people know how to acquire either the virtue
or the reward; their idea is, simply to kill out their
feelings—a process so unalluring that few wish to
practise it—whereas they ought to *transmute* their
feelings instead. Kill out a feeling, and there is
nothing but tedium left; transmute it, and you
transmute it into joy. Even the killing-out process is seldom a success, for the war is usually made
on the gratification of the desire instead of on the
desire itself. A man has only overcome the drink
habit when he no longer desires to drink, not when
he merely refrains from drinking. Now, a lower

desire can only be overcome by replacing it with a
higher one, the higher desire being in reality pro-
ductive of greater happiness than the lower. You,
for instance, prefer to talk philosophy with me here
than to sit in the Carlton every night till twelve
o'clock drinking champagne. In one sense you
renounce drinking for philosophy, but for the
simple reason that philosophy is more attractive:
the renunciation is therefore not painful."

"But I thought the whole point of renunciation
was its painfulness?" I inferred.

"Only spurious renunciation is painful," he
answered; "*true* renunciation is always utterly
pain*less*. And why? Because painful renunciation merely means renouncing the action, but not
the desire, whereas painless renunciation means
being rid of the desire itself, because it has lost all
its attractiveness. Just as love is more attractive
than hatred, happiness than misery, so is spirituality
more attractive than vice. In short, let a man once
taste of genuine good, and he loses all interest in
evil."

"But you spoke of *transmuting* one's feelings?"
I questioned; "but you can't transmute drinking."

He laughed. "I did not mean that simile to
be carried further," was his reply; "transmuting
can only be applied to certain activities, and
especially the feelings I spoke of. Now, the world

wrongly looks upon feelings and love-passions as inherently bad. That is erroneous; feelings are good just *because* you can transmute them : people with no feelings at all are furthest from the ' Kingdom ' than anybody, for, if you can't feel anything at all, you can't feel bliss; moreover, you have nothing to transmute into bliss. As to Flossy, it is just because she can feel that she is far nearer to spiritual emancipation than the most virtuous person who has never felt anything in his life. Virtues which are purely negative are not virtues. Could one talk of the virtue of a stone? "

" And may I ask how you have set to work with Flossy? " I questioned.

" I have started from above downwards," he answered a little cryptically, " not *vice-versa*, as many people do. I have not said, ' Give up your vices, then I will try to show you how to be spiritual.' I have tried to show her how *to be* spiritual, so that her vices might drop away from her of their own accord."

But the short story of Flossy's emancipation is best told as I got it later on from Flossy herself. When I decided to write this book I approached her, and the following is what she related, for Moreward had already left London.

Flossy Macdonald, although of quite humble origin, had an inherent touch of refinement which

showed itself both in her manners and speech. Her
mother and father were both very devout Wes-
leyans—so devout and so narrow at the same time
that from her childhood they had subjected her to
such a strict religious discipline that the very name
of religion had almost become abhorrent to her,
for they had contrived to make religion a synonym
for abysmal gloom. Flossy was of a passionate
nature, and evidently of quite a different temperament from her two parents, so that about the age
of eighteen she fell a victim to an unscrupulous
man, who not only deserted her, but deserted her
with a child to bring up and no means of sustenance
whatever. Her parents, looking upon her character as inherently vicious—having not a glimmer
of understanding concerning such matters—cast
her without the slightest hesitation forth from their
little home, and, after a time of struggle and utter
misery, she found herself—as so many others do—
walking the streets. She had, however, an aunt,
who endeavoured with the utmost kindness to
assist her and to persuade her parents (but with no
success) to soften their attitude. This aunt lived
in respectable but abject poverty, and, although she
wished to extend a widow's mite of hospitality to
her niece, Flossy was too noble to take advantage
of it, but, as Moreward related, repaid the intention a thousandfold later on. It seems that after

her period of great misery, a certain amount of
good luck—if there is such a thing—drifted her
way, and it was during this particular time that she
and Moreward came together one late summer
evening.

"I remember it all so well," she told me. "I
was just near the Marble Arch at the time, and I
saw him coming along. So I said something to
him, and he smiled at me—ah! what a smile he
has!—and began to ask me all sorts of questions
about myself and my life. Somehow, he was quite
different from anybody I had ever come across; he
seemed to take such an interest, and then he treated
me with as much respect as if I had been a lady—
that was the extraordinary part of it. We went
into the park at his suggestion, and we sat down
there, overlooking Park Lane, and then he just
talked to me all the time : such wonderful things
he told me that I really began to love him then and
there. We must have sat talking for an hour or
more—how well I remember it all—and then he
asked me where I lived, and said he would come
home with me for just a little while.

"Then it all seemed so strange. When we got to
my place, he simply sat in a chair opposite to me
and went on talking, talking, talking—always wonderful things—till about one o'clock, when he got
up to go. 'You have plenty of lovers,' he said ;

' what you want is a friend.   Now, men come to
you for pleasure, don't they?   Well, I have come
for pleasure, too, but it is of a different sort from
theirs.   I am a solitary man, and I like a nice
friend to talk to and to take an interest in.   But
you have to live, and with you, like many others,
time is money ' (he put a ten-pound note on the
mantlepiece), ' so, one of the great pleasures I shall
get out of this is to think that my tired little friend
will have a good night's rest.'

"I looked at him, so surprised.   'I couldn't
take it,' I said, ' I really couldn't.'   Then he took
one of my hands in his, and he stroked it with his
other one, as if he wanted to persuade me.   'I am
very sensitive about some things,' he said, ' and if
you won't take it you will place me in a dreadful
position.'

"But I couldn't bring myself to take it, and told
him so.   And then he looked so disappointed that
I gave in.   And after that he seemed so happy
again I was awfully glad about it.   And fancy, he
asked me to lunch the next day at his house.
Wasn't it wonderful?   And oh, he has been so
good to me.   Why has he gone?" she said passionately; "and will he ever come back?"

I told her I hoped he would, to reassure her, and
then I asked her to relate some more about it all.

"Well, I saw a lot of him after that," she went

on, " and, of course, I was in love with him; but
I don't know whether you understand us creatures.
I never wanted anything from *him*—it would have
seemed a sort of sacrilege (I think that's the word,
isn't it?). I know he never wanted anything from
me. Oh, I realise I'm a very passionate girl, but
somehow it doesn't go along with that sort of love.
If I could just hold his hand or stroke his hair, I
was quite happy. It was just heaven to sit close
to him and to hear him talk and teach me wonderful things. He's gone now, but he gave me something that nothing can take away. Besides, he
helped me to get out of it all and to make me
respectable."

" But I understand," said I " that he never
asked you to give it up? "

" That's just the wonderful part of it," she
returned; " he just taught me things that made me
want to give it up of my own accord. Oh, don't
think me a saint," she hastened to add. " I am not
a hypocrite, and I'd do things for love even now,
but I'll never do them for money again—never.
He used to say, ' Love purifies everything as long
as you don't go and get people into trouble, though
of course, if you don't mind about that, it simply
means you don't really love them '—at least,
that's what he used to say. But he said that one
day even when one *was* in love, one didn't want

passion any more. And then he used to tell me about Jesus and the woman of Samaria who had got rid of five husbands and who was living with a man who wasn't her husband. He said that Jesus taught her lovely spiritual things, but He never asked her to give up the man she was living with first, because He could tell she loved him, and that made it all right really. And then he taught me to forgive the man who got me into trouble, because he said it was really silly and like a child to be hating him all the time, and did harm to myself. Of course, he said that man had never really loved me, because, if he had, he'd surely have put me before his own pleasure—you know what I mean— but then, he said, that was why I ought to try and not hate him all the more, but pity him instead, because one day he would have to pay up for it all—poor devil. And I tell you, when I gave up hating him, I felt quite different, and so happy. And I gave up being angry with mother and father as well, and everybody, and it felt just lovely never to feel angry any more. Somehow it seems so silly to hate people and get one's monkey up about them, now. . . . Ah! what a wonderful man he is."

" But how did you manage to give up the life?" I asked.

" Haven't you heard? " she said with child-like astonishment.   " Didn't he ever tell you? "

I told her I had heard nothing.

"Why, don't you know he settled two hundred pounds a year on me for life before he went away?"

"He never told me," I said with genuine surprise.

"Ah! that's just like him," she exclaimed with enthusiasm, and yet with a touch of sadness. "He went about doing good to everybody, but he never let on—that was him all over."

"Tell me some more," I said. "I want all I can get for my book. What else did he teach you?"

She thought for a moment, dreamily looking on the ground. "I'm not much good at telling stories," she answered with simplicity, "but somehow there are times when I could talk about him all day, and those happy times. And yet they were not *always* happy: I used to get awfully blue some days; the sort of life I was leading used to get dreadfully on my mind, and I used to ask him whatever would happen to one like me when I was dead. Oh, that was an awful thought to have to live with. And then he would comfort me by telling me there was so much good in me, that in the end the other wouldn't count much; besides, he says, there are much worse things than doing what I did, which a lot of people don't seem to think bad at all. He used to say, a man who could prostitute his talents (those were his exact words) to get a lot of money just for himself was far worse than I was, because, he said, your mind was a far more sacred thing than your body, and your talents still more sacred than your mind even; but there were thousands of people doing this, and nobody thought a thing about it. Aye, how comforted I used to feel, especially when he just used to smile and say : ' Don't you worry, my child; you'll get out of this sort of life you're leading almost as easy as a butterfly gets out of its cocoon.' And fancy, he was quite right, and one day I felt I would rather live in a garret and sew all day than go on with it, in spite of its good dinners and music halls and plenty of fun. Yes, I gave it up, even when I was having a run of good luck, because I had caught sight of another sort of life—you know, in my imagination like—which seemed to me so much happier and better; just lovely, in fact."

" And what did you do then ? " I asked.

" Well, I just thought of my aunt and the kids, and I hung on a bit longer for their sakes—that's how it was." She paused for a minute, and then added sadly : " It was an awful day, the day he told me he would soon have to leave London, and go far away; and oh, Mr Broadbent, how I dreaded having to say good-bye. I've never been able to say good-bye to people : it nearly breaks my heart, and him of all others.   All the same, he used to comfort me wonderfully, and tell me even if his body was the other end of nowhere, he could still come to me and see me whenever he wanted, although I might not be able to see him.   And then, when he went, what did he do?   Why, he just didn't say good-bye, to spare me, but wrote me the loveliest letter instead, and sent me a beautiful gold cross to wear always.   Of course, I cried dreadfully much, but not half so much as if he had come himself to give me a last kiss.   But the wonderful part was, two hours after, I got the letter from the lawyers to tell me I was to have the two hundred a year."

"And does he write to you now?" I asked.

"Oh, yes, he writes sometimes.   And, isn't it wonderful, he knows all about everything I'm doing without me telling him; and, oh, I know he's in the room so often; whenever I feel I want him very badly, he's there.   God bless him for ever!"

And this ended the story of Flossy's conversion: a conversion achieved in such a generous and original way.   And as I made my way home I wondered how many more 'Flossys' there were in the world, and understood in a way I had never realised before, why the sinners are nearer to Heaven than the Pharisees.

CHAPTER XVII

THE PRELUDE TO THE STORY

I HAD been out of London for six weeks, visiting friends as was my custom during the summer months, and so I had not seen Moreward for some time, nor even heard from him. As might be expected, however, he was the first friend I called upon on my return, and although I called several times in vain, I finally found him late one evening, and in the midst of a litter of papers and documents, which had evidently just arrived in a large box.

His greeting was tinctured with that true and genuine affection which was so characteristic of his entire personality; in other words, he embraced me. "I will not ask," he said, "whether you have enjoyed your visits; I know you have, for I have been conscious of many of your happiest moments."

Then he pointed to a litter of papers. "My daughter has passed over, and these are certain documents of mine which I left with her; they have just arrived from Italy."

I was about to express my condolences with considerable warmth of sympathy, but his smile nipped them in the bud, and made them seem as insignificant and childish as the giving of a sticky sweetmeat on the part of a two-year-old to one of its

elders. This man was, in fact, beyond any necessity for sympathy, for to die evidently meant as
little to him as to go to sleep; not even death could
perturb his eternal serenitude.   And so I made no
further attempt to talk about his bereavement—if
so, under the circumstances it can be called—and
entered upon various topics of conversation of
interest to us both instead; while he, on his part,
gave himself solely to me, as the phrase goes,
investing his whole manner with that sympathy
and attentiveness he knew so well how to adopt.

We must have conversed for some two hours,
when he looked at his watch, and remarked, if I
didn't mind, he would go on with the sorting of his
papers, as certain legal matters had to be gone into
without delay.   But he added, " As the task is
more or less a mechanical one, you will enliven it
by your conversation; at any rate, don't go home
yet awhile."

Nor had I any intention of going home, for to
be once more in the company of Moreward after
so long an absence was to enjoy a spiritual bath—
if I may so express myself—I was glad to prolong.
Nevertheless, our conversational faculties had come
for the time being to an end, or at most grown
intermittent and tempered with long pauses.   I
had, in fact, occasionally relapsed into what were
very near brown studies, as I watched my com-

panion bending over his papers, a task which was the aftermath of death and loss. And yet his face was as calm and untroubled as ever it had been, nor, as I came to reflect on the matter, had it grown one month older in appearance since the time I met its remarkable owner some ten years ago. Then he had looked thirty-five, not a day older, though the thoughtfulness of his face had suggested the wisdom of greater maturity. But had not that unforgettable stout lady said he was well over fifty-five, and now add ten years to that, and here was this imposing riddle of a man, sixty-five years of age, yet still looking well under forty. And I thought to myself, surely it can't be true, and that good lady must have been the victim of idle gossip. And then even this possible solution was knocked on the head, for I reflected further: if he was thirty-five then, he is now forty-five, and this seems to me almost as impossible, taking his appearance into account, as if he were sixty-five. And finally I got into a perfect maze of numerical speculations, leading me to wonder why I never sought to set the matter at rest long ago, simply by putting a direct question.

Then all of a sudden my companion gave a little laugh. " After all, my friend," he said, " I would give it up; you know it wouldn't profit you *very* much if you *did* know my age."

" What? " I said, laughing a little shamefacedly.
" You have been aware of my thoughts? "

" Well," he replied, " you know if you put as
much vim into them as all that, what else can I
do? Especially as all the time they were directed
towards myself. Why! if such concentratedness
had been attached to a loftier subject, my good
friend, you would have achieved something great.
However," and he laughed again a little to himself, as he resumed his work.

" All the same," I said, I think you must
praise my utter lack of curiosity, considering,
somehow or other, I have always refrained from
asking your age before."

" Oh, certainly you shall have the palm for your
discretion," he answered, smiling, "but, you know,
there is a little method known to occultists to prevent people from asking awkward questions—for
their own good."

" But," I urged, " what could it matter if I *did*
know your age? "

" Those who have no secrets need tell no lies,"
he said, " to adjust an old proverb to our present
purpose. In other words, I don't want to place
you in the position of having to tell a falsehood,
should anyone question you respecting my age.
The fact is, as you know, I fear the hampering
influences of notoriety. Besides, there would

hardly be one old, elderly, or trifle-faded lady, who would leave me in peace, though my secret were practically useless to her. It is hardly so simple as rubbing cold cream on the face every night before going to bed, and yet it is more natural. Let a man but lead a certain sort of life, the life indicated by the rules of the Order, and prolongation of youth accrues quite naturally of its own accord."

I stroked my iron-grey hair, and wished I knew those precious rules and how to live up to them. But aloud I said, " Well, it is as I expected, because after all I hardly think a totally unvain man would bother whether he looked young or old, let alone take infinite pains to appear the former— like a society woman."

And Moreward merely smiled. Then suddenly he tossed a manuscript towards me. " One of my few literary efforts," he remarked, " and written in my extreme youth. I had quite forgotten my daughter possessed it." The ink had faded to sepia, the paper on which it was written was musty; it must have been fifty years old if a day.

" You see, I rely on your discretion, my friend," he observed, " for I am aware you are regarding it as a rather tell-tale document."

" More thought reading," I said, laughing.

" Oh, come; deduction might account for that," he corrected.

" Well, never mind," I said; " but may I read it? "

He nodded. " But you will throw it in the waste-paper basket afterwards."

" Oh, surely not," I objected.

He laughed. " Well, if you want to read it, do so now, and then return it."

And then I read one of the most poetic things I have ever encountered in the domain of occult literature. There was a compelling flow and musicality about the language which spoke direct to the soul, as well as a certain quaintness of phraseology. Indeed, as pure sound, it had a flavour of that exquisite fragment of Edgar Allan Poe, called, if I remember rightly, " Silence, a Fable," but the contents were entirely different, of course, and its expressiveness totally original. It also seemed to me as if the writer must have known Sanscrit, or at any rate Sanscrit literature to a considerable extent, for it was tempered here and there with oriental parable. In fact, the impression on me was so great that, as I came to the end, I thought how deplorable it was that a man with such literary powers should be content to refrain from using them to his utmost. Indeed, such a thing totally surpassed my understanding. I had finished it in about five minutes, and it had lifted me, like music often does, strangely out of myself, so much

so that for several minutes I said nothing. I was
merely sensible that I entered into a thought-realm
I had never entered before. And I felt suddenly
possessed of ideas so lofty that it seemed almost
impossible I could think them of my own accord.
Moreover, they came into my mind with a profusion, but at the same time a clearness and intensity,
which astounded me.

Then it was Moreward who broke the silence.
" Come," he said, " that is enough for the present."

I looked at him askance. My soul and body
felt absolutely jubilant and vitalised. " Wonderful! " I exclaimed. " It lifted me into a new
spiritual world."

He laughed. " Not quite," he said.

" How, not quite? " I asked. " You do talk
in enigmas sometimes."

" You flatter my literary capacities," he observed,
smiling, "but they are not as great as you suppose."

But I objected. " My dear friend, I've never
had such ideas as after reading that manuscript; it
simply worked magic."

" That is just your delusion," he said simply.
" Suppose it were possible for you to read *my*
thoughts? "

" But it isn't," I returned.

" Not if I directed them towards you, and you
were in a receptive mood? " he insinuated.

I looked at him, astonished. " Ah, I hadn't thought of that."

He laughed gently. " You see," he continued, " the manuscript *made* you receptive."

" Splendid! " I cried enthusiastically. " But for Heaven's sake do that again, and often—the effect is indescribable."

" Ah, but that would be to spoil you," he objected smiling.

" To spoil me? "

" Well, there must be a good reason."

" Oh, then we must certainly make a good reason," I declared with renewed enthusiasm.

His face became more serious. " The projecting of thoughts," he explained, " requires a certain energy; that energy with us is not absolutely limitless, therefore we must not waste it, but see that it is spent in such a way as to ensure the largest possible results. A moment ago, you lamented the fact that I did not write more. Very good; but there are ways of ' writing ' without putting pen to paper; that is to say, ways of writing *through others;* putting ideas into their heads and leaving them to elaborate those ideas and set them in a framework of their own choosing. Now, if you were to write a story, for instance. . . ."

I began to comprehend. " You would impress the ideas upon me, you mean? "

" Precisely : that is, I would do so now and then, and you would work them out in your own way."

" But would you have to be present ? " I asked.

He smiled patiently. " I wonder you put that question with the knowledge you have acquired."

" It *was* foolish," I admitted, sensible of the gentle rebuke. " But how can I hold myself receptive ? "

" Partly by an effort of will," he replied, " which you could greatly aid by reading something of a certain mantramistic value, as you did a moment ago."

I looked at him questioningly.

" The sound of a certain combination of words," he explained, " has a magical value, and so can awaken receptive or clairvoyant states. Why, there are certain words so sacred and so powerful in their effect that I dare not tell them to one person in ten millions. However, that is more or less another matter. But take poetry, for instance: has it ever struck you why a poem which you realise contains fine ideas, makes no effect, and seems to fall short of its object altogether ? "

I admitted it had never struck me to ask the reason.

" Well, the reason is because its wording, or music, so to say, has no mantramistic value, and therefore does not touch the soul. I must add,

however, that the way people read poetry aloud
destroys its magical value, even if it possesses one :
for the majority of persons either read verse as
they read the newspaper, or else as if they were
announcing somebody's death. The fact is, poetry
ought to be almost intoned, and when this is done
properly the results may be considerable. . . . Now,
that manuscript you read contained an attempt on
my part to compose a mantramistic prose; hence its
effect on you."

" But," I interrupted, " why don't you write
more ? Surely it were better than to use me,
although I appreciate the honour."

He smiled. " We seldom write," he said;
" time is too precious, and we have other things to
do. As I already implied, we prefer to deal with
ideas solely, and not with penmanship. To help
others to help Humanity is our object, and in this
particular matter we chose to give that help
indirectly—through poets and authors and dramatists." He paused for a moment, then he said :
" So now, my friend, earn the right to receive the
help of the Brothers by helping Humanity yourself. The time has come when an occult story of
a particular nature is needed, and since ingratitude
is not one of our weaknesses, assist us and we will
assist you."

" You mean," I corrected, " *you* will assist me, and perhaps others as well? But I can't go and foist something on to the public, making them believe *I* have produced it, when all the time I have been stealing, or I should say accepting, *your* ideas."

He left his papers and came and stood in front of me, looking down at me with his earnestly gentle eyes.   Then he said: " The wisest author leaves his own personality out of the matter altogether—he gives merely for the sake of giving, and doesn't care whether he gets praise or blame. He is anonymous, because anonymity is, for a certain species of moral philosophical literature, the most expedient course, precluding all prejudice on the part of the public at large. Don't you see, for instance, that if the Bishop of London writes a book, all the Church of England adherents will read it, and not one Roman Catholic, whereas if nobody knew that the Bishop of London had anything to do with the matter, it is possible that ' everybody ' might read it."

" How marvellously practical you are," I exclaimed enthusiastically.

" Well, be that as it may, you see my point? But," he continued, " that is not all, for every author has his admirers and detractors, and these read and avoid his works as the case may be. And

yet what about the contents of the works themselves—the ideas, the arguments, everything?
Why, their effect is always flavoured by the fame
and name of the author, or conversely his absence
of fame and name. ' Ah,' thinks Mrs. Smith, ' So
and So wrote that, therefore it must be all right or
all wrong '; for, trite as the saying is, humanity in
mass is like a flock of sheep: it follows the dog it
thinks barks the loudest."

He sat down in a chair opposite me, placing the
tips of his fingers together and his elbows on the
arm-rests. " True altruism," he observed, meditatively, " must ever be divorced from vanity, and
the more this maxim is carried out the greater will
be the result. For there is yet another factor in
the matter! Inspiration, which is really recep-
tivity, is a thing of the heart, and the purer the
instrument the greater the inspiration. Now, the
type of soul who can say, ' What does it signify if
my name is attached to my work, for in reality the
work is not mine, but I am merely a medium,' this
type of soul ever calls to himself the noblest ideas.
And so, my beloved friend, your difficulty is
solved, and you need have no qualms in using *our*
ideas, if you will adopt the expedient of anonymity.
And I assure you, you will be well repaid for your
renunciation in other ways."

" I shall be repaid by the pleasant feeling of gratitude," I said.

" And you forgive me for having read your thoughts, seeing I had a good object? "

" Indeed, I do."

*   *   *   *

And so this is how I came to write the story which constitutes Part II of these impressions, and which I wrote after Justin Moreward Haig's departure, thus receiving his ideas despite the intervenention of thousands of miles of space : a fact, going to demonstrate at least the possibility of telepathy—if nothing else.

CHAPTER XVIII

THE DEPARTURE OF JUSTIN MOREWARD HAIG

AND now I reluctantly come to relate the manner in which my most precious of all friends left London for activities in another part of the world: activities of which I cannot speak, however, for I am requested not to do so, and that reason is a sufficient one.

From the first moment I met Justin Moreward Haig, I regarded him as an extraordinary man; but if our meeting forcibly impressed me, our parting impressed me even more: for it showed me a side of his personality I had not perceived hitherto, although, from our various discussions on occult subjects, I was fully persuaded it existed. It will be remembered that the letter written to me by my sister and inserted in this book referred to Moreward's extensive travels in India and elsewhere and the wonders he had seen in that most romantic and mystic empire. And it was evident from that letter he had acquired secret knowledge over there for which only the very few were ripe. And yet I recollect he remarked to me one day that it was a great mistake to suppose that Initiates and Adepts in occult wisdom existed only in India; as a matter of truth, there were adepts all over the world, England included.

I asked him why we knew so little about them if that was the case, and I remember he smiled that indulgent and slightly amused smile of his, and replied that it usually takes a genius to fully comprehend another genius, and that only a very advanced occultist could recognise an adept when he saw one, for no person of such high attainment either advertised himself or was advertised by circumstances. " Your butcher and your baker," he explained, " only bow down before a king because they know he is a king; let him but walk the streets incognito, and nobody would take any notice of him. I am personally acquainted with a man who has been alive three hundred years, strange though it may seem, but, as he looks more like forty than three hundred, only a very few people are any the wiser when they see him. And that is just his protection, for if people really knew the truth, he would be subjected to an amount of curiosity which would render his whole life a burden, and considerably hamper his highly important activities."

" If a man could manage to live for so long," I said, " I take it he could manage to perform other miracles, so-called ? "

" He certainly could, but he doesn't," was the answer.

"But if he could convince humanity of some great truth by doing so, it seems to me he ought to," I urged.

Again he smiled with that patient indulgence which showed he had heard my observation all too often. "You are apt to confound mere belief and spirituality," he said; "an exhibition of phenomena can never make people spiritual. I daresay Mr Paderewski could play blindfold with the greatest ease, but by showing off in that manner could he ever make an unmusical person musical? The answer is obvious. You forget that to gratify idle curiosity is to gratify one's own vanity. Would it not be extremely *infra dig.* for Paderewski to play blindfold? Hence it is equally *infra dig.* for an Adept to perform miracles so-called."

"But Jesus Christ is said to have done so," I insisted.

"The Nazarene Adept never performed miracles without an adequate reason. He cured because people were ill; He materialised food because people were hungry; He calmed the tempest because His disciples were afraid; but He neither ' showed off ' nor gratified idle curiosity, neither did another Adept, Apolonius of Tyana."

I asked him if anyone could acquire the necessary knowledge to work miracles?

" Yes, and no," was his answer. " Yes, because
it is only essential to possess the right qualifications; no, because most people cannot be bothered
to acquire them.   You yourself are on the way to
acquire them, and perhaps in a later incarnation you
will have progressed far enough to perform miracles
if you wish to do so."

" And you? " I asked.   " Can you materialise
things? "

" You ask me a straight question," he replied,
smiling, " and I cannot very well tell a lie; but
when I answer in the affirmative, I beg you not to
mention the fact as long as I am in London."

I promised absolute discretion.

" Of course," he went on, " there is no such
thing as a miracle. We of the Brotherhood merely
utilise laws of nature which most people are not
acquainted with; that is all."

" But why is the knowledge not given forth? "
I asked.

" Because humanity is not spiritually developed
enough to use it in the right way.   Give it to
people who have not the necessary qualifications,
and they would wreck the Universe almost."

" And the qualifications are? " I asked.

" Perfect selflessness, perfect tolerance, complete
absence of vanity, absolute self-control, and all
other spiritual qualities."

" In a word, *perfection*," I said.

" Practically speaking, perfection," he assented.

" Then I am out of the running," I observed.

He laughed. " You forget you have Eternity in front of you," he said, " and therefore plenty of time."

But this conversation, if I remember rightly, took place a short time after I had made Moreward's acquaintance, and since then, what with the books he put in my hands, I have acquired knowledge which causes me to review the thing in a different light. All the same, I had enough curiosity to wish very ardently for a display of those powers which he admitted the possession of, and frequently I asked him to give me even the most trifling manifestation, but he always—though with great gentleness, refused. And then at the very moment of parting he granted my request.

He had prepared me to some extent for his departure, for he told me that the time of his stay in London was drawing to a close and that I must not expect to have him with me very much longer, as far as his physical presence was concerned, though in spirit and love we could never be separated.

Well, it happened in this way. It is a habit of mine to lock my door at night owing to the fact that I have lived for a certain period of my life in hotels. On the night in question, I had not deviated from my usual custom. Retiring to bed about midnight, and sleeping soundly for some eight hours, my first dim consciousness the following morning caused me to be aware of a most exquisite perfume of roses. It seemed, in fact, that I was dreaming of roses, and then to my great astonishment when I opened my eyes I found on the pillow, just by my head, a letter on which was placed a large red rose. My first thought was that I had left the door unlocked, and that my servant had quietly entered the room; but, being so unlike her to do such a thing, I began to think there must be something of deeper import in the matter. My speculations, however, were soon set at rest, for I opened the letter and began to read. It ran :—

"Beloved Friend,—By the time you receive these few lines I shall already be on my way to a place which for the time being must be nameless. My life in London is now over, and for the purpose of my own development it is essential I should retire from the outside world for a span of a few months. In future, another kind of work is allotted to me, and you and I will not be able to meet in the flesh for some time to come : though whenever you need my help, I shall be aware of the fact and shall answer to your call. I have avoided the useless

sadness of saying good-bye in person, because,
my friend, I know you possess a tender heart,
and I wish to spare you pain. Nevertheless, in
reality, there is no such thing as the parting of
souls who are truly in sympathy, for those who
love one another are nearer together, though
thousands of miles of material space intervene,
than two beings out of sympathy living in closest
proximity. Thus, in saying farewell, let us not
regard it as a parting at all, since only when love
and memory are dead can separation come into
being; but in that this love between you and me
I now realise can never die—having existed
through so many incarnations—to feel the pangs
of farewell is to feel the pangs of an illusion
rather than the joy of a reality. As to these last
few years in which we have worked so sympa·
thetically together, let me thank you for that
sympathy which has made them so truly happy,
and for that open-mindedness on your part which
has rendered it possible for me to instil into you
a little knowledge from the Brotherhood. For
it is we who thank those who *permit* us to help
them a stretch along the evolutionary pathway,
thus giving us an opportunity of doing what we
desire to do the most of all things, and not they
who need to thank us. For the rest, may things

be always well with you, and may you live neither in the past nor the future, but ever in the serene and unchanging happiness of the Great Eternal.

"Always your devoted friend,

J. M. H.

"P.S.—Do not fail to write that occult story, and I on my part shall not fail to impress on you the necessary ideas."

As soon as I had finished reading this letter, I went to my door, and found it exactly as I had left it on going to bed, namely, locked on the inside and the key in the lock. Then I realised that, at last, Moreward had granted my request and shown me an example of materialisation. For at any rate that is my personal interpretation of the incident, though others may endeavour to find a more mun dane one, regarding me as imaginative and credulous.

And that ended, needless to say, my participation in the philanthropic work of Justin Moreward Haig. Although I see him from time to time in what is known as the Astral Body, and hence am in touch with him, yet he only appears to me when I am in need of certain instruction connected with my own psychic and spiritual development; and thus, whatever his activities may be, I am in no position to follow them.

My " History," therefore, has come to its
natural end, and when I look back at it, and the
people it attempts to depict, one fact strikes me
indeed very forcibly, and I allude to the entirely
commonplace nature of all its characters, barring,
of course, the central figure himself. For their
ordinariness showed me how inherently true was
the essence of Moreward's philosophy, namely,
that " a thing is tedious or pleasant according to
what one brings to it oneself." Indeed, as he
remarked on one occasion when he had been confronted with a particularly unbending and arid type
of humanity : " The more difficult a problem is,
the more interesting it becomes; for no people
are more difficult to deal with than the essentially
ordinary ones." And that is why so large a part
of his energies was spent on Pharisees, and types of
a like nature, " the poets, artists, philosophers have
mentalities so receptive (he informed me) that they
do not need our personal contact, and the Brotherhood can impress upon their minds ideas and ideals
from a far higher plane than the physical ; but the
man in the street is entirely different : only by the
more clumsy method of conversing with him can
something be achieved." And so one of the objects
of this book is to show that, however jejune and
commonplace the externalities of life may be, he

who cares to cultivate a certain peace-inspiring point of view may shed a happiness on all around him, and by so doing bring the only true and never-to-be-taken-away happiness to his own soul.

PART II

How The Circuitous Journey came to be written has been stated in the episode headed " The Prelude to the Story," but a few words of explanation must be added. The process known as " writing through " a receptive person is one recognised by those who possess any knowledge of occultism or occult methods, but the general public is unenlightened respecting this, and probably for the most part sceptical, and, in spite of what I may relate, is likely to remain so. Scepticism, however, does not alter facts, nor can the oratory of the unseeing annihilate the convictions of those who see, for, as Mrs Besant pithily puts it, " Ignorance can never convince knowledge." But be that as it may, for those at any rate who have ears to hear, I am constrained to express my conviction that the ideas, ethical, philosophical and mystical, contained in the following pages have been impressed on me by the Initiate I may now rightly call my Master.

True it is, in some cases I may unwittingly have distorted certain of those ideas, and so " brought them through " incorrectly, but should this be, then I alone am to blame, and not he who used me as an instrument.

With regard to the " manner " adopted for the writing of the story, I was given certain instructions by Justin Moreward Haig before he finally left London.   " Let the English be quaint, flowing, and as poetical as possible," he had said, " for occult truths impress themselves more readily on the reader if they be clothed in melodious language. Also endeavour to decorate the large story by a number of smaller stories, and do not fail to be lavish with simile and parable."

Thus I have attempted to carry out these instructions to the best of my ability, and I need but mention one significant fact in addition: When Haig told a certain kind of story or discoursed on ethics, I noticed his language took on a particular sound and flow which was exceedingly striking and compelling.   Well, strange to say, as I started writing my story, I found myself unconsciously imitating that very musicality of language.   Then one day when I was particularly conscious of Haig's presence, I mentally put the question, " Did you impress on me the style of writing as well as the ideas ? "   And the answer came : " I did not actually impress it on you, but you got a certain flavour of the way I *might* write, simply because we are in such close rapport."

I

LONG ago, in a past generation, and in a distant mountainous country, there lived a rich man, Antonius by name, who had partaken of all the enjoyment his riches could offer, and then grown weary and satiated, as a child wearies of a toy which has lost all its attractiveness. And finding life unendurable by reason of the utter tedium he felt within his pleasure-wasted mind, he turned to the study of ancient books and ancient lore, endeavouring to while away the long hours in the acquirement of knowledge, living alone and seeing no one; for the visits of his former companions only disturbed him in the pursuit of his studies. So as he sat one day reading, as was his wont, in the shade of his garden, it chanced that an old beggar came through the gate, and stood before him asking for alms. And being of a kindly disposition and void of all parsimony, he drew forth his purse and gave that old beggar a handful of coins, bidding him, with a word of good cheer, go on his way, and let fortune attend him. But that old beggar, having thanked him for his unusual liberality, said, " Be not so hasty to dismiss me, O Generous One, lest I go without repaying you for what you have done; for that were ungracious indeed, since you have given me more than ever I expected to receive." So then Antonius, thinking within himself, " What

can this ignorant old beggar possess that he talks
of repayment? " smiled indulgently, and suffered
him to remain, looking at him the while askance,
and waiting for what he might have to say.   But
that old beggar smiled indulgently in return and
said, " O, would-be Philosopher, know that appearances are deceptive, and wisdom is oftentimes
clothed in very modest garments, being the
property of the poor as well as the rich; and know
also that Chance is but a phantom word which has
no place in Truth, and that what brings me here is
not chance at all, as you supposed, but the result of
desire working unseen through the forces of
Nature.   For truly my coming is but the outcome
of your thirst for knowledge, and your generosity
is the sesame which permits me to let you pass
the first doorway towards the secret path to Truth,
since the Truth I have in view for you can only be
attained by the large-hearted and generous-minded,
and by none else—verily, by none else."   Then
Antonius began to prick up his ears, and to think
within himself, " Truly I have been mistaken in
this old mendicant, for, in spite of everything, he
appears to be somewhat of a sage, and talks with the
voice of learning rather than with ignorance, therefore I shall do well to listen to him and pay heed
to what he has to impart."   But aloud he said,
" O Stranger, so rich in wisdom yet so poor in pos-

sessions, think not I wish to dismiss you without giving you a hearing; on the contrary, I beg you to be seated, and my servant shall bring refreshment ere you depart on your way, for you have the air of one who is travelling, and I take it also you are very old?" And so that aged mendicant sat down, folding his two hands on the top of his knobbed staff, while Antonius went to the house and gave orders that fruit and bread and wine should be brought into the garden: and then he returned and waited for what the old man should say. And that old man, after thanking him courteously, looked searchingly and steadfastly into his eyes, and said: O Seeker! only the very beginnings of knowledge are to be culled from the pages of books, and, although your reading has been long and steadfast, yet unless you have already learnt this much, your study has been well-nigh in vain. For know that true knowledge is alone to be found in your own soul, and the way to your soul is through the passage of the heart, from which all darkness must be banished by the light of selflessness. And, this being so, it behoves you to lay aside your books, and seek for knowledge elsewhere, leaving your house and possessions to the care of your servants until your return. For what you seek is not to be found here, but on the summit of yonder snow-clad mountain, where dwell the

Masters of Wisdom, ever waiting to impart their
inestimable treasures of Enlightenment to those
who are courageous and persistent enough to
achieve the great ascent.   But, as only the selfless
can earn the right to receive that knowledge, so one
of their conditions is, that you journey not alone,
but lead others to their Temple of Wisdom as well;
and even if they on their part should weary of the
climb and retrace their steps, leaving you to pursue
the remainder of the way in solitude, will the
Masters nevertheless receive you and give you your
reward.   But know that the journey is long, as
you can see by measuring the distance of yonder
mountain range, and the task is difficult and
arduous, but there are many halting places on the
way, in the shape of towns and villages, where you
must sojourn and rest.   And yet, in each of these
halting places you will learn not only a further
stretch of the on-leading path, but also a fragment
of knowledge, which shall prepare you as a preliminary initiation, so to say, for the enlightenment
of your final goal; and that goal itself is none other
than the finding of the Philosophers' Stone—as in
the language of allegory it is expressed*—by
which you shall attain the vanquishment of death
and the possession of unending Bliss."

---

* Research has shown that the Philosopher's Stone was never intended to be other than a purely symbolical term.

Then said Antonius: "O venerable old man, although your body is emaciated with long years, your speech has retained the energy of youth, and words flow from you as a rivulet rushing swiftly to the sea of Wisdom, and therefore ring true within my ears. But nevertheless you ask the impossible, in demanding that I should find others to bear me company on so long and arduous a journey, for where am I to seek for those who desire knowledge, not only strange in itself, but purchased by so strange and difficult a price? And moreover, who will believe me if I tell them on yonder summit lies, in the custody of a few Anchorites, the Philosophers' Stone, about which they have never heard, and of which, in all probability, they will not care to hear either? Do you think my former boon companions would do anything but laugh me to scorn, were I to lay before them so fantastic and unverifiable a proposal? Truly, your integrity may be indubitable, but your conditions were hard indeed to carry out."

Then that old mendicant suffered the suspicion of a smile to play upon his wrinkled face, and answered: "O Nescient One! were the conditions the Great Ones impose impossible of carrying out, either in your case or in that of another, truly would I not have come here to waste my breath in unprofitable discourse, and the telling of falsehoods; for have I not said that I came by the inexorable decrees of fate in answer to your aspirations, and not by the illusion of Chance or for- tuitous circumstance? Therefore, before you tell me of the impossible, take heed and hear what I have further to say, for unbeknown to yourself you are already a little way along the road to know- ledge, and have already fulfilled, unconsciously to yourself, a few conditions of the Great Ones which hitherto I have not defined." And as he was speaking, servants emerged from the house and came across the green sward, bearing in their hands a tray laden with fruits and bread and wine; so he hesitated, and waited to continue, until they had gone back into the house, courteously ignoring a gesture on the part of his host that he should refresh himself with the proffered repast. Then he continued: "And now I will tell you in what way you are already a little stretch along the path- way to knowledge, for have you not wearied of your eating and drinking and your fondness for women, and all the enjoyments which your riches have purchased for you; and did you not turn from them because they sickened you, and cloyed your senses, as a surfeit of honey sickens the palate; renouncing them all without effort, in that they no longer afforded you any delight?"

Then Antonius looked at the old man and answered: " Truly, I have done as you say, but indeed what other course could I have pursued, seeing that to cling to delights which are no longer delights were the summit of folly, and equivalent to embracing the form of a phantom which has no substance coarser than air? Nor in casting away willingly that of which I was weary can I see anything of merit, for rather had there been merit only if my action had been contrary to my desire, and not in accord with it instead."

Then that old mendicant smiled with a sapient smile, and said: " O Innocent One! yet tinctured with a drop of Wisdom! Only he who renounces without effort has truly renounced at all; for to refrain from that which the mind still desires is to walk on the edge of a precipice, for ever in the danger of falling into the abyss; and what were the use of a shattered corpse to those who would impart knowledge; for just as a corpse cannot hear, being deaf to all sound, so he who is gnawed by the worms of desire cannot hear either, being deaf to all Wisdom. And now reflect and delve into the recesses of your memory, lest among your companions there be not a few you can take on your journey to Truth; and if there be none that you love, perhaps there be those who still love *you*, and because of that love, if for nothing else, will follow

you along the great Road." And then that old
beggar, after having partaken of a little refreshment, slowly arose from his seat, and, bidding his
bewildered host farewell, departed and went on
his way.

II

Now Antonius possessed a friend, who stood as
it were apart from his other companions, and whom
he loved with a tender and steadfast devotion, seeing in him an example of learning, benevolence,
and love. And he dwelt not far away, in a
cypress-girded villa by the sea : a man, it was said,
of vast wealth, yet, unlike the wealthy, choosing to
live a life of simplicity and moderation rather than
extravagance and revelry. And Antonius thought
within himself : " I will repair to my friend Pallomides, and at any rate ask his advice concerning
the proposition of this mysterious old mendicant,
for was it not he himself who lent me those books
I have been so long studying, and therefore it is
not unlikely he may be able to tell me which course
to pursue—if indeed I should pursue any at all."
And so, immediately the thought had come into his
mind, he set out along the white shady road, over-
hung by the intertwining branches of the trees,
planted like sentinels on either side, and suffering
the deep blue of the cloudless sky to peep through

the interstices of their green leaves. And as he drew near the villa in which his friend lived, he could discern his tall and beautiful figure wandering to and fro on the terrace overlooking the calm, noiseless sea; and his head was bent down over a book, from which now and then he looked up, as if to inhale the scent of innumerable roses lifting their pale faces to the morning sun. Then when he saw Antonius approaching, a smile of joyful welcome overspread his calm and classic countenance, and he went forward to meet him and give him a welcoming embrace, as was the custom in those long-ago days. And then Antonius told him for what purpose he had come, and of the mysterious old beggar who sought to persuade him to embark on so strange and unfathomable a journey, begging him to extricate his bewildered mind from the dilemma of its inclination and doubt. And Pallomides looked at him with impenetrable smiling eyes and said: "Are you not a little easy of credulity, O friend, seeing that a disreputable old beggar-man coming to ask alms of you can so dexterously impress your mind with a project which may turn out to be nothing more than the very height of folly, so that your journey, if you decide to undertake it, may end only in disappointment and regret? Nevertheless, I also have heard that on yonder mountain summit is a monastery of mysterious monks, possessed of an incalculable treasure of knowledge, and that to reach them through that long and laborious ascent is to earn a reward outweighing all the material riches of the world. And yet to persuade you to go were a responsibility I am indeed loth to undertake, and to persuade you to remain were equally a responsibility; for who knows, that the old mendicant may not be sincere in his gratitude and wish to do you a good turn, and let you profit by a knowledge of which he is too old to avail himself on his own part? Moreover, even if your journey turn out to be in vain, you have little to keep you here in our world below, and therefore it seems no great harm could accrue one way or the other, for you are in the prime of life, and have many years before you as yet, and on your return could still pursue your studies, aye, perhaps the better for your travel and adventure."

Then said Antonius: "You say well, but the conditions imposed are difficult of carrying out, and where am I to seek for a friend to bear me company on so strange and seemingly chimerical a quest; for apart from you, who are patient of my scheme by reason of your large-mindedness and learning, what other can I persuade to believe in my integrity, instead of regarding me as a madman or a fool?"

Then said Pallomides: " Surely you flatter one
who is unworthy of flattery, since my large-mindedness is nothing but a little worldly wisdom, realising that no opportunity placed on the path of man
is to be wholly disdained and let slip away. Nor
is it so hard as you suppose to find a companion
for your journey, for, if a man is not forthcoming,
perhaps a woman might be found in his stead."

Then replied Antonius: " But what woman do
I know other than those with whom I have amused
myself in former days, and who are unsuited to my
quest; for even if I could induce them to follow
me, the Wise Ones would hardly receive them as
pupils for a knowledge so high? Moreover, I
have neglected them, and let them melt like dreams
away from my life, forgetting almost their names,
so that I could not find them now even if I would."

Then Pallomides looked at his friend with the
gaze of a father, as he said: " The seekers of
wisdom do not disdain even their dreams, lest
underlying their diaphanous texture there be some
meaning of import and weight; and even should
there be nothing, yet to essay their retention were
an exercise for the memory not to be despised; for
surely your own must be of the shortest if you
cannot recall at least one of your many loves; or
surely you spoke without forethought, or are seeking an excuse to hide from me your disinclination

to take one of the weaker sex as your companion,
lest she should prove a hindrance to you rather than
a help."

And then Antonius laughed a little shamefacedly,
and said: " O, reader of character! You have
divined somewhat of the truth, for I fear to burden
myself with a woman who may for ever desire to
repose or linger or turn back, being as whimsical
and capricious as the breeze, and as lavish of her
tears as a moisture-laden cloud of its rain at the
change of the moon."

But Pallomides answered him gravely, and said:
" Yet are you not thus forgetting the conditions
imposed, and seeking to consider your own ease,
avoiding the very first task you must undertake, to
achieve your reward; for verily, did not that old
man tell you that selflessness alone could give you
entry into the Temple, and for that reason it was
you should be accompanied by others, but not for
the gratification of your own comfort or to mitigate
the irksomeness of your journey upon the long
road? Nevertheless, take heed, I would not persuade you to go, as I would not dissuade you
either; but if you are fain to try your fortune on
the strength of the words of that old sage, then
folly were it to try it half-heartedly, ignoring one
portion of his so unequivocal directions, and only
obeying the other instead; for it seems truly the

portion you would discard has every whit as much value as the portion you would obey."

Then Antonius smiled a little sadly, and said: "No doubt you are right in this case, as you have been to my knowledge in most others, for truly a thing that is worth doing in part is worth doing altogether; and, although I will seek first for a man-companion to go along with me, yet should I fail in this, I will do as you say and take a woman instead." And he hesitated for a moment, looking a trifle appealingly at his friend, then added: "Vain were it, I opine, to ask you to come with me yourself?"

And Pallomides laughed with kindly amusement, and answered: "Yes, I fear it were vain indeed."

So then Antonius departed and went back to his home, steeping himself in his troubled reflections, and trying to devise some plan for the search of a companion and some oratory to convince him, if he should find one, of the value of the quest. And he reflected for several hours, until the twilight was beginning to settle upon his garden, and then set forth in the direction of the town, intending to visit many of his former comrades, though hopeful of little success for the object on which he was bent. And so, after going from one to the other, and receiving nothing but laughter and good-natured mockery for his pains, he was compelled to give up his search, which, as he correctly presaged, had come to nought. Then said he to himself: " With the men I have utterly failed, as I expected, for after all they only liked me for the good food and wine I lavished upon them in former days, and not for myself; since when I ask of them aught in return, they one and all refuse and laugh me to scorn, deeming me a fool. So now will I try with the women instead, for one at least loved me and vowed she would always love me, though I treated her badly, and turned my own life away from hers without further ado. So who knows but that she may love me still; and even if chary of believing in the object I have in view, she may go with me because of love, if for nothing more; for what ties have courtesans to tether them to this place or that, and, seeing I have money and to spare for both of us and many more, surely there can be few other obstacles in the way? "

And so Antonius at length came to the house of one, Cynara, his former mistress; and to her he laid bare the project he had so close to his soul, while she on her part listened with wide-open eyes, full of wonderment and also full of a love which had never died. But as he was telling the tale, he noticed that she had aged, and much of her former beauty had faded away with the passage of years, and her body had grown thinner, and her eyes a little sunken with a weariness of soul which, on the one hand, touched his heart with something of pity, and, on the other, caused him to shrink a little from her away. And he thought to himself, as he looked at her and talked to her in the gloaming of the rushlight: " Truly I wish she seemed to love me a little less, for surely she will embarrass me with her devotion, and perhaps I shall need to feign that which I no longer feel. And yet, if she loved me no more, certainly she would not do as I ask her, and come with me on my journey: therefore, the importunity of her love I must accept as the price of her companionship, and so endure it as best I can."

And then, when he had finished speaking, and come to the end of his tale, she looked into his eyes, and answered playfully: " O faithless, yet beloved one! Although thou hast left me these long years with never a message nor an inquiry after my welfare, and only now when thou dost want something of me, seekest me at last, as, who knows, a final resource; yet, because I still love thee, I will go along by thy side on this strange journey, being glad to have recovered thee when I thought thou wast gone for evermore. For just as thou art enwearied by thy riches, so am I wearied by my amours, and would fain make an end to them all

and seek for something better on the roadway of
life; the more so, as my loves existed in name only
and not in truth, since, glimmering through every
one of them, was thy imperishable image, and the
undying memory of thee and thy love; and
although I know full well thou dost care for me
no longer, yet nevertheless I will companion thee
faithfully and ask nothing in return."

So then Antonius rejoiced in his heart, saying
to himself: "At last I have found someone to go
with me on my way; and now my doubts are set at
rest, and I can prepare for my journey without
further ado." But to Cynara he said: "Thou
wast ever noble, and didst treat others better than
they ever treated thee, making of my own delin-
quent self no exception to the rule of thy soft-
heartedness. Yet in this instance thou shalt be
repaid a thousandfold by a reward of which thou
canst not even dream until thou dost learn a little
further of what is in store. But now I will depart,
and will send for thee at the appointed hour, when
I shall have made all the essential preparations for
our journey; and until then, farewell."

III

So then Antonius began to trace his steps to his
own home once more, with a light heart and a mind
full of expectation and an enthusiasm which he

made no efforts to suppress. And as he walked along, plunged in his own felicitous meditations, suddenly a thought darted like an arrow into his brain, causing him for a moment to feel as if all his project had burst like a bubble floating in the air For as he turned the bend of the road along which he was walking, a view of the far-off mountain-range suddenly came upon him, as the full moon, just rising above its highest peak, silhouetted it against the fathomless dark blue of the immeasurable sky. And he said to himself : " Surely I am mad to think I can ever ascend to that cloud-kissing height, where certainly to my knowledge no footstep has ever trod and no traveller has returned to tell his tale. And surely that beggar must have been laughing at me in his heart, the more so as he gave me no directions how to discover the way, telling me only of the conditions under which I was to journey instead. And did I not let that mysterious old mendicant depart without exacting a promise that he would return and enlighten me further how to proceed? And now in all likelihood he has gone away for ever, and to try to discover him were as vain almost as the attempt to discover a particular shell at the bottom of the sea."

Then suddenly as he turned the final bend of the road before his own house, there, as if in direct contradiction to his thoughts, he saw that very old beggar seated waiting just outside his garden by the gate; and his heart gave a great bound in the intensity of his expectation, so that he hastened his steps until he confronted him where he sat.

Then that old beggar arose and bowed, but without any preamble and without waiting for Antonius to speak, said with measured accents, as is the custom with those who are old: " And now, since you have decided to go, and since you have found someone to go with you, listen well to what I have to impart, for without my directions difficult were it indeed for you to find the way, as also the guides and halting places at each juncture of your journey. But first let me deliver you this little amulet, which you must wear attached round your neck and hidden beneath your garments, for it is a symbol whereby your prospective instructor shall know who you are and what is your quest; nor must you fail to show it whenever demanded of you, otherwise you can receive no instruction, and so will have your journey in vain."

But Antonius in his astonishment interrupted him and said: " Old man so enshrouded in mystery! how came you to know I have decided to embark on this strange journey at all, let alone that I had found a companion? "

But the old man put up his hand to silence him.
saying : " I have no excess of time for the solving
of idle questions; so take this amulet as I have
said, and listen further to what I have to impart."
So as Antonius took the amulet from his hands,
he continued immediately : " And now learn that
your first destination is a village lying on yonder
lowest slope at the foot of the two great over-
hanging rocks, which you will discern on your
approach, after a day or so of journey on foot.
And at the very last house at the further end of
that village, which you must know, consists of but
one long street, you will knock, and the owner of
the house will receive you and instruct you further
how to proceed. But take with you but little in
the way of money, and wear but modest apparel,
looking as a beggar rather than as a wealthy man;
and of servants you must take none at all, but only
a weapon to guard yourself against attack and a
staff to assist you in your ascent. And now farewell, and may the gods guide you and protect you
on your way."   And without another word or
look, that old beggar turned and was gone round
the bend of the road out of sight.

Then Antonius, tantalised by perplexity on the
one hand, yet, utterly convinced as to that old
man's integrity on the other, turned into his gate
and so into his house, determined to set out on his

journey without protracted delay.   And he called
to him his servants, saying: " I am soon about to
travel for a while on some business of importance
to myself, not knowing how long it will be before
I shall return; but as during my travels I shall be
the guest of friends, I therefore desire to take
no servants with me, intending to journey without
baggage and retinue and encumbrance of any kind;
and I have fixed the day after tomorrow for the
day of my departure."   Then having said this and
partaken of the supper that was awaiting him, he
went to bed and slept far into the dawn, dreaming
of that mysterious old sage, and Pallomides, and
Cynara, and snow-capped mountains all in one, as
is the way of dreams.

IV

AND on the appointed day Antonius and Cynara
set out on their journey together, for he had
despatched a message to her respecting their meeting place and the hour of setting forth.   Nor had
he failed to take a farewell of Pallomides in his
villa by the sea, deeming, who knows, a long
separation might be between them, or even one
that would never have an end at all.

And so those two wayfarers plodded for many
hours along the dusty roads, now resting, now

walking on again, now taking a little refreshment at a wayside inn or throwing themselves on the grass for repose by the edge of a stream; and sometimes they bathed their hot and aching feet in the cool waters of a river, splashing their faces to wash away the dust and sweat engendered through the burning sun. And yet as Antonius grew more tired with the passage of time, he thought to himself: "Woe is me for my folly in choosing to travel thus without horse or servant like a beggar, dragging my legs after me as if they were stones increasing in weight at every step. And here am I, with all my wealth, because of the babbling of an old beggar-man, leaving everything of comfort behind, and going in search of I hardly know what." But as he looked at his companion bravely tramping along by his side, her face was calm and without complaint, though the lines under her eyes had deepened with fatigue. And in response to his look she smiled with a smile in which weariness and encouragement, as it were, seemed blended in one, but she did not speak, for she was too tired to find any words to say. And Antonius thought to himself: "Ah, if I could but love her as she loves me, my road were disburdened of much of its weariness and brightened by so small a thing as a smile, as hers seems to be brightened by my even taking notice of her at all. For truly she must

have a noble heart to place such implicit faith in
me and love me these long years even through the
glamour of so many other amours; and if she were
not so faded, who knows I might have loved her a
little in return?" And he looked again at her,
but this time smiling with a kindliness in his
glance he had not shown hitherto, so that as she
smiled back at him with a furtive joy in her eyes,
he felt he could play on her soul as the hand of a
bard plays on his lyre seeking to bring forth joyful
sounds. And straightway a thought shot into his
mind which made him very glad, for he said to
himself: " Have I got a new game to play which
will while away the hours of my tramping, and so
bring me all the quicker to my destination? And
the very simplicity of the game is half the attractiveness, in that it can be played anywhere almost,
and not only between my present companion and
myself. And yet it is strange that I never thought
of it before, and that the look in the eyes of a jaded
girl who loves me, yet whom I cannot pretend to
love in return, should be the very first to open my
own eyes to its existence. Although had it been
otherwise, and had I loved her in return, most
likely all of it would have escaped my mind,
intoxicated as it would be with love and passion,
and hence blind to the subtler things of the heart.
And now I will look at her again with a glance even

kinder than before, and take note of her response,
for somehow or other to give her a little joy, and
watch its effect on her countenance, gives me not
only a little joy in return, but opens the shutters of
my heart as it were to let in a tiny beam of some
vast immeasurable and mysterious ocean of joy
vibrating outside." And he looked at her once
again, this time with a smile of compassion, and
taking her arm to help her climb the little ascent of
the road on which they walked. And she turned a
gaze upon him mingled with gladness, affection
and gratitude, pressing his arm a little against her
body in response, but uttered no word. And he
said solicitously · " When we get to the top of
this incline we will rest for a while before going on
to yonder village and seek an inn to shelter us
for the night, for thou hast walked far enough and
done thy task bravely, and without a murmur, even
though the heat has been very intense and the day
interminably long. But now I feel the cool breeze
springing up from the sea over there on the right,
and we have reached higher ground, as thou canst
see, and I hope thy limbs, as mine, are beginning to
feel a little lighter in consequence, for the air is freer
up here on the hill among the pines." And she
answered him : " Truly, the weariness of my limbs
is almost forgotten in the lightness of my heart, and
even if weariness seems to chain my feet to the

earth, my spirit is free, and has cast off chains far
heavier than any that can bind my body; and all
this I owe unto thee, seeing that thou didst choose
me as a companion out of others more suited to go
with thee on thy strange venture." And he said :
" Not so, for as to this I would not delude thee, in
that everyone of those others laughed me to scorn,
and utterly refused to go; and thus had it not been
for thee I could not have gone at all, and must
needs have given up my project altogether. And
yet, now I am glad thou art my companion rather
than one of the others, so that I think destiny has
chosen for me better than I could have chosen for
myself; for where could I find a comrade so long-
suffering and trustful as thee? And who knows but
much of my instruction will not come from thee
also, since this journey is none other than a journey
of knowledge, and every factor therein has its
message for him who is perspicacious enough to
understand." And she looked at him with a gaze
of such dulcitude in return that for a moment her
fadedness was eclipsed by the deep soulfulness of
her eyes, so that he thought within himself : Who
knows but that I may still love her a little after all,
for though she be faded, her eyes are inex-
pressibly tender, and her voice as soft as ever it
was before? And he pressed her arm a little tighter
and helped her tenderly to the top of the hill.

V

AND that night, as he promised, they slept at an inn, and when the morning came, arose early and went on their way, which meandered by the side of garrulous streams, and through woods of umbrella pines and orange groves and olive trees, and every variety of luxuriance illumined by a resplendent sun. And all around them were un-lating hills and verdant valleys, flower-prinked and songful with the carols of countless birds, accompanied by an undertone of myriad humming insects intoxicated by the early morning air. And the whole day long, although the sun rose in all its intensity and poured down on the hill tops, yet the way of these two wanderers lay through shaded cuttings, between wooded slopes, cool and moistened by the running rills. And their hearts were joyful and unified as they walked side by side, exhilarated by the breezes which gently swept through the valleys, and braced their nerves almost to the point of ecstasy. And Antonius had thought as he started out: To-day I will play my newly discovered game even more than yesterday, and watch its effect on my companion as we walk along. And so sometimes he would stray into one of the meadows in order to pick her out a special flower which he espied lifting its head from amongst the floral profusion, composing the capricious pattern

on the carpet of blossoms overspreading the grass.
And then he would give it to her, watching the
while the expression in her hazel eyes as she took
it from his hand.   And as he scrutinised her,
softening his own eyes with the sweetness of
fraternal affection he thought to himself: All
these years have I lived and yet not learned so
simple a thing as to give a little of my heart with
the gift of my hand; for although I gathered my
companions around me, lavishing on them food,
and wine of the choicest vintage, yet not for the
delight of giving did I do these things, but only
that I might enjoy their society and divert myself
with ribaldry and jest.   And no wonder I wearied
of riotousness and folly, seeing it left me no delight
in my heart, but only a reaction of insufferable
aridness instead, goading me to more riotousness
and folly, so that I might drown and forget that
reaction with further excess.

And when it came to twilight-tide, and the red
disc of the sinking sun was slowly disappearing
behind the now far-distant sea, they came finally in
sight of their destination, the village nestling at the
foot of two great rocks which the old beggar had
described.   And then as they passed through the
one long street as directed, the wondering inhabitants looking the while with some curiosity upon
them, they at length descried the last house

situated a little apart from the others in a garden surrounded by trees. And Antonius knocked with his staff at the door, which was opened by a man of calm and dignified appearance, and a benignity of countenance which went straight to the heart.

And he said: " Welcome, O strangers, and yet not strangers, for I have awaited your coming— unless indeed I be mistaken, and you are not the travellers I expected? " But immediately Antonius brought from beneath his garment the amulet he was instructed to show, saying: " Your surmises are in truth correct, as you can see by the scrutiny of this sign. And yet how did you know we were coming, for surely no messenger on horse- back preceded us and advised you of our arrival?"

But the man in the doorway only smiled and said: " Enter first and refresh yourselves, and ask me what you will afterwards, for you must be weary after so long a journey on foot these hot summer days, and my wife awaits your companion (on the verandah overlooking the garden) ready to take her to her room and attend to her wants, as I on my part will attend to yours."

Then later on in the evening, after they both had refreshed themselves and partaken of supper in the company of their host and his wife (whose names were respectively Aristion and Portia, and who were adepts in the art of hospitality as well as

beautiful to look upon) Aristion took his two
guests into another room, and, begging them be
seated, sat down confronting them. And he turned
to Antonius with a kindly smile, and said : " And
so you are seeking the great Arcanum, and the
Masters of Wisdom have directed you to me that
I may give you your first initiation ? " And
Antonius replied : " I know little of these Masters
of whom you speak, having obtained my grain of
knowledge from a few ancient books and from an
old sage masquerading in the form of a decrepit
beggar, who, after admonishing me to discard my
studying as practically worthless, sent me to you.
And yet I was not permitted to come alone, but
was directed to bring a companion—as you see—
so that she also might share such knowledge as I
might obtain; for that was the condition imposed,
and to ignore that condition was inevitably to fail."

And Aristion said : " You have done well, and
have fulfilled the first behest of the great one who
sent you; and that being so, I am prepared and
happy to act as your instructor, at any rate up to a
certain stage, and then if you prove yourself
willing, to pass you on to one yet higher in the
scale than myself." Then Antonius said : " So that
old beggar was after all no beggar, but one you call
a great one in disguise ? And I thought as much,
for his learning was incompatible with his mendi-

cancy, and his speech betrayed him, savouring not
of ignorance, but of refinement instead!" And
Aristion laughed and answered: "Your surmise is
not altogether at fault, nor yet is it the truth either,
for that old mendicant is but as yet a pupil, and
was sent by his master, it is true coming willingly
to enlighten you, yet nevertheless not entirely of
his own accord. Nor was it he who sent you here,
but his master, using him merely as a mouthpiece
and an emissary, and nothing beyond. And indeed
it lay within your reception of him whether your
heart was ready for our order of knowledge or no;
and if you had sent him away, then would you
with your own hands have closed the very first
gate on the path, for truly the key to the beginning
of all enlightenment is faith and a discerning
credulity, without which no knowledge could be
acquired at all."

And then having finished, he turned to Cynara
and said: "And you, are you also willing to be
instructed, like to your companion?—if so, tell
me a little of yourself, seeing that although I know
already something of him, by a method of which at
the moment I may not speak, yet of you I know
nothing at all."

And Cynara blushed a little, and said shyly:
"Truly I desire to go along with him wherever
he may go, and learn with him whatever he may

learn, for I have given my promise that this should
be so; but I am doubtful whether you will be ready
to teach me so exalted a science, for my life has
been evil, and I have gone the way of the flesh
instead of the spirit, having been a courtesan, and
so in all likelihood a person quite unfitted to be
taught at your hands." And Aristion smiled kindly
upon her and said: "And have you loved very
much, and is he your last love, inspiring you to
surrender your former ways of living and search
for wisdom instead, alongside of him?"

And Cynara answered: "Although I have loved
many a little, yet truly I have loved him the most;
and he is not the last, as you suppose, but rather
the first, whom I have never forgotten and of whom
I never ceased to think, though we were long
parted, and I was amusing myself with others in
his place."

And Antonius interrupted her and said: "It 's
true we were long parted, as she told you, but the
parting was my doing, and no fault of hers, for
when I wearied of my boon companions and my
riotous living, and sent them all away, I sent her
along with them, and told her I would see her no
more. And so I am to blame, and truly not she."

And Aristion looked at her with benevolence,
and smiled as he answered: "Nay, of blame we do
not speak, for who am I to blame those who have

done me no wrong? Moreover, though the saying be trite, yet verily experience is the best of teachers, and those who have lived not at all are unfit candidates for the science of the soul, since what they have never tasted they may yearn to taste in the future; if it be but out of curiosity, and for no other reason. And so for some, the surest foundation for the path of knowledge is satiety, and not inexperience, for only those who have known desire themselves, can understand and condone desire in others, thus acquiring forbearance and sympathy, without which no true wisdom and happiness can ever be attained.* For in evil there is always lurking something of good for him who knows how to seek, and therefore on the plane of appearance the difference between good and evil is one of degree rather than one of kind; a sublime truth, yet of which the wise alone are aware. And so, far from blaming you for having tasted of the fruits of the senses, I think, on the contrary, you have both a point in your favour, for the lesson thereby you have learnt could in your case not have been achieved in any other way. Moreover the cold and the passionless, being deficient in force and vitality, are useless as aspirants to the science of the

---

* Let those who think that Aristion was too tolerant, or did wrong in condoning Cynara's former life, remember that "the sinners and harlots are nearer to the Kingdom of Heaven than the Pharisees"—as the New Testament has it.

soul, which requires emotion and warmth and power in place of weakness and impotence; for how can a lower desire be transmuted into a higher one if it does not exist at all, seeing that the quint-essence of wisdom is the transmutation of the baser into the more exalted, without which the attainment of the final goal were utterly impossible, and hence its undertaking practically in vain? And now, as the night is approaching and the mind is too weary for the understanding of divine philosophies and the learning of lessons, let us seek the cool of the garden and refresh our souls with the sight of the moon, which, as you see through the window, is rising over the brow of the hill and flooding the landscape with its sublimating beams. But to-morrow we shall discourse again, and so day after day until the time comes for you to seek another teacher; though until then you are my guests, and welcome to remain as long as you wish."

VI

AND in the morning Antonius rose betimes, full of a joyful expectancy and a calm delight which he had never experienced heretofore. And he thought within himself: there is a peacefulness about this household surpassing any I have entered, save perhaps that of Pallomides, my friend, in his villa by the sea; and I am so full of contentment here

that I think when the time comes I shall be very
loth to depart. Moreover my host and his wife
have around their entire persons a serenitude and
benignity which render them lovable at first sight,
causing me to feel as if I had known them many a
long year, instead of but a few hours. And now I
wonder what sort of learning this paragon of
charity and tolerance has to impart, for meseems
he will be no hard taskmaster, judging from his
discourse last night and the manner in which he
condoned our delinquencies, a procedure quite at
variance with the stern maxims I have read in my
various books. And as he was engaged in these
reflections a servant came to his room and said :
" My master awaits you at your convenience for
the morning meal in the garden by the fountain."
So then Antonius, after completing his toilet, went
down into the garden as he was requested, and
together with Aristion, his wife, and Cynara,
partook of a light repast in the shadow of the trees,
while the trickling notes of a melodious fountain
played a soft accompaniment to their conversation
and cooled the air with its diaphanous opalescent
spray, wafted by the morning breeze. And after
the meal was over Aristion said : " In yonder little
temple at the foot of the garden, among the pines,
we will pursue our morning studies, and I shall
await you both there in an hour from now, when

my other duties are fulfilled." And as in the interval Antonius, together with Cynara, loitered about, exploring beyond the garden-close the surrounding slopes, Antonius thought to himself: Far away and inaccessible indeed does that snow-crowned summit look which one day I am destined to climb, and whether I shall ever reach it is a matter filling me with doubt, for somehow, now I am nearer, it seems to be further away rather than the reverse, and its whole contour looks more formidable from this spot than it does from my own town. And he turned to Cynara and said: "The problem of how thy little feet are to climb yonder lofty mountain troubles me sore, unless indeed we learn some magical method of transport, defying the laws of nature, and carrying us on the wings of the wind up into the snowy air." And Cynara looked at him and smiled as one who worries not over the future, but is content to wait without questioning. And she said: "To-day is too sweet to be marred by the anxieties of to-morrow, and why weigh down a light heart with the burden of fears which may be nothing but phantoms, having no reality at all?" Then Antonius laughed and answered approvingly: "Thou speakest already after the way of the wise, seeming to be gifted with a natural philosophy without the labour of study, as a bird is gifted with song; and I think Aristion is likely to find thee an apter pupil than I am with all my reading, so that unless I bestir myself thou wilt surely outstrip me and attain the goal first. But now we must go to the little temple and seek our teacher, for I think an hour must have gone by, and to keep him waiting were inexcusable and wanting in courtesy, seeing he gives us everything and asks nothing in return."

And as they came round the bend of the garden path facing their place of meeting they saw the tall figure of Aristion already crossing the sward. And he greeted them with a smile, and bade them be seated on a stone bench between two of the pillars supporting the domed roof, round which the roses twined in rich profusion. And Aristion sat himself opposite to them on another bench, and reflected for a moment ere he began to speak.

And then he said slowly : " If it were possible to enjoy the aggregate of all earth's delights and rid them of every drawback and every reaction, yet would their pleasure not compare a thousandth part with the Bliss arising from proficiency in the Science of the Soul, for that Science is the art of striking the very fountain-head of all Bliss, which is, as it were, *within* man himself, and not *without*. Nay verily, as all joy coming from without is conditional, so all Bliss coming from within is

unconditional, and hence eternally present whether
we know it or not. And yet, even the joy which as
I have said comes from without, does so in appearance only, and not in reality, for neither wealth
nor lands, nor delicious food, nor gorgeous apparel
contain joy in themselves, but only serve to draw
out a minute portion of that infinite joy latent in
the soul of every being. Nor can this be otherwise,
seeing that, to one man rich apparel affords delight
yet not to another, and to a second man great
possessions afford delight yet not to a third, and to
a third man delicious food affords delight yet not
to a fourth; and so on it goes well nigh to infinity;
for if joy lay inherent in all these things rather than
in man himself, truly there would be no diversity
of taste, but utter uniformity instead. Nay, the
objects of sense are as nothing more than a number
of reeds, and the Mind is the player, and Joy the
wind which produces the sound; for verily the
wind is put into the pipes by the player himself,
and certainly cannot proceed from them of its own
accord, since were the skill and the breath of the
minstrel absent, the instrument could emit no
sound at all, and thus were as useless as any stone."
And Aristion paused for a moment to look
questioningly at his pupils so as to ensure that they
understood, and then he continued: "And now
learn, that the Science of Wisdom is to make the

mind one with the *unconditional* joy that lies
within, and which is the Reality in contrast to the
Illusion; and yet, not only with unconditional joy,
but also with its concomitants unconditional Beauty
and unconditional Love, without which two other
qualities perfect Joy were impossible to attain. But
to this end, the mind must be purified of all dross
by an effort of will, as a dewdrop must be free of
dust in order to contain a perfect reflection of the
sun : seeing the Soul is as the sun of infinite Joy,
and the purified mind is that which reflects it;
though indeed the simile is but arbitrary, and at
best a halting attempt to bring the truth to your
understandings. Nay, rather is it, that the mind
must be saturated with the joy of the soul, and
every feeling hostile to that ineffable joy removed
by the will, as the dust from the mirror is removed
by the hand of the polisher. For the particles of
dust on the mirror of the mind are none other than
the vices and sorrow-bearing emotions of
humanity, which are illusions, containing in reality
no sorrow at all, though seeming to do so by
reason of that very illusion. For what else is
sorrow than the absence of joy, as darkness is
nought but the absence of light, when the sun is
excluded by the closing of the shutters, though it
be shining outside all the time? And know therefore that as he who opens the shutters of his room

to the light of the sun, banishes all darkness, so does he who opens the shutters of his mind to the joy of the soul, banish all sorrow, which falls away from him then as easily as water from the feathery back of the swan, or the transient frets of childhood from a grown-up man. For just as no object, whatever it be, contains joy in itself, so no object nor train of circumstances, whatever it be, contains sorrow in itself: and to know this is the first and most valuable of all lessons, which rids a man of every illusion and eventually sets him free." And here Aristion smiled with affection upon his two pupils, and arose from his chair, saying · " And now enough philosophy for one day. For although the instructor may be ever ready to teach, the pupils are apt to grow weary, and so lose the capacity to learn. Moreover he has other duties which must not be neglected, and which demand his attention elsewhere, so that he must leave you awhile to your pursuits." And with this Aristion departed, and did not return till the evening in time for supper. But at the advice of his wife, Antonius and Cynara wandered about in the adjoining woods, in perfect contentment, listening to the chatter of the streams and the song of the birds, reflecting on all they had heard, and wondering what new lesson was in store for them on the morrow.

VII

AND again at the same hour of day those three
met once more in the little temple among the pines.
And after they were all seated Aristion smiled upon
them with the suspicion of a twinkle in his eye,
and began : " Once there was a goose who lived
among his own kind in a farm on the hillside,
passing his monotonous existence as every other
goose does, waddling about and quacking incessantly, adding to the general hubbub and chatter
of the yard.   And his owner was a man who, as it
would seem, was not content to breed a number of
animals merely, but needs must breed a number of
children as well; for these children were to be seen
rampaging around the farmyard at all hours of the
day, and making every bit as much noise as the
animals themselves, ever on the alert to discover
some new prank they might play and some new
excuse for making a greater noise.   And one day
the eldest, who was a boy, said to his brothers and
sisters : ' I have learnt from my comrades at school
a prank we may play on yonder goose, which
requires nothing more than a bit of chalk wherewith to make a circle on the ground; for if we do
this and place that old goose in the centre, it will
remain there, deluded into the belief it is a
prisoner and so we will have considerable fun
watching its antics.' And no sooner had he said

this than he drew from his pocket a piece of chalk, making therewith a large circle on the ground, meanwhile telling his brothers to catch the goose and place it in the centre. And no sooner was this done than happened exactly as has been said, for that foolish old bird waddled about and round its imaginary enclosure, seeming utterly unable to find a way out. And it thought to itself: Woe is me, for here I am imprisoned in this enclosure which these intolerable children have made, and now I can no longer wander about picking up bits of food, so that, who knows, I may be left to starve and meet my death in this ignominious fashion, while my jailers look on and laugh me to scorn. And it quacked and flapped its wings in its extremity, deploring its bondage, yet never realising for one instant that all the time it was free."

And Aristion paused for a moment and smiled, and then he said slowly: "And now know that that goose is none other than a parallel of the mind of mankind deluded by ignorance, and pestered by fears which are purely imaginary and relative, having no substance in actual fact. For just as in reality that deluded old goose was absolutely free, and at any moment could have stepped over its imaginary boundary, so is mankind in reality eternally happy, and needs only to realise its happiness in order to become what in all truth it already

is. For its sorrows are lesser illusions proceeding
entirely from the greater illusion, and are susceptible of banishment by the realisation of truth,
seeing that Truth and Illusion cannot exist at the
same time, any more than fire and water can exist
in the same place. For know that once there was a
timid woman, who walking one night in the dark
along a lonely lane, espied, as she thought, a man
standing immovable by the roadside, so that she
was overcome by fear, but on approaching,
discovered it was merely a tree; and with the realisation of the fact of the tree, the illusion of the
man vanished, together with all her fears, which
were based on illusion, as was the man himself.
And now, as I said yesterday, the way to banish
illusion is to make the mind one with truth, which
is the essence of bliss; for theory without practice
is of little avail, as merely to cry out Art! Art!
were of little avail for the painting of a picture.
And so the science of the soul consists, among other
things, in the practice of concentration, by which
the vicissitudes of the mind are brought under
control, and no longer permitted to jump like a
monkey in unending restlessness, willy nilly, from
one thing to another; for like a pond is the mind
covered with innumerable ripples, set in motion by
the wind of desire and the vagaries of desultory
thought; and not until those ripples are calmed can

the smooth bedrock of the pond be seen, which is
the soul itself." And then Aristion arose from his
seat and said: "But enough for to-day, and
to-morrow, at the same hour, we will continue our
lessons; meanwhile you are welcome to amuse
yourselves in whatever way you will." And there-
upon he went into the house.

VIII

AND on the following day those three went for
the third time to the little temple among the pines,
and after they were all seated Aristion smiled
benignly upon his two pupils and said: "All
virtues come hard to those who have not identified
themselves with unconditional happiness, and
sought first the things of the spirit; for as only he
who has perfect health feels no fatigue in the taking
of exercise, so he who has unconditional happiness
feels no effort in the practice of virtue. And so the
wise ponder unceasingly on the bliss of the soul,
willing themselves to feel it eternally, in that by
so doing, all unselfish and noble actions become a
joy in themselves, and never a hardship. But the
foolish, on the other hand, pondering not on the
Bliss of the soul but on the pleasure of the senses,
lament continually, saying: 'Woe is me, for how
difficult it is to be virtuous, and how tedious is life
without a little vice to flavour the food of existence,

which sickens my palate with its utter insipidness and poverty of taste.' And so they go around seeking for means to put an end to their tedium, and yet never find it, seeing the means is in themselves, and nowhere beyond. And yet, hardly less foolish are those who say : ' I will seek for virtue by suppressing all my emotions and making myself like to a stone, which feels nothing at all, and therefore can do no harm; and if I gain no happiness in this world I shall at least gain it in the next, and in this way shall reap my reward. And Ariston paused for a moment to reflect, and then went on : " Know that there are two ways to be rid of vice, a right way and a wrong way, the one being slow and uncertain, the other being speedy and sure; for just as the foolish physician studies disease in order to bring about health, so the wise physician studies health in order to annihilate disease, saying to his patients : ' Fulfill the condition of health, and diseases will fall away from you of their own accord. And if this is so with the body, in like manner is it also with the mind, which is full of maladies in the shape of hatred and jealousy and sensuality, and anger and other excrescences full of pain and bitter sensations, aching incessantly, and allowing us no respite at all.' Then asks the sufferer : ' How am I to rid myself of these evil humours which torment me and leave me no peace ? ' And the physician of

souls in the shape of a priest answers: ' Kill them
by poison, so that they die and harass thee no more.'
And so then the sufferer endeavours to kill them,
sometimes succeeding after great effort, and sometimes not succeeding at all. And when they are
dead, having kicked and screamed in the process,
flickering at the end like a candle on the point of
expiration, he thinks to himself: Now I have
annihilated my weaknesses, and yet somehow I am
not much the happier, and the process was
intolerably painful and hardly worth the effort
after all, and surely there must be something
wrong, for it was less tedious to feel a little hatred
or jealousy or passion than to feel nothing
whatever? And then peradventure a wise physician
of souls chances his way, saying: ' My friend
thou hast endeavoured to cure diseases by the study
of disease, instead of by the study and fulfilment
of the conditions of health, and so thy second
plight is little better than thy first, since now thou
hast neither disease nor health, but something
which stands midway between the two, and is
utterly negative and neutral; a body as it were
without a soul. For although thou hast got rid of
thine evils, Good is not there to take their place,
neither is Happiness to take the place of thy pains,
but merely the thing which is neither good nor
evil, pain nor happiness, being tedium, and nothing

beyond. Nay thy whole procedure was at fault, and thou didst commence at the wrong end of the undertaking, destroying evil instead of building up good; for unlike everything else, spirituality begins at the top, and not at the bottom, and the purest happiness is to be found in the rarefied air of the azure welkin, into which the mind must soar like a bird, and not in the murky atmosphere of a slum. And as it is with the air, so it is with virtue and happiness, seeing that a man can only oust the bad air in his lungs by filling them with pure air, and not by depleting them altogether, as thou, meta-phorically speaking, hast done, and become well nigh suffocated in the attempt. And so as I said, the only way to be rid of sorrow from the mind is to oust it by the incessant concentration on Happiness, as the way to be rid of hatred is to ponder on Love, and of evil on good, and of vice on virtue; for verily it is better to love good than merely hate evil, seeing that hatred in whatever form it exists, is an evil in itself.' And now our lesson is over until to-morrow, and the rest of the day is yours to amuse yourselves according to your own inclinations." And with this, Aristion arose, and smiled, and walked across the garden, and so out of the gate.

IX

AND the next day those three met for the fourth
and last time in the little temple among the pines.
And when Aristion had greeted them with his
usual smile, and they were all seated, he began :

" He who would reach wisdom must learn to
grow up out of childhood and become a man, seeing
that the majority of mankind are but children,
though they deem themselves adults. For the
indications of a child are its likes and dislikes, its
capacity for lamenting over things unsuited for
lamentation, as also its capacity for rejoicing over
other things which call for hardly any rejoicing at
all. And yet, as the adult smiles with indulgence
at the childishness of children, so does the sage
smile with indulgence at the childishness of
Humanity, seeing the majority are but large
children in disguise, rejoicing and lamenting over
circumstances unworthy of either the one or the
other. For one man is angered by the evil ways of
his fellow saying : ' Cursed be he and his wrong-
doing, let him get out of my sight, for he is
abhorrent to me in his folly,' forgetting all the time
that his own anger and curses are nothing but
folly also, and that he is merely adding folly to
folly, which is nothing but childishness. And
another laments over the loss of a trinket, saying :
' Woe is me for I have lost my jewel, and now I

can no longer adorn myself with it and make
myself beautiful'; and yet this also is childishness,
for what after all is a trinket to an adult but the
equivalent of a toy to a child? And another one
worries and frets, saying: 'I have heard that
people spread this or that report about me, or relate
I am one thing or the other, and as all they say is
untrue, therefore let me revenge myself upon them
by spreading evil reports in return'; and this also
is childishness, for how can the chattering of a few
parrots disturb the serenitude of a mind other
than that of a child? Moreover this anger and
desire for revenge is nothing but wounded vanity,
which belongs to the occupants of the nursery
rather than to the hall of the adults. And to
impress this on your minds I will tell you a story:
For once there was a married man who possessed a
friend he loved so dearly that he took him to live
for a time at his own house, treating him almost
as a brother. But as his wife was very beautiful
that friend conceived a romantic passion for her,
and, unable to withstand the temptation, committed
adultery with her one night when his host was
away, and then realising what he had done, deemed
the only way to make amends was to put an end
to the amour by departing, never to come back;
and so before the husband returned he quitted the
house and went a long journey, but falling in with

a band of thieves, was robbed and murdered, and
so never seen any more. But the husband, when he
came home discovered by accident what had
occurred in his absence, and being overcome with
anger and jealousy and mortification, conceived in
his heart a terrible lust for what he foolishly
deemed the heroism and dignity of revenge, so that
he started out, almost then and there, in search of
his ' friend,' but could never find him, seeing he
was dead. And he pursued his search for weeks,
which lengthened into months, and months which
lengthened into years, putting himself to an infinitude of trouble, yet ever goaded on to new efforts
by one inextinguishable idea which he made no
attempt whatever to expel from his mind. And
then finally, when at last he came to see that all
his wanderings throughout the entire country were
proving utterly in vain, and he was getting old and
ill and worn out in consequence, he returned home,
for all the money he took with him was exhausted,
and so he had no other course left. But in the
meanwhile his wife, whom he had abandoned and
left without even the sending of a letter or a
message of any kind, finding herself deserted by
her lover, and forsaken by her husband, and torn
by feelings of grief and remorse and yearning all
blended into one, grew ill of a mortal sickness, and
finally died. So when her husband returned he came

back to a deserted house, covered with dust and cobwebs, and falling into disrepair; for his wife had been dead for a score of moons, and the priest had buried her in the burial ground near by. And then when that culprit in the shape of a husband saw what had occurred, although he had not a trace of pity for his wife, he had an abundance of pity for himself, and for his own loneliness, and for the wrongs done, as he thought, to his own heart; and longing for consolation, he repaired to the house of that very priest who had buried his wife, pouring out his woes in a torrent of fretful words. But that old priest, after listening to him for a while, looked at him coldly and said: 'Childish and evil man! what avails it to rail at woes and miseries which thou hast brought on thyself by thine own wicked ness and folly, and by thine unquenchable thirst to do a thing that is not worth even thinking about, even wandering the world over to carry out? For only a fool or a child in the nursery were so utterly lacking in discernment as to pit the pain and trouble and botheration lasting over months or years, against a very doubtful pleasure, which at most could only last but a few moments, and even when obtained, would in all probability be followed by years of more pain and more trouble in the shape of remorse, and inappeasable regret. Moreover, whose but the mind of a fool or a child

could be so utterly void of weightier ideas or
matter of import, as to conceive of, and ponder
over, a pleasure which any person with the smallest
grain of discernment could not account a pleasure
at all. For even if thy friend *did* possess thy wife,
he did so not in order to spite thee, or wilfully to
injure thee, but simply because he could not resist;
a fact which is self-evident from the sequence of
events, in that he quitted thy house the very next
day, so that he should be removed from a temptation he was totally unable to withstand. And thus
does thine own folly outweigh his in every respect,
seeing that in absolutely cold blood thou didst
ponder over and rejoice in the contemplation of a
terrible injury, while he on his part never desired
to injure thee at all. And now, what is the outcome
of thine inconceivable childishness, which through
the collective yet fatuous notions of the ignorant
and undiscerning, thou wast deluded into regarding
as heroic and grand? For, firstly, thou hast wasted
years of thy life in an utterly fruitless search,
giving thyself an infinitude of trouble for nothing;
and, secondly, thou hast lost thy wife, who died of
a grief which could easily have been prevented by
thy forgiveness; and, thirdly, if thou hadst found
thy friend thou wouldst have killed him, and so
deprived thyself of his existence as well; thereby
losing everything and gaining absolutely nothing

whatever. Moreover, just as thy evil intention was undeniably childish and fatuous, so was the notion that gave it birth nothing but childishness also, seeing it was solely the outcome of delusion and vanity, attributes both belonging to infancy rather than to manhood. For only the foolish think to possess the devotion of another entirely for themselves, totally blind to the possibility of losing it. or a part of it, through circumstances over which they have no control, as was the case with thy wife and thyself. Nor do any but children and misers clutch and snatch at a thing, saying, "This is mine, and nobody else is to have it but me." Besides, both thy love for thy wife and thy affection for thy friend were impure, and tainted with selfishness and vanity and reprehensible egotism, for had it been otherwise thou wouldst have placed their happiness before thine own, and if not heroic and magnanimous enough to condone their amour, wouldst have at least forgiven it, which had in all truth cost thee infinitely less trouble than journeying the world over in the way thou didst. So that altogether thy conduct has been such as to smirch thy soul with so grievous a taint that only a life of penance and benevolence and self-sacrifice can save it from consequences which were horrible in the extreme, and which, apart from this, nothing whatever could avert, seeing that as a man sows so must he reap, without the palest shadow of a doubt.' "

And here Aristion paused for a moment, having come to the end of his story, and then he said slowly and with emphasis: "Know therefore that the vices and weaknesses of mankind are nothing but childishness in disguise, and that only the glamour cast upon them by the ignorance of folly and of conventionality causes them to be endowed with a fictitious dignity which is no dignity at all; as is the case with resentment and jealousy and every species of revenge or backbiting. For, as that old priest rightly said, it is less trouble to forgive than to seek for revenge, and only he whose mind is utterly void of weightier matters would give such a thing a moment's consideration. And so, to be rid of weaknesses, we must behold them in their true light, and not in their fictitious one, as the woman in yesterday's story beheld the tree, which at first she thought to be a man. But, above all, we must identify our minds with that Uncon-ditional happiness which is within, for by so doing we shall grow up into a manhood of the soul, which shall render all wrongs as insignificant and remote as the bleating of a few sheep in a far-away fold.

"And now I have taught you all I am authorised to teach, your next instructor* being a hermit

---

* Both the long journey and the various teachers at each stage are purely symbolical of the aspirant's gradual development

dwelling at the top of yonder distant hill in his hermitage among the trees. And to him I will give you a word, Antonius, although he already awaits you both; while, as to a lodging place, there is a cottage near by where you can obtain food and shelter, seeing he has no room for you in his little hut. Nevertheless, remain here until the morrow, or as long as you will, for the journey is greater than it looks, and it will take you a whole day to arrive at your destination, even if you start very early in the morning." And Aristion arose and smiled, saying : " Until we meet this evening— and may peace be with you both." Then he crossed the garden and went out by the gate.

X

AND the next day Antonius and Cynara arose very early, and bidding farewell with a feeling of regret to their host and his wife, set out on their further journey, being directed how to proceed by Aristion himself. And for long hours they walked on a road, which was a ledge running along the side of a hill, and affording a view very beautiful to behold. For beneath them was a broad valley containing a wide serpent-like river, blue as the sky above, yet fringed with the shadows of poplars, dyeing it with a light green just beneath its banks. And in the valley were picturesque villages dotted here and there, as also on the great slopes of the mountains opposite, which were covered with patches of woodland and meadowland, and on which the herds grazed, wafting the tinkle of their little bells across the valley with the sighs of the breeze. And sometimes the notes of a shepherd's pipe were just audible far away in the distance, coming from who knows where, while at others strains of a song floated upward from the voice of a happy boatman, slowly paddling along the river in his boat. And Antonius said, as they turned a bend of the road, coming upon a solitary cow lazing on the grass: " I wonder what yonder cow sees of all this loveliness, for although its eyes no doubt are as ours, and thus these mountains and woods and the river down below must look in one sense the same, yet nevertheless they must be utterly devoid of meaning, or possess a different one altogether, and one we could never divine? Nay, are not beauty, colour, and poeticalness surrounding us on all sides, and yet there is a creature endowed with consciousness, yet utterly unconscious of these things, as a fish is unconscious of all outside its own element? And so did not Aristion say rightly when he said: ' Nothing in itself contains Beauty or Happiness, but only serves to draw out a particle of that infinite Beauty and Happiness latent in the mind, or better said in the soul'? And no doubt yonder cowherd emerging from that little hut over there is well-nigh as blind to all this loveliness as his cow itself; for although he sees the same contour of the mountains and the same unfathomable blue of the welkin, yet the poetry of it all, this is lacking altogether in his perception, for he has none in his mind." And Cynara answered playfully: "Meseems thou hast profited quickly by thy lessons, the more so as even a cow can teach thee something in spite of all thy long study and learning; but as to yonder cowherd, who knows but what wisdom he may not have learnt in his communing with nature, being perhaps a sage in disguise, as thy old beggar-man, to whom we owe a debt it were hard indeed to repay. And therefore let us not be too ready to cast aspersions on our humbler fellows, seeing that appearances are so deceptive, especially, as strange to say, I feel an unaccountable affection for yonder cowherd, even though he be dirty and ugly and altogether ungainly; and thus am loth to hear thee say he has no poetry in his soul." And Antonius laughed and answered: "It seems thou hast also profited by thy instructions, for surely thou dost feel a suspicion of *Unconditional* Love in thy heart for yonder fellow, who has nothing whatever in his favour to call forth a more personal feeling; and as I have learnt something from the

cow, and thou hast learnt something from his
master, we are now quits." And Cynara laughed
in return, but replied: "Not so, for if my love
were really unconditional yonder fellow would have
little to do with it, and I should have been
conscious of it all the time, even before I had seen
him at all. And now I will tell thee a little secret,
which thou canst believe or not, according to thy
inclination; but she who has love in her heart must
needs exhale it all around, for such is the nature
of true love, being like the sun, which, when it is
once admitted into the room, illumines everything,
even the ugly things as well as the beautiful. Nor
is love which fails to do this real love at all, but
only selfishness masquerading under its name."
And Antonius smiled at her with approval, saying:
" Little philosopher, thou art indeed worthy of so
exalted a title, and did I not tell thee I was destined
to learn much wisdom from thy lips, which act, it
would seem as a mouthpiece to thy lofty intuition."
And then they both fell to talking of Aristion and
his teachings, and his serenitude and his charm,
wondering at the same time what their next teacher
would be like, and what strange lessons he had in
store for them. And they walked on all the day,
only resting once to take a meal at a little village
situated at the top of a gorge, down which a
thunderous torrent flowed, rushing impetuously to

the broad river below. And after their meal they were compelled to descend this gorge, amid great boulders and moss-covered rocks, splashed by particles of cool spray, but they were unable to converse owing to the resounding music of the waters, which drowned their voices with its own. Then late in the afternoon they arrived in the valley by the side of the broad river, on which white swans glided mid the shadows of cypress and poplar trees; and in front of them stood the hill they were to ascend in order to reach their destination, a hill covered with woods. Then after a slow and arduous climb, they reached the top, at sundown, finding a little cottage nestling among the trees, at which they asked their way of an old woman standing on the threshold. And in reply, she asked quaintly: " Be ye the twain that Petrius the hermit is expecting? for if so, your lodging be here in this house, and he will await you in the morning." And Antonius answered in the affirmative, thinking to himself: these people seem to know everything; by what magic do they acquaint themselves of the doings of others? But to her he said: " Be it so, and now, good dame, provide us, I pray you, some food, and also water wherewith to refresh ourselves, for our journey has been long, and we are very tired."

So the next morning they arose early, and

having bathed and broken their fast, they were directed by the old woman to go a few hundred paces down the right side of the hill, where the forest was especially dense and the path almost overgrown and difficult to discover. And, following her instructions, full of expectation and enthusiasm not altogether unmingled with a little awe, they finally came out at a space in the shape of a greensward, containing a round tarn of pellucid water, and a stone hut, over which wild creepers clambered in verdant profusion. And in the hut was seated a man of calm aspect, with a pointed black beard and a long robe suggestive of a monk's habit, though of a less sombre colour, being a beautiful rich blue, a shade darker than the sky. And when he saw them approaching he rose and smiled, and came forward to give them welcome with a few well-chosen affable words. And he said : " It is a long time since I have had a new pupil, for the teacher is more ready to teach than the pupil to learn; and yet we cannot go a-seeking for neophytes, since in our Science, the rule is different from other Sciences, and the pupils cannot be *sent* to school by their elders, but must come entirely of their own accord." And he smiled again, saying : " My accommodation is of the meanest, but the green grass affords the softest of seats, and so let us sit down under the shadow of

these trees by the little pond, which is always
fragrant and cool, issuing from a spring in the
middle of the wood." And when they were seated
Antonius looked at the hermit and said : " Father,
I am struck by the seeming unchangeable happiness
and serenitude of not only Aristion, who sent us
both here, but also of yourself, who in spite of your
utter solitariness and choice to live away from the
world, have nothing of austerity in your countenance at all." And the hermit laughed a little, and
answered : " A sad philosopher, O brother! were
indeed a contradiction in terms, and quite
unworthy of the title, since what were the value of
philosophy unless it brought us peace?" And
yet," replied Antonius, " I have heard tell of many
a philosopher who was austere and sad, pulling a
lengthy face and appearing lonely and misan-
thropic, and out of tune with the world." And
again the hermit laughed gently, and replied :
" Then it seems your philosophers were such in
name only, but not in fact, for to him who realises
the oneness of life and all beings, there can be no
loneliness nor misanthropy nor discontent, but
completely the reverse instead. And yet to bring
this about is the very first aim of philosophy, which
diffuses within us a divine indifference, making it
utterly immaterial whether we live in the world or
out of the world, or in a palace or in a hovel, or in

one place or another. For know there are two kinds
of indifference—a divine indifference arising from
unchanging happiness, and a profane indifference
arising from unchanging tedium; and the one
pertains to the sage and the other merely to the
cynic. For just as the former declares: I am too
happy already ever to feel sorrow, so the latter
declares: I am too sorrowful already ever to feel
more sorrow, or ever to feel joy at all; so that the
attitude of the one is positive and of the other
entirely negative instead. And thus the true
philosopher cultivates a divine indifference, which
is brought about by an unwavering contemplation
of the bliss of the soul, and which I am authorised
to impart to such pupils as are willing to learn."
And Petrius smiled and stroked his beard for a few
moments, looking from one to the other of his two
prospective disciples with a glance of affection.
And then suddenly his face became grave, and he
said: "But there are secrets in the process of
instruction which must not be divulged to the
profane, for to those who practice diligently great
powers accrue, which if placed in the hands of the
evil would be grievous instruments of destruction,
and therefore a menace to the welfare of Humanity.
And so I am compelled to take steps to insure
secrecy from the lips of those I teach, for should
they fail me in this respect, then the speedy way

of knowledge must be closed to them, leaving no
choice but that they should take the tardy way
instead.   Nor is this secrecy all, but faith and
tolerance must be added as well, since tolerance is
the great security against misuse of power for
erroneous purposes, glamoured by the semblance of
good.   For once, long ago, out of a misguided
kind-heartedness, I relaxed the rules of our order,
allowing one of my disciples to acquire a few
powers before he possessed the necessary tolerance
in his heart to use them aright.   And this disciple
entertained a great affection for a friend, fanatically
desiring him to pursue the same path to knowledge
as he himself, seeing it had brought him
happiness; but that friend would have none
of it, returning angry responses to all his
entreaties, declining finally to hear any more.
Then   my   disciple   in   his   fanaticism   said:
'Well, seeing you are utterly blind to everything that is for your own good, I will make use
of my powers, and so compel you to comply with
my wishes'; but the matter coming to my
knowledge, I banished that foolish disciple for
three years, telling him to learn the virtue of
tolerance before his return, seeing that all fanatics
were dangerous to the community, as well as
totally lacking in discrimination and wisdom.   For
know that all people, whoever they be, are going

along the pathway to knowledge best suited to themselves and their characters and temperaments, and to endeavour to coerce them into taking speedier or more direct routes is not only wasted activity, but is also nothing short of folly, and likely to accomplish their downfall. For the incen tive to all action is the search for Happiness, and the only difference between the saint and the sinner is that the former searches the direct way and the latter the indirect way. And yet, just as only the brave and strong can hope to climb perpendicu- larly up the mountain side without coming to grief, while the weaker must needs take the winding and longer spiral path; so only the brave and the strong in spirit can hope to climb the precipitous mountain-side to Divine knowledge, the weaker ones having to take the slower path, in that any other course would inevitably result in their destruction." And Petrius the hermit paused again, allowing his eyes to wander for a moment to the blue sky as if in reflection, and then his gravity of expression melted once more into that of a smile, and he said: "The object of Divine Science is the transformation of ordinary conscious- ness into one which no words can portray, and which alone can be experienced but never described. And yet this is no argument against its possibility and existence—as many wiseacres and

learned ignoramuses would have us believe—for
who could describe sweetness to one who had never
tasted honey, or love to one who had never loved,
or the faculty of seeing to one born blind, tho'
all these things are capable of being experienced
nevertheless? But as in order to experiece many
a mundane thing, certain conditions must be
fulfilled, so to experience God-consciousness
certain conditions must be fulfilled also; the first
being knowledge *what* to practice, the second being
knowledge *how* to practice, and the third being
practice itself, for without this trinity of pre-
requisites nothing can be attained. And now my
task is to enlighten you respecting all these things,
and after a preliminary explanation, which
to-morrow, at the same hour, I will give, your
practices will begin, and may fortune attend you."*
And then Antonius and Cynara, deeming these
words to be an intimation that their instructor
desired to be left to his meditations, arose to
depart; returning, after a little ramble in the
woods, to their own habitation.

And it so happened that the air of the hills made
them unusually hungry, prompting them to ask
the old dame who kept the cottage what she could

* The practices here referred to are those of Yog Vidya : a secret
science which came from India, and spread throughout the
whole World in the course of time. It has been in England
for over 300 years, though kept very secret.

provide for their mid-day meal. But in reply she looked as if the question had never been put before, answering: " What else would ye expect to find on a lonely hillside but bread and milk and cheese and butter, seeing I have nothing but my cows down yonder to supply me with food?"* And Antonius looked meaningly at Cynara, saying, when the old dame had departed: " It seems our hardships are beginning, for how am I to contrive to sustain my body on such meagre and monotonous nourishment, being totally unused to fare comprising neither meat nor wine? And yet I suppose I must console myself with the thought that many a poor mortal is compelled to live on even less, having but water and bread, and nothing beyond, while not a few luckless fellows are starving altogether. And Cynara laughed and said: " It is as thou sayest, but, nevertheless, thy consolation is but a poor one; and certainly not very noble, and perhaps not really a consolation at all; since how can the sufferings of others ever act as a comfort to oneself, seeing they ought rather to act as the reverse? Nay, a better and more exalted consolation were in the reflection : If I myself have to undergo deprivations, thank Fortune I am the only one, and at any rate, my fellow creatures are

---

* Abstinence from all stimulating food is advised for beginners in the Science of Yog. Besides, killing animals is incompatible with the high degree of compassion exercised by Adepts.

happy and totally free from my own particular woes." Then Antonius laughed in return, and said : " Little philosopher, thou art indeed quick with thy wise and witty repartee, pricking the bubble of the false and foolish catch-phrases of the unreflecting, which fall from our lips carelessly, without our taking the trouble to enquire what they may mean, or whether they contain a particle of truth at all. But now, with thine aggravating wisdom, thou hast robbed me of consolation altogether, seeing my own lesser deprivations bring home to me the greater ones of others, which I had never thought on before; and the only way to undo the wrong thou hast done is for us to go into the woods and gather wild berries and herbs, so that we may augment the meanness of our meal; the extra trouble being thy punishment for outwitting me with thy bothersome repartee."

XI

AND the rest of that day those two wayfarers spent in the search for berries and sorrel and many varieties of edible herbs good to the taste; but when the morrow came, after a night of dreamless and refreshing slumber, they repaired again to the Hermit's hut a little way down the hill.

And when he had greeted them kindly he said : " Yesterday I hinted to you that all life is in

reality *one*, and the highest Consciousness is that
of Unity, in contradistinction to separateness; the
former engendering Bliss and the latter engendering pain. And now learn how this is the truth;
for just as the wave is one with the ocean, its
separateness consisting in name and form only, and
not in actual fact, so is each living creature one
with the Universal Consciousness; though in name
and form he appears to be separate. And yet not
only is the wave one with the ocean, but consequently conjoined with other waves, though
possessing an individuality of its own; no two
waves being exactly alike. And similarly is it with
Humanity, for although each unit of consciousness
possesses an individuality, yet it is conjoined to
all the other units, in that, as already implied, all
consciousness is *one*. And for this reason it is that
every high precept declares: Love thy neighbour
and do him no injury, for to injure thy neighbour
is to injure thyself, seeing that in this great ocean
of Universal Consciousness the law of eternal
Recurrence obtains, and that which a man projects
from himself eventually comes back to himself in
accordance with the great law of Cause and Effect
or Sequence and Consequence." And Petrius
paused, and smiled and asked : " Do I make myself
clear to your understandings? " And Cynara
replied: " Indeed, Father, who could fail to

comprehend one who assists his pupils with such simple and well-chosen similes? " Then Petrius continued, and said: " And the object of the Divine Science is to realise this oneness with all Life, so that, as I already said, a transformation of consciousness takes place, and the individual comes to know himself unified with the Universal, and so attains to unconditional Bliss here and now; and not merely in the future, as the ignorant suppose. And as a preliminary to this end he should project a feeling of perfect love towards all beings, yet at the same time, paradoxical though it may sound, catch that very feeling, as it were, in the net of his own mind, holding it there for ever, and never letting it escape. For this incomparable practice opens the door of Realisation, though the method be tardy in its results, however certain those results in the end. But the speedy method of achieving this realisation is a secret, or rather a series of secret practices, which in part I will divulge to you, disclosing to you more and more if you should prove yourselves worthy, but witholding them if you prove yourselves the reverse. And now go home to your cottage, returning to me in the morning; but in future come separately, the one coming an hour after the other; nor must you divulge to each other what I teach until I give you permission; for how should a person expect that another should keep a secret he is unable to keep himself? And yet even secrecy is the thing that requires a little practice, being a good exercise for the control of the tongue, which is ever too ready to babble when it were best silent. But now, farewell until to-morrow, and may peace go with you."

XII

AND for many weeks Antonius and Cynara practised the great Science under the tuition of Petrius the Hermit, pursuing their task diligently, and employing the mornings to that end, wandering over the hills and amusing themselves the rest of the day. And, strange to relate, they both began to look younger and healthier and more beautiful. And Cynara lost all her fadedness,*regaining her youth, but with an expression of countenance which had never been there before, and which straightway went to the heart of any of her beholders, as also the added mellowness of her voice, full of sympathy, benevolence, and love. And Antonius thought to himself: Truly Cynara's attractions may become a menace to my peace of mind, and stand in the way of my advancement along the path of knowledge, for surely my Instructor would disapprove of any form of

---

* This is not fiction, but fact, in that some who practise the science of Yog Vidya regain their youthfulness.

passion, and if I succumb, instruct me no more, so
that I shall be undone altogether. And yet I cannot
desert Cynara just to reinstate my peace of mind,
leaving her to live without a companion or
protector. Besides, she seems to love me more
than ever, and I would rather do anything than
let her suffer, after all she has done for me. For
in this manner did Antonius reflect and question
and ponder, wondering what the outcome would be
in the end, yet saying nothing either to Petrius
or to Cynara herself.

And one afternoon, having on previous days
exhausted all the other walks in the vicinity of the
cottage, and chosing for a change to wander
farther afield, Antonius and his companion came to
a little village situated in a valley some few miles
away. And the day being hot, and both being a
little tired after their walk, they made their way
to an inn, thinking to take there their evening
meal and walk home in the light of the moon. So
as they sat in the garden of that hostelry eating
their supper they overheard a conversation going
on between a few other guests hidden behind a
leafy partition, and so out of sight yet perfectly
audible. And one said, " Ah, yes, he practises
magic up there in the wood, and waylays the
innocent, pretending to give them valuable
secrets." " Aye," said another, " and all to get

them into his power and have his will of them
afterwards." "And that is why," said a third, "he
dare not live in any of the villages, but up there
all by himself, because he knows full well the people
would drive him out of any respectable place, with
his sorcery and evil doings." "And now," said the
first again, " I learn he's got another woman in his
clutches, a good-for-nought who came with a man;
but I know full well what the end will be, for the
man will be sent off and the woman will remain,
and when he's had his fill of her he'll send her off
too; and so on it will go, until one day he calls
down vengeance on his evil head." " Aye, and
what is more," said the second, " he's not alone in
his wickedness, for there's a whole black brotherhood of them, assisting each other in their nefarious
designs, and bringing the innocent to perdition."
And then there was a shuffling of feet and a few
remarks which could not be overheard, as the
speakers got up to move away. But Antonius and
Cynara looked at one another, feeling a strange
misgiving in their hearts, though it lasted but a
moment, leaving, nevertheless, the faint adumbration of a doubt behind in its wake. And as they
walked home they treated each other to the
substance of their reflections, yet never once
expressed a doubt as to the integrity of their
teacher, whom they now loved and venerated,

seeing the proofs of his teachings had been made
manifest in their own selves. But the next
morning, although Cynara said never a word to
her instructor concerning this, yet Antonius
broached a subject which he knew might lead to
the throwing of some light on what he had heard.
And he said: "Father, as every day Cynara
becomes more and more beautiful, I fear lest the
ashes of my old desire should be fanned once again
into flame, all the more so, as this time, contrary
to the last, love and admiration would be the
winnowers, two forces hard to be overcome, even
if it be desirable to overcome them at all. And yet,
if what I fear should come to pass, I am at a loss to
know the course I ought to pursue, and whether it
were best for me to depart altogether from her,
which certainly would solve the difficulty in a way
no other procedure could bring about." And then
Petrius pondered for a moment, and replied
musingly: "That course were always a possibility,
for separation is as a rule the best remedy for
passion, though why forestall things which, who
knows, may never materialise, and so allow the
mind to embrace all manner of apprehensions
totally futile in themselves? Nay, to fear a thing
is the most likely way of giving it birth, seeing
that the mind is creative, and what a man thinks,
that does he create sooner or later; while con-

versely, that on which a man refuses to think at all he starves, so that the very germ of it dies for want of sustenance." And Petrius smiled and added: " So now go home and be happy, and think no more of the matter one way or the other, for that is the best advice I can give."

So then Antonius went back to his cottage, thrust deep into the labyrinth of a variety of reflections in which faith and doubt swung like a pendulum from one point to another. For he reasoned: if my master were false, as those voices in the garden maintained, then why did he not jump at once at the opportunity I offered him, and so banish me, retaining Cynara for himself; and yet, on the other hand, why did he allow me even to entertain the notion for one instant of deserting her and leaving her in the lurch, instead of commanding me to restrain my desires on pain of some evil penalty, which he easily could have done? Nevertheless, to doubt him seems totally reprehensible on my part, seeing all he has accomplished for me; for truly the proof of the fruit is in the sweetness of its flavour; and everything connected with my practices has come about exactly as he foretold. And then Antonius grew angry with himself and thought: I will put an end to all this, and confess my doubts to-morrow, telling the whole story without further ado. And so the next day he carried out his design, and related the incident of the walk and the hostel, and the slanderous voices in the garden, and all that followed as the result. And when he had finished speaking Petrius looked at him with a smile, which conveyed the adumbration of disappointment, but nothing more, though it went to the heart of Antonius, afflicting it with sorrow and shame and regret, as no anger nor scolding nor resentment could ever have done. And Petrius said: " My brother, the ignorant explain away all things according to their ignorance, knowing no better, and if they be evil at the same time then their explanations are evil as well. For those speakers of whom you relate are confronted by a puzzle they are unable to solve without taking slander and uncharitableness to their assistance, and that being so, they clutch at an uncharitable falsehood in place of a charitable truth, never troubling for a moment to reflect whether they be right or wrong, being only too glad for an excuse to indulge in slanderous talk. For the world at large is totally incapable of understanding altruism and selflessness in connection with motive, believing in no motive at all rather than an altruistic one. And yet those speakers were but the instruments of the powers of evil known as the Black Brotherhood, and ever working to turn the disciple from the Right Hand

Path as soon as he shows signs of becoming a force
for good. For it was they who unbeknown to
yourself prompted you to go to yonder tavern,
so that you might overhear what you did. And
although I knew this to be so, in that these evil
brothers are perceptible to the subtler senses of the
initiate, nevertheless I did not warn you, thinking
it advisable you should both be put to the test,
and your faith should be tried in the way it
undoubtedly was, such tests being necessary for
your advancement, and a prelude to the receiving
of greater spiritual truths. For learn, that we of
the White Brotherhood strive to turn even evil
into good, taking the very tools of our opponents
and using them for loftier purposes ourselves; and
although the poisoned edge of these tools as used
in their hands had done you no harm, yet the
cleaner and sharper edge, as used by us, scratched
you just a little, seeing that you came through the
assay victorious, it is true, but not entirely
unscathed. For the first and very best course is
never to doubt at all, and the second is to doubt
your own doubts, as you did, while the third and
wrong course is to doubt altogether; and that
means retardation, or even failure in the end."

Then Antonius looked sadly at his teacher, and
said : " O, Master, I am reproved by your kindness
as well as your power to convince, making me

ashamed of my doubts and sorry for what seems
to me now my ingratitude; nevertheless, were it
right if I were to go blindly forward without ever
questioning anything at all? " And Petrius replied
with a smile of affection : " Nay, that were uncalled
for indeed, though your very query undoubtedly
shows me you confound questioning with doubt,
thinking them to be one and the same thing, which
truly they are not, possessing on the contrary a
very subtle distinction; for to question is to have
faith and to believe in the validity of that which
one questions, and so is positive and constructive,
but to doubt is to disbelieve in the utility of the
question itself, and so is negative and destructive
Or to propound the matter in other words : the
act of questioning is the method whereby we seek
to construct something on a foundation we know
to be sound—as one who having found a firm rock
busies himself with the design and construction of
the house he desires to build; but the act of
doubting is to disbelieve in the possibility of
constructing any house at all, deeming the
foundation to be rotten and unsound in itself, and
so unable to support any structure whatever. And
yet, think not that doubt in itself is a sin, but
merely an indication, showing the amount of
ignorance, or, if you will, knowledge, in the mind
of him who doubts, for he who must needs be

shown two pairs of pebbles to convince him that
two and two make four—doubting its possibility
—at once indicates to his teacher his lack of intelligence, in that he is unable to realise the simple
fact without being confronted by the material
proof. And now go home, and think no more on
the subject in a remorseful way, for truly remorse
is a waste of good activity, identifying the mind
with sadness and depression instead of joy, which
is its divine inheritage.' And when he had finished
speaking Antonius seized his hand and kissed it,
turning away without another word.

XIII

AND many more weeks went past, each week
bringing a little more knowledge and happiness
and power, and, in addition, beauty of body and
beauty of soul.   And one day Petrius said to
Antonius: "And now a few hidden powers are
on the verge of waking, and merely a touch, as it
were, is necessary to bring them into manifestation,
and then a portion of the subtler realms of nature
will be visible to your now etherialised senses
And yet before this course I have a commission to
give you, necessitating a journey of a few hours on
foot, which you will take alone. For I have here
a package of value, which I wish you to deliver to
a brother living in a village on the crest of that

hill which we can see from a little opening there
in the trees." And he led Antonius to the spot he
had mentioned, taking at the same time a small
packet from his breast, and giving it to him, with
sundry instructions. And so the next day Antonius
set forth on his errand, happy to be rendering a
service to the teacher he loved, yet at the same time
regretting the instruction he had to forego as a
consequence. And the sky as he started, was
covered with dense clouds, which broke into
torrents of rain, rushing soon in rivulets down the
side of the paths, and carrying mud and pebbles
and gravel along with them, so that Antonius got
wet to the skin as he picked his way along, as best
he could, with the aid of his staff. But when he
got down into the broad valley below the rain
ceased and the great vapoury curtains rolled aside,
giving here and there a vista of the firmament, like
blue lakes surrounded by grey indefinable foliage.
And then, in one clearing, he could see the snowy
mountain peak which was some day to be his
destination, projecting its great chin into the sky,
enveloped by a grey misty beard of clouds. And
he thought to himself: ' How long will it be
before I ascend that great summit, and indeed
shall I ever ascend it at all, being content to remain
here below, for am I not becoming happy enough
without venturing forth any further? And yet if

the joy to be encountered up there rs proportionate
in increase to that I have already encountered, then
were it folly to abide where I am now for ever."
And with such-like reflections he got across the
broad valley, and began ascending the hill on the
other side: hastening his steps so as to reach his
goal before the sun sank down, leaving him no
light to guide him on his way. For the evil
weather had retarded him sorely, and as to
returning to Petrius that same day, it had now
become impossible, seeing it would be nightfall
ere he could fulfill the object of his mission. And
the climb was steep and slippery, by reason of the
recent heavy rains, so that he felt as if his journey
would never end, although as twilight approached,
he could see the light of his destined village
twinkling in the damp air above. And then
suddenly as he climbed, apprehensive of nothing
but making a false step in the dark, there sprang
out from among the trees a man, who threw himself
upon the wayfarer without a word, trying to wrest
the packet from the folds of his garment, so that a
struggle ensued, which had indeed proved disas-
trous had not Antonius been the stronger man.
And at the moment of attack Antonius had thought
to strike his assailant with his staff, but, swift as
lightening, there came the counter-thought to stay
his hand lest he should do the man injury. And

then, all at once the man wrenched himself free, and Antonius saw the gleam of a dagger in his hand as he stood menacingly a few paces off. And he said " Give me that packet or else I will plunge this dagger into your breast." But Antonius answered : " That may not be, for this packet is not mine to give." Then the man said : " I will be merciful and let you keep the packet if you will open it and read out to me the secret which it contains, for only on that condition will I spare your life." Then said Antonius : " Alas, if my life goes, then the secret goes also, for there will be no one to prevent you from seizing it; and yet if we fight I on my part will only attempt to disarm you, and not kill you, seeing I am filled with pity for one who is driven to such a plight as to be tempted to rob the innocent, who have done him no wrong. And look, I too have a weapon on my person with which no doubt i could destroy you, being the stronger man, but to use it against you were evil, and not to be thought of on that account." " Then," said his opponent, " cowardly fellow, you are afraid of your own skin, and are but hiding your cowardice under the guise of magnanimity, and although I am the weaker man, yet nevertheless I would fight for the posses- sion of that secret, which means more to me than life." Then at so unjust a taunt, a flame of anger shot into the heart of Antonius, taking all his strength to subdue its force; and yet the very next instant an impulse arose to throw the dagger away (and so be beyond temptation), which he followed without another thought. And then, to his astonishment, suddenly a voice of unspeakable gentleness said: "My brother, the conquest is yours, and the ordeal is over, and truly you did well; for in reality I am no thief at all, but am the very brother for whom the packet was destined, having come to meet you, that I might help your teacher in the carrying out of the test, which had to be applied solely for your own good. And now pick up your dagger and put it back into its place; though some day not very long hence, you will need it no more, for he who acquires perfect Love is freed from all attack, seeing he learns to protect himself with weapons mightier than swords." And so then Antonius, overcome with joy and relief and astonishment blended into one, picked up his dagger, too overtaken with surprise to speak, but his enemy, transformed into a friend, came forward and took his arm, saying: " And now let me assist you the rest of the way, for this night you will spend with me in my house, where indeed you are thrice welcome; and shall have food and warmth and rest, which you well deserve." And Antonius followed him, and felt strangely at peace through

the very gentleness of his voice, though of his
face he could hardly see anything at all, because of
the darkness and the density of the wood. And his
companion said: " The ordeal was severe, and
even more so than you divined yourself, not
knowing how deep it was calculated to probe into
your heart. But of that we will speak later, when
you have put on dry clothes, and eaten, and
refreshed yourself; for in a few minutes we shall
be at my own door."

So then a little while and Antonius stood in the
house of his new friend, being thus enabled to look
on the face corresponding to that gentle voice; and
the light of the lamp showed a man of some
thirty-five years of age, spare and slender, but fu¹l
of activity, vitality, and strength, and void of all
femininity in spite of so marked a gentleness whenever he spoke. And his house, though modest and
free from luxury, was neat and full of taste, and
apparently tended by one male servant, who
prepared a bath for Antonius and provided ı
change of clothes, for which he felt indeed
grateful, seeing he was wet and weary and a little
cold. Then when he had bathed and changed and
eaten, he said to his new companion: " And now,
I beg you, tell me more of the meaning of all that
has occurred, for although I realise I have been
subjected to a test, yet I am unclear as to all that

test implies, and what is its exact value and import." And his companion said: " Know that the time has come, as no doubt Petrius already told you, for your initiation into the method of attaining powers which are denied to the profane, but before this can be, the teacher must have assured himself that the pupil can be trusted with forces so potent, lest he be placing fire, as it were, in the hands of a child. For know that the heart must be purified of all temptation to take revenge, or bear resentment under any provocation what· ever, as also to be free of angry impulses, leading to lack of control, and any form of retaliation and smiting back. And yet this is not all, for respecting these powers absolute secrecy must be retained, so that the pupil would sooner lose his body almost than give his secret away. And so, I being one of the brotherhood, was instructed to put you through this severe test, attacking you to discover whether you would strike back, and then trying to wrest a secret from you in addition, in order that I might probe your integrity to the full." " Then," said Antonius," all this I now understand, but on one point I need further enlightenment, for why when I refused to fight to the death, telling you even if I had you in my power, I would only protect myself, never striving to injure you fatally or even at all— why, in the face of all that, did you call me a

coward, seeing that to fight you at such odds
hardly merited the taunt? " Then his companion
smiled upon him very benignly, and said : " My
brother, that was the very climax of the test, aimed
at unearthing in your heart the absolute finesse of
bravery, which is more essential to the neophyte
than that of any other kind. For learn that bravery
(and conversely cowardice) are of two orders, the
lesser being physical and the greater moral; and
whereas the former is dependent merely on health
and general well-being, the latter is dependent on
something far higher altogether, and therefore
rarer as well. Nay, strange to say, the one often
seems to contradict the other, as it did in your own
case, for truly he who refuses to fight must
ofttimes be accounted more heroic than he who
stands up to face the fray. And this is so, because
to the moral hero the taunts of friends and foes
mean as little as the blows of the adversary to the
physical hero, who thinks alone of conquest, and
nothing beyond. And yet how can that compare
with the generosity of one who says ' Truly my
adversary! in the face of being deemed a coward
by the whole world, I will not risk taking thy life,
even though thou hast done me a multitude of
wrongs; for what is the death of my reputation in
comparison to the death of thy body, which would
surely plunge thy mother and brethren into

mourning and woe!' And so now, my friend, you realise why I called you a coward, when in truth you were nothing of the kind, for it was solely to probe the depths of your moral bravery; and the test was indeed severe, seeing that for a fraction of a moment you wavered, and needs must throw away your weapon lest you had been tempted to succumb." Then his companion ceased speaking, and looked approvingly on Antonius, but the latter said: "Then the victory was not altogether complete after all, for had it been otherwise I should never have needed to cast the dagger away?" And his companion answered smiling: "Nay, were everyone of us absolutely perfect, then the necessity for these ordeals would not exist at all; and yet think no more of that, for if the heart be right the hand is stayed from doing wrong, and the impulse which you felt was nothing but a little flicker of the expiring fire of habit, brought over from hundreds of previous lives, and not to be utterly quenched in a moment of time. And now give me the packet entrusted to you by our brother, and I will give you one in return, which you will deliver to him in its stead."

And in the morning Antonius set out to walk back to his temporary home, his mind full of joy and love and felicitous expectation. For the rains had departed, leaving an aftermath of snow-white curly clouds in the turquoise sky and a moist fragrance on the earth, refreshing to the senses, and even to the very soul itself. And hundreds of little flowers had come forth in the night, mingling their motley colours with the laved and brightened verdure of the woods and lanes and meads, so that the love-laden soul of Antonius sang, as it were, a hymn of adoration to Nature, as he walked on his way. And he thought to himself: " I have been parted from Cynara but a whole day and night, and yet I am longing to get back to the sight of her beautiful face, which somehow mingles itself with all this loveliness and enriches its very essence in a mystic unaccountable way. And not only that, but the calm face of my beloved teacher is also blended with it all; and the more I love Cynara the more I love him, and the more I love him the more I love Cynara, and all are one, commingled in a great unity of joy." And he hastened his steps, carried along by the exhilaration of his thoughts, making him feel as if he were treading on air, replete with mere shadows of flowers and grass and mossy paths, offering no resistance whatsoever.

Then, as evening approached, he neared his home, and as he was some few hundred paces away, he saw the figure of Petrius coming to meet him down the hill. And he took the packet from his

breast in readiness to hand it over, but when
Petrius saw it, as they came quite close, he
embraced his pupil and said: " My brother, thou
hast done well, and I am glad to see thee back,
carrying the palm of victory. And now yonder, at
my hut, Cynara awaits thee, impatiently having
longed for thy return; and yet say nothing of all
this to her, for to do so would frustrate my designs,
seeing she also has her ordeals as well as thee." So
Antonius gave his promise as they went together
towards the hut, where on seeing Cynara once
again, he kissed her with a joy in his heart he was
at no pains to conceal; while Petrius standing by
their sides, regarded them as a benign father might
look on two happy children at play.

XIV

AND the following day, after each had received
their usual hours of instruction, Cynara and
Antonius rambled about in the woods, as was their
custom in the afternoons, especially towards the
cool of evening, whiling away the time with happy
talk. But this day the face of Antonius looked a
little sad and museful, so that Cynara commented
upon his silence, asking him the reason, and
begging him not to withhold from her what lay
in his heart. And he looked on her with a sad
intensity, saying: " O, Cynara, I have progressed

a little along the path of knowledge, having
conquered a few obstacles with some success, little
dreaming that the most formidable one lay slum-
bering within my very heart all the time, only
waiting to awaken and come to life." And Cynara
said : " And pray what is it? " And he answered :
" O, Cynara, it is thyself, and my love for thee,
which all these weeks has lain dormant, and now of
a sudden has woken up, knocking at the door of
my realisation like one who will not be denied! "
And Cynara smiled at him a sagacious smile, and
said : " And yet why is it an obstacle, seeing my
own love has been awake for thee all the time? "
And he answered : " Alas, that makes it in one
sense the worse for me, and not the better, for the
very barrier to my passion which thy unrequital
would have erected is thus removed, and so my
asceticism of the body stands on the brink of an
abyss, with no railing whatever to prevent its fall,
which unless something totally unforseen happens
must sooner or later come about, do what I will."
Then Cynara smiled again a sapient smile, and
replied : " Art thou so very sure that absolute
ascetism, as thou dost call it, is demanded of those
that love, seeing that love itself transforms the
lower into the higher, and so makes it pure? And
was not our former teacher Aristion married, so
disproving by his example what thou hast just

said? " Then Antonius replied: " O, temptress!
art thou also a test in disguise? for if so, then this
is surely the worst so far, and methinks I shall fail."
And Cynara replied: " Nay, to my knowledge at
least, I am no test, though who knows what is in
the mind of our teacher, for I may be a test quite
different from what thou dost think, and not one of
an order to try thy asceticism, but to try thy selflessness instead, seeing it is sweeter to be loved in
return when one loves as I love thee, than not to
be loved at all." Then Antonius answered: " But
have I not just told thee I love thee very much? "
And Cynara replied: " But what is the good of
love if it be never expressed? For to hide one's
love in one's heart, withholding its happiness from
those who desire to receive it, is to ignore the very
first principle of true love, which is nothing else
but to give happiness unto others, placing them
always before one's own self."

Then said Antonius passionately: " O, my
Beloved, an ocean of gems would I give to render
thee happy, and thy words stab me like a knife in
the heart; and yet I am torn 'twixt my love for thee
and its yearning to give thee all the happiness
lying in my power, and my yearning for knowledge, which certainly will be withheld if I fall a
prey to passion, for so I read in the ancient books
And yet this is not all, and my terrible dilemma

does not end here, seeing that if I remain by thy
side I shall certainly succumb to thy loveliness, and
if I go away I shall be tortured with yearning to
come back, not only because of desire to see thee
again, but also because of pity for thy sadness,
which would almost break my heart." And then
Cynara, beholding the extremity of his woe, took
his head to her breast and stroked his hair,
kissing his head repeatedly and soothing him as
one soothes a child. And he complained, " Woe is
me, who thought I had reached happiness
dependent on nothing but the soul, and yet now,
that happiness seems covered by a veil, and I am
utterly undone, yearning for thy kisses as I have
never yearned before,* the more so because I long
to make thee happy, and realise how thou must
have suffered all this time when I hardly loved thee
at all. And yet thou art stronger than I, never
once complaining nor reproaching me for my
selfishness, although all the time thou didst know
that when I first met thee I only made love to thee
to amuse myself and gratify my passions, and for
no higher motive whatever. For in those days
love was unknown to me, a mere dream and folly
at which I used to laugh with the cynicism of
ignorance and inexperience. And now this is my

---

* This appears to be another tendency during occult development,
viz. : the birth of a deep passion for a high type of soul.

punishment, coming by the hand of nature through the law of sequence and consequence, which is, as it were, avenging thee for the wrongs I did."

And then Antonius suddenly lifted his head from her breast, as a thought flashed like lightning through his brain, and he cried: "Once I selfishly sent thee away by reason of my desire to obtain knowledge, thinking solely of myself, and not of thee; but fate has been kind, allowing me the chance to repair my error, sending thee back again for that very reason; and now, for a moment, I thought to leave thee once more, or deny thee my love, about to commit the very same error I had committed before, totally discarding the lesson I was no doubt intended to learn. And yet this cannot be, and to deny thee my love seems now as reprehensible as it seemed right a moment ago, for have we not learnt all along that knowledge may not be purchased by selfishness and the sufferings of others; and even if I be deluded, and that knowledge be withheld as the result, then it were better to wait for it a little longer than to buy it at so fatal a price. So now my mind is made up, and to-morrow I will tell Petrius my difficulty and my resolve, knowing he will bear with me in his charity and tolerance, and *understand*, as perhaps no one else in the world can do." And as he finished speaking, Cynara flung her arms around him in a transport of joy, pressing him close to her breast as if she were unwilling ever to let him go.

And on the morrow Antonius went down to his master at the wonted hour, full of reflections and speculations as to what he would say, and in what manner he would receive his resolve, remembering how one day not so very long ago that self-same master had advised him on the very subject he was now going to approach. And yet, as he recollected that advice, one thing troubled and puzzled him a little whit, seeing that Petrius had said in effect: " Separation is the best remedy for passion." And to leave his beloved therefore was not utterly beyond the boundaries of consideration. But verily now, after so many more weeks together in the sweetest and closest companionship, even the mere thought itself stung him like a poisoned arrow shot into the very centre of compassion, namely, his large and loving heart. And then of a sudden his reflections came to a pause, for the bend of the path brought him within sight of Petrius, who waved his hand in welcome as he approached.

And after the usual greetings Antonius told him his tale, and his difficulties and fears, and the resolve he had in view, begging his guidance and the fruit of his wisdom, as well as his comfort and forgiveness, for he knew himself to be weak and still tainted by desire, longing all the time to be

strong. And so, as he came to the end, he said:
"And if this be another test you have devised for
me, O father, then it seems I must fail." And
Petrius looked at him lovingly and compassion-
ately for a moment without speaking, and then,
with deliberation, he said : " My brother! the wise
go slowly and with dispassion, exacting not too
much from themselves, and being content to walk
ere they can hope to run, not to say fly. And the
wise also having learnt in their tolerance and
charity to exact nothing from others, have at least
earned the right to demand not the totally
impossible from themselves, which is practically
what you are doing, seeing you would attempt to
thwart altogether the strongest force of Nature,
without the necessary knowledge and power to
achieve so prodigious a task. And so, if you will
forgive me the simile, you are like a child who,
thinking to fight a giant, laments on being confronted with so formidable an opponent, over his
own helplessness and weakness, instead of over
thinking to fight him at all. For your error does
not consist in your defeat, but rather in your lack
of humility, prompting you to deem yourself
stronger than in all truth you are as yet, seeing
perfection cannot be attained in a few weeks, or
even months or years, and more than often not in
a whole lifetime. Moreover, you have misunder-

stood the nature of the problem, which does not consist in the total annihilation of all passion by a process of killing out, but rather its purification and control. For learn that passion is of three kinds : the selfish gratification of one's own desire for the mere sake of obtaining sexual pleasure, without taking into account the welfare of one's partner in the act; and that is the first and lowest kind, since it is devoid not only of unselfishness, but also of the purifying influence of love. And the second form is the desire for union with the body of a woman for whom one entertains affection and devotion, yet nevertheless in the act of passion thinks of one's own pleasure rather than hers. And the third and highest is when one thinks no more of self at all, but solely of the welfare and enjoyment of the beloved, performing the act of passion not for the gratification of the senses, but solely as an expression of love on the physical plane, or in other words, to bring another being into the world of men.

" And so, now you must see, that this is no test of my own devising, but one which exists through the very nature of things, and one by which you can learn an invaluable lesson, and so adjust the debt between yourself and the beloved. For, although a little while ago, solely to test your faith, I hinted that the treatment of passion with the oblivion of unremembrance were in some cases to effect a cure, yet in the present instance to resolve on such a procedure would be altogether reprehensible, seeing the desertion of your beloved a second time were not only to ignore the debt already incurred, but to incur a greater one as well. For learn, that although the fullest knowledge cannot be purchased until passion be purified to the very highest degree, yet neither can it be purchased by the pains and woes of others—just as Heaven cannot be reached by climbing a ladder composed of dead men's bones. So that altogether your resolve was right, and the test which Nature imposed has been withstood. Nevertheless, see that you learn its lesson to the full, tempering passion by the purifying waters of moderation, unselfishness, and control, for by so doing will you gain instead of lose, and thus prepare the way to that Happiness which is too continuous to suffer passion or any form of desire to find therein a place at all."

Then said Antonius : " O, master, I am consoled and enlightened by your words, and also full of gratitude; and yet tell me why did I read in those ancient books, that complete asceticism of the body was essential to the pursuit of the highest wisdom ? " And Petrius smiled and said : " The way of the world is actually to make a pursuit of

Desire, seeking every means to increase it rather than let it run its natural course. And this is altogether hostile to the Science of God, for who *can*, or even *cares*, to think of the things of spirit when he is altogether engrossed in the things of the flesh? So that knowing this to be the case, those ancient writers emphasised the necessity for the practice of continence, meaning thereby moderation and clean living, but not torture of the body in the shape of attempting to oppose the natural appetites altogether. For to do this would mean not to be rid of them, but rather to drive them into the mind itself, which were the height of folly, seeing they are then liable to become an obsession, torturing their victims unceasingly and distracting them from all nobler thoughts and deeds. Nay, let me tell you how once there lived a high-minded and altruistic but simple man, who went about doing good and meditating on Love and the Divine Consciousness, seeking to bring consolation and happiness and enlightenment to all people he met. And one day an emaciated old devotee chanced across his path, and after expounding the felicities of devotion, said to him : ' But to attain to the highest and purest state of the mind, it is necessary to fast, refraining altogether from food for several days on end, for this advice I have given to many, and the results that accrued were wonderful in the extreme, as I know from my own experience.' So then, that unsuspecting and over credulous altruist immediately followed this advice without any further questioning, beginning his fast that very same day. But alas, far from any miracles in the form of ecstatic visions or transports of joy accruing as a result, something of an entirely different order came about instead; for the sensation of hunger took complete possession of his mind, suffering him to think of nothing else whatever, and making him weak and ailing in addition, so that he had neither the strength to do any more good works nor the concentration to think exalted thoughts. And then, while he was in this deplorable condition, a friendly old priest, who was at the same time a physician, called at his house, having heard that he was ill, and so unable any longer to perform his good works. And he said to him kindly: ' My son! what is the nature of thy complaint, and how didst thou come by this emaciating malady, which so grievously stands in the way of thy numerous and merciful duties?' And then he told his confessor the whole tale, so that that old priest hardly knew whether to laugh or to chide, doing a little of both in the end. And he said: ' One thing is simple, and that is the remedy, which is to eat, and at once, without any further ado. But this is not the whole of my

advice, which further consists in counselling thee
not to be led astray by desire to emulate others
in methods which may be applicable to one man's
condition, but may be highly inapplicable to
another, for a feat which an acrobat can perform
with ease the ordinary man cannot perform at all;
or again, the fruits which to twenty persons may
taste good, to the twenty-first may taste bad:
seeing that nothing whatever applies to the whole
world, there being in all things exceptions by
reason of individual circumstances, environment,
and state.' "

Then Petrius paused for a moment, and smiled,
adding : " And now, do you understand the moral
of my story, and in what way it applies to yourself
and the question you asked ? For, as that old
priest said, this is something which each man must
discover for himself through his own perspicacity,
knowing the rules set down in all books are
indications for the general mass of students and
humanity itself, and not laws blindly to be followed
by all. Nay, the speediest progress is ever attained
by doing good to others, and not merely refraining
from evil, and spending a whole lifetime in eradi-
cating one particular vice or attribute from one's
character, especially when it acts as an obstacle to
that very doing of good. For truly he who thinks
least of his own character benefits it the most." And

Antonius answered : " I have understood : for just
as food is a means arranged by Nature to perpetuate
the life of the body, so is passion a similar means
to perpetuate the life of the race; and therefore
to deny oneself passion altogether is like denying
oneself food; a denial which instead of aiding one
to progress, acts instead as an obstacle to the doing
of good, by reason of the obsessing thought of
hunger which ensues, as in the case of the over-
credulous altruist of your story. For both food
and passion are right if used for their rightful
purposes, namely, to appease hunger; and only if
they be turned into a hobby as it were, do they
become evil, placing as formidable an obstacle on
the path of progress, as the opposite extreme of
attempting to discard them altogether."

And then Petrius interrupted him, saying :
"And now I will confide to you another little morsel
of wisdom, but one which perhaps you have already
guessed from the result of your practices; for
without a doubt purity of the heart affects the
body, and hence all the bodily functions as well,
so that he who embraces his beloved as an act of
devotion, having no selfishness in his heart, loses
nothing in the form of spiritual power by that
embrace, feeling no reaction or weariness as a
result; but he, on the other hand, who embraces
his mistress out of lust, and nothing beyond,

having an impure and loveless heart, weakens and injures both body and mind. And so the moral is: Into everything whatsoever it be, bring purity and love, which is the secret of health and harmony of the body as well as of the soul."

Then Antonius arose, kissing the hand of Petrius, as he said with gratitude: "Truly the ways of the wise are wonderful and replete with comfort, never demanding the impossible nor the totally impractical, as does the so-called wisdom of the world, which is but emptiness and hypocrisy in a mask. And now my heart is lightened and encouraged to proceed with the great work;" and so saying he turned away, walking homewards up the hill.

And in front of the cottage Cynara sat awaiting him with impatience, wondering what he would say. And as he approached with joy on his face, he exclaimed rapturously: "O, Beloved, once more have I profited by thy wisdom and intuition, and indeed thou wast no temptress, but the mouthpiece of truth, and altogether my resolve was correct." And he led her away to a little bench among the trees in the garden close, kissing her repeatedly when they had sat down. And she said: "Now is the cup of my happiness full to the brim, the more so for the long waiting, for which I am now altogether glad instead of sorry." And he replied, with the very quintessence of love shining from his eyes : "Thou wast ever the most generous of souls, never once reproaching me for my misdeeds, and even now I believe thou didst help me to my resolve, not for thy sake so much as for mine own, knowing that any other way spelt misery for me, as undoubtedly it did." But for answer, she merely pressed his hand to her heart, her silence giving consent. And he said : " I knew it was so, seeing thou dost answer me nothing." Then suddenly he added : " O, Cynara, where didst thou learn thy nobility, for as many a time I have repeated, thou art more advanced than myself." And she replied, smiling : " Not so, for thou hast what I have not, and maybe I have a little something thou hast not, and yet that would make us quits rather than me superior to thee. Nevertheless, if I have learnt any nobility at all, thou knowest my life has been far from exemplary, being by many considered totally evil, yet from evil is always to be learned a little good, as the result of experience, if from nothing else. For, through that very experience, and the woes attendant thereon, I acquired a few things I could never have acquired otherwise ; being battered, as it were, into gaining a little wisdom by the painful knocks of a self-imposed fate. Aye, as one after another deserted me, I learned not to grieve, but to take things as they came, realising the futility of resentment and the value of resigna-

tion instead. And when I saw their hearts turned
away from me to other more graceful and attractive
women, I learned not to be jealous, but to be rid
of my vanity and pride, as also not to reproach my
errant lovers for leaving me in the lurch. And now
I am glad of all this, seeing I will make thee a
better mistress and friend than otherwise I ever
could have done." And Antonius exclaimed:
" Talk not of mistress, but rather of wife, for now
I will never let thee leave me again unless it be of
thine own choice." But Cynara answered quickly :
" Not so, since a man of thy station must not marry
one like unto me, who in the eyes of the world
possesses no virtue at all, and who may act as a
millstone round thy neck when thou dost return
as a great sage to that very world thou hast now
renounced. For when the time comes, thy mission
is to teach and help others towards wisdom, yet
who will listen to thee, and believe in the integrity
of a philosopher who takes not a goddess of
learning, in the form of some high-born lady, for
his partner in life, but merely a despised and
ignorant courtesan instead? "

And Antonius cried in ecstatic admiration : " O,
Cynara, truly thou art even nobler than I thought
thee all along, if indeed that were possible, and
never have I loved thee as I love thee now, feeling
as if my heart would break with a transport of

devotion. And yet thy words sadden me, seeing they imply thou canst even *think* for a moment of a separation which were utterly intolerable to me, as I had hoped also to thee. And as to thy high-born lady, curses be on her and the impotent chatter of the world, which could put her absolutely negative virtue against thy adorable nobility of soul. For truly the much praised innocence and virtue of most women, is nothing but a fortuitous restraint, resulting in a total lack of experience, and therefore entirely negative, as the tameness of a caged bird, which, were it let loose for a moment, would immediately fly away." Then said Cynara with a playful laugh, "Thy arguments no doubt are ingenious, and worthy of an orator; nevertheless, what I said is true, and so I will be all in all to thee,* yet at the same time leave thee thy liberty; for so long as thou art glamoured by the intoxication of love, thou art in no fit condition to decide whether I be a fitting wife for thee or not, and thy wits have forsaken thee just a little, requiring the passage of time to bring them back. But now I will close thy further arguments with kisses, and take thee deeper into the wood, where we may think of nothing else but love."

* This is symbolic of the fact that conventional morals are not of necessity an indication of spirituality at all, nay, often the reverse, seeing in many cases they are based upon selfishness and vanity.

XVI

Now after a few more weeks had gone by, the
time came for the undertaking of a further step
on the journey, which led to a town situated some
days' march away, higher up in the hills. So that
one morning Petrius told his two disciples they
must bid him farewell and fare forth to newer
fields. " And from now on," he said, " your lives
must be different for a time, and no longer secluded
from your fellows, but rather must you be as
missionaries, seeking to spread a little enlightenment abroad, though at the same time sedulously
guarding the secret of those practices I have
entrusted to your care. And to this end you will
need money and more clothing and equipment
generally, taking a house which shall be ready for
you, having been arranged for your coming at my
request; while as to the money and clothes, I will
notify one of the Brothers living near your own
house to despatch a servant on horseback, so that
you can give him all the needful instructions
yourself. For we of the Brotherhood have a means
of communicating with one another across space,
as you in the near future will learn, realising that
space is no obstacle to the power of thought or the
transplanting of consciousness from one place to
another. And so to-morrow evening your servant

will be here, and on the following day you will set forth for the doing of new deeds. Moreover, in the town which is your destination, and known as Marbletown (since all the buildings are composed of white marble), you will find another teacher, Florian the Sage by name, a man of venerable appearance and renowned for his wisdom. And yet you will only go to him once in a while, though you will seek him at the moment of your arrival, seeing that he will indicate to you the place of your abode; also the work you shall undertake."

So then, all happened as Petrius had said, his own servant arriving the following evening with money and equipment, and also mules on which to ride for the journey, for it was long and steep. But as the hour for departure approached Antonius's heart was moved to sorrow, and touched with the pathos of saying farewell, so that he could scarce keep back the tears which uncontrollably welled up into his eyes. And he said brokenly, as he approached Petrius for the last time: "Much have I learned from your lips, O Master! but one thing I have failed to learn, and that is to feel no grief at parting from one whom I love. And now I am totally overcome with sorrow, born of a devotion and gratitude which can find no expression in words, but only in tears instead."

And Petrius looked at him with unspeakable
dulcitude and compassion in his gaze, and, taking
his hand, said, in the most soothing tones : " Be
not ashamed of thy tears, my Brother, which flow
from the poetry of thy nature, and are more
eloquent of gratitude than many a well chosen
word. And yet it is rather I who should be
grateful to *thee*, for thy implicit faith and patience
and diligence and aptitude; and if I too do not
weep it is because thy departure means no separation from thee at all, seeing I will follow thee with
my consciousness to the very ends of the world :
as also my beloved Cynara " (and he drew her to
him, as she stood close by sorrowfully looking on).
" For know that the link between master and pupil
can never be broken, and that your consciousness
has now become a part of my own, eternally
blended in the great world-soul. And so, sweet
friends ! be not sorrowful over an illusion, and
think not you can leave me in reality, merely
because the body goes away. For the time will
soon come when you can actually see me, and
commune with me whenever you will, having
acquired, as it were, the eyes to perceive that which
is still denied you to perceive now. Nay, a farewell
is but a wasted sadness, although, until the eyes
have become incapable of tears, dried for ever by
the pure sunshine of joy emanating from the soul,

it needs must be. Nevertheless, if my love could dry you tears, assuredly it would, but seeing it cannot, then know this separation will only be short, because your internal sight will awaken very soon, and you will see your old teacher standing lovingly by your side as if you had never parted from him at all." And then he embraced them both long and tenderly, saying : " And now, sweet friends, go! for to protract this parting were but to prolong your sadness. And may my blessings and peace go with you on your way." Then Cynara, with streaming eyes, led the now sobbing Antonius away up the hills, and Petrius looked after them with a smile, in which love and compassion and paternity were all blended into one, until he could see them no more.

So from then onwards the life of the two way-farers underwent a change, beginning by their journey to the town of Marble, then a long sojourn amid its white walls. But this time the journey was neither long nor arduous, by reason of the mules which Antonius was permitted to take. Nevertheless, for a little while his heart was sorrowful, and the scenery and incidents of the journey all passed before him almost unnoticed ; his thoughts all the time remaining with Petrius, and the pathos of that leave-taking, which had so touched his soul. And yet this sorrow was but

of short duration, and disappeared so quickly that
he was moved to say to his companion : " Truly
wonderful is this Science of God, which dispels
dolefulness so rapidly, causing it to fall from one
like water off the feathery back of a swan, as our
teacher Aristion said.   And somehow I feel as if
even its sorrows were more beautiful than the most
beautiful pleasures of the world; if indeed they be
beautiful at all, for everything becomes sublimated,
no matter what it be, and the most of all does love,
my sweet companion of the soul."   And Cynara
looked at him tenderly, wafting him a kiss as she
rode on her mule by his side.   And then, as the
late afternoon approached, and they came to the
crest of a hill, they saw the white loveliness of
Marbletown below them in a large hollow, over-
shadowed by enormous mountains on the further
side.   And the reddening sun dyed its domes and
cupolas and towers with orange, causing it to look
like an enchanted pleasance hidden away from the
profane travail of mankind among the hills.   For
large cypress trees arose here and there amid its
buildings like great sentinels keeping an endless
vigil; so that Cynara exclaimed : " Never have I
beheld   anything   so   impressively   silent   and
beautiful before ! "

And then a little later on, after much enquiry
and seeking, the travellers found themselves before

Florian the Sage, who answered to the title in the
fullest meaning of the word. For his hair was
white and long, thrown back from a lofty broad
forehead, which, however, was totally free from
lines; and his beard was snow white, pointed, and
flowing down well-nigh to the region of the heart,
while his eyes were strangely deep set, and gazed
forth at his beholders as if they could penetrate
into the very soul itself. Furthermore, he had the
bearing and dignity of a courtier, with a gravity
seldom tempered even by a smile, though when he
did smile his face transformed itself into something so totally benign and dulcet as to change
him into another being, as it were, altogether.
Nor was his voice out of keeping with his general
mien, being deep and resonant and impressive, for
he spoke with deliberation and emphasis, yet
interspersed his conversation with a suspicion of
wittiness, which was rendered all the more
humorous by reason of the fact that he seemed
totally oblivious of it himself; accompanying his
most pithy remarks with scarcely a shadow of a
smile.

And as Cynara and Antonius were ushered by a
servant into his awe-awakening presence he rose
from a chair, in which he had been seated reading a
scroll, and bowed, making a gesture with his long
thin white hand, praying them to sit down. And

he said, as he resumed his seat: " From my friend
Petrius you come, I believe? And it is well. And
your house is prepared, lying close by here, to
which my pupil Leonidas shall presently conduct
you." And then he paused for a moment, while
Antonius thanked him for his courtesy, after which
he continued: " The gods have sent you to assist
me in our work; for this town is full of budding
philosophers in need of instruction, being for the
most part but learned idlers, working within the
precincts of a circle, thinking to discover truth
therein, and totally blind to the fact that the very
truth is outside their circle altogether." Then
Antonius said: " O, venerable Father! with such
a one as yourself in their midst, surely they do not
lack a redeemer, and can scarcely be starving for
want of enlightenment." And the sage answered:
" I, as you see, carry a weight of years, and so am
deemed old-fashioned and out of date, being
treated by these younger ones with mere indulgence, mingled with somewhat of scorn and an
abundance of irreverence. And yet, that is my
protection, leaving me unmolested to remain, as
it were, the power behind the throne. For they
say: ' He is but an old man who shuffles along
the tumbledown slums of antiquated philosophies,
and therefore his opinion is of no value.' And so
they leave me entirely in peace, which is what I

desire, thus enabling me to direct my younger disciples to work for our cause, without seeming myself to come into the matter at all, which is ever the most expedient manner to work and influence mankind, and give a pauper's mite towards the improvement of humanity. For alas, the present age in which we live is plunging headlong into the morass of materialism and ignorant unbelief, a fact arising from that meagre knowledge, which is a dangerous thing, by reason of its total lack of humility, and its consequent fertilisation of pride instead. And thus our philosophers erect a fictitious knowledge based upon nothing but nescience, denying, as a result, the immortality of the soul and the existence of any consciousness outside and above the physical envelope, trying to convince even those whose psychic eyes are open to the perception of superphysical beings, that all such perception is imagination, and nothing beyond. And yet assuredly ignorance can never convince knowledge, as also inexperience can never negate the fruits of experience; which, by the way, recalls to me a story I will tell you, seeing it may prove useful one day in argument. For once long ago there was a certain city filled with ignorant and superstitious people, who angered the gods by reason of some unholy and sacrilegious rites which they performed, involving horrible cruelty and torture in the shape of human sacrifices. And not only were innocent men and women offered up to demons, but first their eyes were put out, while the populace looked on intoxicated by the spectacle and the sounds of the screams of agony which filled the air. And then at length, as I said, the gods grew angry, and vowing to put an end to such monstrous activities unless they ceased forthwith, never to be resumed, sent a proclamation to the city by the mouth of a holy man, who came from afar and took up his stand in the market place, exhorting them to mend their ways. But as they would not listen to him, all with the exception of five or six turning a deaf and scornful ear, at last he exclaimed, ' Seeing ye are deaf and obdurate, it now falls on me to carry out the behests of the gods, my masters, which is to curse this city in such wise that all its inhabitants, save those who heed me, and their children and grandchildren and great-grandchildren, shall be stricken with blindness. And this I now do in the name of the Almighty.' And his voice rang out, terrible and overwhelming in the awfulness of the curse. Then, with the exception of those five or six repentant ones, all the inhabitants of that city began to lose their sight, so that their children and grandchildren and great-grandchildren were born

blind, having no memory or idea of what it meant
to see at all; but the progeny of those few repentant
ones were born, as are the rest of the world, with
their visible faculty unimpaired.   And so it came
about that from time to time great discussions
arose between those congenital blind ones and
those who could see; and the former argued:
'Aye, fools, why this thing ye call seeing is all
imagination and trickery and nonsense, having no
foundation in fact, and ye prate to us about it
solely to give yourselves airs and make yourselves
conspicuous and important, and to endeavour to
get the better of us ordinary but more sensible
mortals.'   Then the latter tried to convince them
by logic and rhetoric, but seeing all arguments
failed, they said: 'Very well, we will convince
you by doing things ye are totally unable to do
yourselves,' which was no difficult matter, seeing
they were unencumbered by the limitations of
blindness, and could perform many a feat the
others could not perform at all.   But again their
opponents said: 'This is no proof, for your
performances are but conjuring tricks and the evil
devices of charlatans and impostors, so away with
them, and let us hear no more.'   And then at
length the time came for the expiration of that
curse, which was brought about by the appearance
of a strange and imposing physician, who suddenly

arrived in that stricken city, creating a sensation
by reason of a wonderful balsam he applied to the
eyes, causing, after repeated application, the blind
to see. And those who suffered themselves to be
treated were cured, but the rest, pronouncing the
man to be a quack and an evil influence, conspired
against him, so that the authorities banished him
from the city on the slanderous pretext that he
obtained fees under pretences that were palpably
false. Then the gods, learning of this, said
amongst themselves: ' The curse we inflicted on
these foolish denizens, in order to punish them,
and so lead them from their iniquitous ways, has
run its course, and is therefore at an end, but if
they choose to inflict a second curse on themselves
in the shape of bigotry and folly, so that they
scorn the opportunities we now afford them, then
that is an affair of their own, and no longer one of
ours;' whereupon those gods went on with their
work. But as a result that city remained stricken
with blindness for another two generations, and
would have remained so until this day, had not
those few enlightened ones who were cured gone
forth, out of pity for their fellows, and brought
back that physician, and many another like him,
so that in the end all were restored."

Then that old sage paused for a moment prior
to expounding the moral of his story, looking the

while at his two listeners with penetrating gaze. And he said : " The meaning of my allegory is not far to seek for those who have understanding, for that stricken city is none other than the world, and its denizens the inhabitants of this globe, who possessed at one time the eyes to see in the shape of clairvoyant faculties and super-physical percep- tion, but by reason of desire for gain, and lust for power, and other wickednesses born of selfishness and materialism, the controllers of Destiny were compelled to deprive them of those extra senses, cursing them as it were with blindness, and making exceptions merely of a few enlightened and more altruistic souls, so that the truth might never fade altogether from the world. And yet the time has now approached for the termination of that curse, and those same controllers of Destiny have sent physicians in the form of Adepts and Prophets and Teachers, to cure the blindness of Humanity; but instead of welcoming their new deliverers, they will have none of them, prolonging the curse of their own accord by reason of bigotry, and pseudo-sapient negation, and intellectual vanity, and such like attributes of ignorance masquerading under the guise of knowledge; so that they persecute those deliverers, endeavouring to banish them altogether from the domain of serious thought. Nevertheless, out of compassion for their persecutors those deliverers remain, instilling into the minds of poets and philosophers and writers little gems of Truth, though unbeknown to those writers themselves. For know that inspiration is nothing less than a glimpse of truth, culled from a higher plane, and put into the heart of the poet or philosopher by favour of intelligences working incessantly for the enlightenment of humanity; so that his capacity to become inspired is commensurate with his capacity for holding himself receptive, and freeing his mind from the obstacles of bigotry and vanity and egoism, which taint the heart as nothing else in the world. And now, my son, as I said, this city is full of budding philosophers, as also of poets and sculptors and minstrels of every kind, for they gravitate here by reason of its beauty and purity of air: and some of them are preaching utter folly, while others catch a glimpse of truth here and there, and so may sooner or later be drawn into the Brotherhood; though seeing, as yet, disciples are few, I am glad to have yourselves to swell the ranks, and say a word for me in the Hall of Discussion, sowing here and there a seed which may fall on good ground . . . . But now I will call my pupil Leonidas, that he may escort you to your dwelling, for it is not well to keep your servant waiting outside with the mules

too long a time." And so he walked slowly from
the room, but with back unbent and a step as firm
as if he were a young man.

And Cynara turned to Antonius with a mis-
chievous smile, saying, beneath her breath like an
indiscreet schoolboy when his master has left for
a moment the class: " I wonder how old he may
be, and why does he look at all old, when the
others are young in comparison, for he is not only
venerable but he inspires me with awe? " And
then, at that very moment, he came back into the
room, bringing with him a young man, medium
in stature, and with an unusually small head, and
a manner denoting an abundance of vitality,
expressing itself in rather quick movements,
though devoid of any agitation. And this new
comer greeted his fellow students with an affili-
ating smile and a few warm words of welcome,
saying he placed himself at their service and was
ready to do for them anything they desired. So
then, having bid goodbye to the sage himself, they
found themselves in a little while at their new
abode, which, though modest, was tasteful and
comfortable, and spotlessly clean; while a twilight
of gold, tempered with the virginal whiteness of
its walls, arose from the dim rays of the now
lighted lamp.

XVII

AND so from then onwards the life of these two underwent a change, and they returned once more to their fellows, making many friends and engaged in all manner of activities.   And as time went on those powers which had been promised to Antonius awoke and came into being, so that, for one thing, he found himself endowed with a flow of language and eloquence which astounded even his own mind; as also the power to heal the sick of many diseases, and, above all, to heal, as it were, the soul of sorrow.   And as a result of this all manner of people collected round him, some to learn, some to discuss, and some to be healed; but enemies* collected as well, for he defied many a convention, and also aroused envy and suspicion by reason of his good works and healing, seeing he took no money for his pains, and so enraged the physicians on the one hand, and the priests on the other, who inquired into his religious convictions, and found them not as their own.   And the doctors said among themselves : " He heals for nothing, there-fore he will ruin us, for all our patients will leave us and go to him instead.   Moreover he sins against our knowledge of medicine, using methods

---

* This is always the case, for the powers of evil seek every means to place obstacles in the path of those who become a force for good.

of which we do not approve, and which must be
quite erroneous; so that if the patient gets well it
must be merely the result of their own credulity,
and nothing else." And the priests said : "He
never takes part in any of our ceremonies, nor
enters our temples, nor praises the gods, therefore
he must be a heretic and an evil influence, and so
a danger to the community; and well it were if we
could accomplish his downfall." And the conven-
tionalists said : "He transgresses against the laws
of society, failing to observe this and that; besides
many of his disciples are women and girls, and
seeing he takes no fee for his instruction, and as
nobody does anything for nothing in this world,
we may be safe in pronouncing him a libertine,
who covers up his immoralities under the pretence
of imparting philosophy." And even the Atheists
condemned him, saying : "He is a charlatan, a
trickster, and an impostor, performing miracles,
which are but conjuring tricks, in order to gain
notoriety; and the very fact that he takes no money
is a proof of what we say, because by this means
he gains even greater notoriety, pretending to be
an original and a philanthropist and a saint. And
yet, when we ask him how he accomplishes his
feats, he evasively replies, ' By a knowledge of
natural laws, the secret of which he is not permitted

to reveal,' showing at once that the entire matter must be trickery, and nothing else." And so, as time went on, although his friends remained steadfast, his enemies increased, hurling at him calumny and slander of every sort, and seeking to thwart and exasperate him by every manner of means.

But he said within himself: " My happiness, which is of the soul, cannot be extinguished by the pitiful folly of these ignorant mortals; and yet it seems, the story of that old sage was something of a prophecy concerning myself, and the end will be that I shall be banished from this city and sent forth on my further journey by the decree of fate, irrespective of my own inclinations; and that very soon." Nay, so it happened; for the priests conspired with the physicians, and the physicians with the atheists, and all three parties went to the authorities demanding that this charlatan be tried and then imprisoned, or else expelled from the community altogether. But in the meanwhile his friends came to him and said: "We have heard that to-morrow or the next day you will be arrested, and therefore beg you to fly from the city while there is yet time, for to go of your free will is better than to be driven forth."

But Antonius said: " Not so, I am content to wait and be taken; for had it been intended that I should do otherwise* my masters would have apprised me of the fact. Nevertheless, I am grateful for your counsel, seeing it prepares me, and so warns me to bid farewell to my friends while yet I may." So that same day he visited Florian the Sage, knowing that from him he would receive instructions as to the next step in the journey; for during his sojourn in Marbletown, Florian was ever his director and counsellor in secret. And this old sage said, as he entered : " My Son! you have done well, and sown much good seed in this city, obtaining many disciples for the Science of the soul; and yet your downfall, though apparently evil, will bear good fruit, for it will weed out the true disciples from the weak and sickly in spirit, showing forth those who are genuine from those who are mere dabblers, and ready to fly at the first sign of danger, losing faith at once. But as to yourself, together with Cynara, the last part of the journey may now be undertaken, seeing you have earned the right to attain your final initiation from the Masters, who, as you know, dwell beneath yonder snowy peak which we can see through this window. But know

---

* This downfall in the eyes of the World is a thing every great
   Initiate has to face : and one of the rules is, that he should
   never defend himself to the extent of vindicating his own char-
   ate r . Even the greatest of Adepts, Jesus, had to face this;
   and, as to lesser initiates, of late years one is reminded of
   Mme. Blavatsky and others.

that the ascent is long and arduous; yet struggle
to your utmost, so that you attain the goal,
allowing yourself never once to think of defeat.
And now the way is clear, since the summit is ever
before you; but should you be uncertain as to the
way, ask your mind, so to say, and the answer
shall be forthcoming." And then Antonius bade
him farewell, and thanked him for his instruction
and the fruit of wisdom he had so freely bestowed,
whereupon the old man embraced and blessed him,
wishing him Peace.

So then Antonius returned to his house, and,
together with Cynara, prepared for departure, not
without a little mild sadness in his heart. And he
said to her: "Hast thou bid farewell to thy
teacher Florian, for who knows what the morrow
may bring forth?" And she answered: "I will go
now." But just as she turned to depart, suddenly,
without any warning, Petrius the Hermit stood
by their side. And a light shone around him of
surpassing beauty, while in his eyes gleamed that
benevolence and love which was ever there, but
now intensified and lovely beyond description. And
a great joy came up into the hearts of Antonius
and Cynara, mingled with adoration and love, so
that they felt like kneeling and worshipping him
then and there; but he said: "I am but mortal,
and come but according to my promise of not

long ago, for rather is it that your own faculties to
perceive have awakened, so that you may see me
almost whenever you will." And then he said:
" And now listen, for to-morrow the authorities
will take you, Antonius, but well I know you will
be faithful to your trust, and divulge no secrets,
making no defence, nor disclosing the fact that
Florian has been your instructor in any way
whatsoever; for your downfall in the eyes of men
is your exaltation in the eyes of the Masters, as
also the indication that your labour in the field of
publicity is over, or at least for the present; being
a matter for your own determining whether you
resume it later on. But know, that those who
suffer disgrace for the Masters and the cause of
Humanity, are rewarded a thousandfold, as you
will learn in due course. And now, my blessing
be upon you both until we meet; " and so saying
he vanished from their sight as suddenly as he had
come.

XVIII

AND in the morning, as predicted, soldiers
arrived at the house and arrested Antonius, taking
him then and there before the tribunal, where
Cynara followed, refusing to be parted from him
at so critical and momentous an hour. And a large
assembly of people was present, for the matter had

got noised abroad, filling the populace with an intensity of curiosity and speculation and excitement and morbid joy. But Antonius, on his part, faced his judges and the spectators with unruffled mind, saying to himself: "I will make this an occasion for endeavouring to do a little good, so striving to follow the Great Ones, and using evil tools, as it were for righteous purposes." And as he stood up with so calm a countenance confronting them all, some of the spectators whispered among themselves: "This is either no impostor at all, or else the very king of impostors, seeing he can invest his face with so much dignity and serenitude at the very moment of his disgrace." Then when all was ready the spokesman said: "We have it against you that you have corrupted the women and maidens of this city, under the pretext of teaching them a secret science, luring them away from the true religion, and imposing on their credulity by pretending to commune with spirits, and perform miracles in the shape of healing diseases. And all this being so, we look upon you as a danger to the community, and as an evil influence, which it behoves us to rid ourselves of, seeing we have the welfare of our citizens at heart." And Antonius smiled and said calmly: "I am apprised of your charges against me, and what then?" And the judges being non-plussed, and thinking themselves about to be deprived of the divertisement they had expected, seeing the prisoner showed no signs of making any defence, conferred with one another in an undertone, scarcely knowing how to proceed; while a great murmur, indicative of disappointment, was audible among the crowd. Then said the spokes-man again : " Should you be unable to prove your innocence, then the penalty is imprisonment or banishment." And again Antonius smiled, and answered with unruffled serenitude : " Be it so; and yet in demanding proofs of my innocence, first state the proofs of my guilt." Then another of the judges said, reading from a scroll : " We have despatched messengers, and ascertained that formerly in the town of your birth, you led an evil life, steeped in profligacy and riotousness and vice of every sort." And Antonius replied with dispassion : " Are then the follies and misdeeds of infancy a criterion of the behaviour of manhood? And must, in your estimation, a human being necessarily conduct himself at ten as he conducted himself at two, or at thirty as he did at twenty, or at seventy as he did at forty?* For is there no such thing as a change and reformation and outgrowing in manhood as well as in youth? Nevertheless,

---

* Those who suppose a riotous early life cannot lead to spirituality let them remember the case of St. Francis of Assisi.

although your statement is no proof, but merely an inference, proceed with your table of charges." And the judge said: " We have learned that the greater part of your so-called pupils are women and young girls, not youths and men, which is significant in itself; but when we learned further that you took no fees for your instruction, which was of suspiciously long duration, it is evident that you were repaid, not by money, but by favours in the form of licentious enjoyments, seeing that no man gives time and services without demanding something in return. Nay, this is evident, knowing as we do your former life." Then Antonius said calmly: " Here again is no proof, but merely an inference; and yet undoubtedly you have me at a disadvantage, knowing that my innocence is as unprovable as my guilt: for were I to summon all my female pupils as witnesses, being assured they would deny the illicit intercourse of which you suspect me, yet the answer on your part would be: ' These witnesses are no proof whatever, seeing certainly no woman would avow her own disgrace.' Nevertheless, nothing would induce me to summon any witness at all, in that by so doing I should place their reputations in jeopardy in order to save my own; for such is the nature of scandal, that even should I be acquitted, people would say, ' his witnesses lied in order to readjust

themselves in the public eye.' " Then the judge
said : " We see you deny nothing, drawing there-
from our own conclusions; and yet this is not all
there is against you, so that I shall now proceed
with the further charges, each one going to
establish your guilt.   For it is known that you
pretended to use secret powers, and worked on
the credulity of the innocent, feigning to cure their
diseases, when all the time the patients would have,
and *did* get well of their own accord.   And this
imposture on your part was doubly reprehensible,
since it went to deprive the physicians of an honest
livelihood, by luring their patients away from
them, and discountenancing the exalted science of
medicine."   Then Antonius allowed the suspicion
of an ironical smile to cross his lips, and said : " An
exalted science is one which is tempered with
altruism and nobility, seeking before all else to
effect a cure, if it be that of therapeutics, and if it
be any other, to enlighten humanity and manifest
Truth.   And the genuine scientist is he who
manipulates his convictions so that they coincide
with facts, and not facts so that they coincide with
his convictions, as your physicians have done
respecting myself.   For, finding I was able to
effect cures by methods unknown to themselves,
and therefore beyond the boundaries of their
knowledge, they dishonestly denied my cures, or

attempted to explain them away, instead of investigating first, and then, if necessary, avowing their own limitations afterwards." Then said the judge sternly : " To slander the physicians will avail you nothing, and only assist in establishing your guilt, for your statement is inconsistent with Truth, seeing that several physicians approached you, requesting you to confide to them your secrets, which you refused to do : and yet from that very fact we draw our conclusion, being assured that there existed no secrets to disclose at all, since the entire matter was one of imposture, and nothing more." Then said Antonius with a gentle smile : " To him who seeks in the proper spirit, truth and knowledge will not be withheld, as also to him who is ready to fulfil the essential conditions, in order to receive instruction; but seeing your physicians came to me utterly in the wrong spirit to begin with, and then totally refused to comply with the conditions I was compelled to impose, what else could I do but send them unenlightened away? For know that certain knowledge can be used for evil as well as for good, just as fire may be employed to destroy as well as to warm; and to place my particular order of knowledge in the hands of the untrustworthy, were not only the height of folly, but also a menace to mankind at large."

And then once more the judges began to confer
in an undertone, while the buzz of subdued talking
was again to be heard from among the assembly.
But after a few moments the spokesman arose and
said : " Nevertheless, in spite of what you have
just declared, there is yet a way for you to
minimise your disgrace, and re-establish your
reputation, for since we believe there are no
secrets, and you declare the contrary (seeking to
evade their disclosure by pretending it were
dangerous for mankind at large), then tell us those
secrets in private, so proving their existence
without further ado. Nay, if we consider them of
value, your integrity will be proven beyond a
doubt, whereas if we do not, then no harm will
have been done." And again a slight hubbub
began to be audible among the crowd, but the
spokesman quelled it, as did also the voice of
Antonius delivering his reply. For he said, with
deliberation : " As to my disgrace and my reputation, these are nothing to me whatever, and to
seek to minimise the former were childish, and not
worth the pains, while as to the latter, well, desire
for a good reputation is born of vanity and
egotism, and nothing beyond. Moreover, in this
instance, to gain my reputation in the eyes of the
world, were to lose it in my own eyes, thus proving
my heart to be vain and egotistical and untrust-

worthy, and ready to endanger Humanity for the worthless prize of public opinion. And so what you demand I am not ready to comply with; therefore proceed with your charges if you have any more to bring."

Then said the judge: "We have it against you that you teach heretical and superstitious doctrines, luring your pupils away from the only true Religion, and pretending to commune with their departed kinsmen and friends, yet knowing all the time that such a thing is impossible, and so totally unsusceptible of proof." And Antonius replied suavely: "Your words convict me of superstition, and yet what greater superstition is there than that which declares nothing is true save that which can be proven, and conversely, all is untrue which is susceptible of apparent disproof? For what son can prove that his father in name is his father in reality, seeing the fact is far easier to disprove than to prove? Nay, once there was a madman who possessed the delusion that his nominal father was not his father at all, and when his physicians and friends remonstrated with him he lacerated them with the keen edge of his argument, so that they had one and all to retire and give up the case. For, he contended, 'I have merely been *told* that my mother's husband is really my father, and, as all men are liars, it is probably untrue. Then one of his friends said : ' But your mother is a virtuous woman, and not an adultress, and it is well known she never possessed a lover.' But that exasperatingly logical madman replied : ' Who is in the position to say whether she possessed a lover or no, since all women with any sense whatever consort with their lovers in secret, and not in the market place or on the roof of the house ? Besides, even if she possessed no lover, who knows but that one day she walked alone in the lanes and encountered a scoundrel or couple of scoundrels, who outraged her then and there ? ' Then another of his friends said : ' But surely if that were the case, seeing she is still alive to tell the tale, she would have apprised the authorities and created an uproar, so that soldiers would have been despatched to catch those ruffians and bring them to justice ? ' And the madman answered : ' Not so for my mother would have been chary of owning her own disgrace, or even if not that, then anxious for the dishonour and chagrin caused to her husband by publicity, and so would have deemed it best to keep silent and suffer her wrongs without complaint.' And in this way did that insane logician argue, having an unanswerable objection to every proposition, though his father was really his father all the time. And yet, though his arguments were perfectly sensible, and might have

applied in one case out of a million, yet my
contention is, they were so extremely unlikely as
to be hardly worth a moment's consideration, being
born of delusion, and nothing less. And now that
is just the case with your own arguments
concerning my guilt, for they likewise are born of
delusion; the delusion of criminality which exists
as a fixed idea in your minds; for as in the case of
that madman, most of your arguments are likewise
based upon suppositions so unlikely that only to
the hyper-credulous could they carry any weight at
all. Nay, learn that the credulity of the sceptic is
every whit as great as that of the believer, affording
indeed matter for astonishment to the reasoning
mind; for the only difference is, that whereas the
believer is credulous about one set of things, the
sceptic is credulous about another, offering
explanations to negate phenomena, which are a
thousand times more difficult to credit than the
phenomena themselves."

And as he said this a slight murmur arose
among the assembly indicative of approval, which
was however immediately quelled by the judge;
but Antonius continued his speech entirely
unmoved. And he said: "What can be proved,
then, and what can be disproved, is no criterion of
Truth nor of untruth; but learn nevertheless that

thinking can be dishonest as well as acting, and he who brings an unlikely and totally far-fetched explanation to bear on the matter, solely to suit his own preconceptions or beliefs, is a dishonest thinker without the shadow of a doubt. And just in this way you have all erred respecting myself (as assuredly respecting others as well); possessing what I term the minds of spies,* and reading criminality and vice and evil into all things which appear strange and foreign to your thoughts, instead of seeking for more charitable and likely explanations first. And so, entirely ignoring the simple truth, which is embodied in the one word altruism, and is the key to the whole matter— seeing that he who has found happiness himself desires that others should be happy also— you bring forward a number of untenable supposi- tions, and credit me with attributes and powers I do not possess at all. For to account for the fact that I take no money from any of my numerous disciples, you endow me with the erotic capabilities of a chanticleer, conveniently forgetting the rake or libertine is discernible from other men, by reason of the signs imprinted on his frame and face, as the result of excess. And to account for my doctrines and clairvoyant faculties, you

---

* This really means the mind of a detective, who is always on the look-out for crime, and so, often sees in the most harmless action something of a criminally suspicious nature.

call me an impostor, again conveniently forgetting that impostors have very good reasons for imposing, namely, in order to obtain money, which I for my part have no desire to obtain at all. And then, finally, you say that I lure my disciples away from the true religion by pretending to commune with the souls of the departed, which you further say is impossible, because totally unsusceptible of proof. Nevertheless, what is the backbone of all religion other than belief in the immortality of the soul? And so if I commune with the departed for the comfort and enlightenment of the bereaved, I am helping to prove Religion, and not to disprove it, and therefore teaching my pupils to *know* that which hitherto they have merely *believed*." And then again a slight disturbance, indicative of some approval and also a little astonishment, was audible among the assembly, while the judges on their part conferred in an undertone at some length, finding the accused inconveniently rich in argument and logic and flow of words.

Then finally the spokesman said : " Although you are endowed with the gift of talking, nevertheless we remain unconvinced, considering you as a bad influence in our midst, a breaker of our sacred traditions, and an inciter of others to do likewise; and yet, after deliberation, we are inclined to be merciful, looking upon you, after listening to your defence, rather as a deluded man than an out-and-out criminal. And this being so, we are willing to minimise the penalty somewhat, which shall not be imprisonment, but merely banishment from this city without permission ever to return." Then Antonius said, with a smile of gentleness: "I am apprised of the sentence, and depart with but one regret, which is of the nature of sorrow and compassion for those mine enemies who conspired to accomplish my downfall; for alas, by the law of Retribution, over which I have no control, these must sooner or later suffer, without a shadow of a doubt; and not so much for the wrong done to me as to those who desire I should remain. For learn, that every moment of unhappiness brought upon others by our misdeeds must be paid for by unhappiness to ourselves in return.* Nor will the fact that I broke your traditions and customs and conventions alter this in the least degree. For traditions are not susceptible of hurt, as are the hearts of human beings as yet unimmune to all suffering, through the sun of Enlightenment and Truth. Moreover, if I went against your traditions, I did so because they stood in the way of altruism and charity and the bringing of comfort and enlightenment to

---

* This in occult literature is called the law of Karma.

others." Then suddenly he turned to the assembly with a smile of surpassing benevolence, and said : " My brothers and sisters! to-morrow I leave this town, as you have just heard, for ever; and yet before I go, will you bear with me for a few moments while I tell you a story? " And a great applause arose, with shoutings of " Aye; tell us a story; " for he had won the sympathy and approbation of the crowd, by reason of his eloquence and benignity.

So then he began : " There lived formerly in a little town among the hills a widower who possessed two sons; and he was much addicted to the pleasures of the chase and athletic games, as no doubt are many of you. But one day while he was out hunting he fell from his horse and injured himself so severely that his comrades were compelled to fetch a bier and carry him home, where he remained for the rest of his life an incurable invalid, never able to go forth any more, nor even to move from his couch. Nevertheless, he made no complaint nor fretted, thus showing himself to be so great a paragon of virtue that the priest, who visited him from time to time, said : ' Truly the sight of this uncomplaining sufferer is a veritable sermon in itself.' And so long years passed away, and those sons grew up, showing themselves to be dutiful and loving towards their

father, albeit reluctantly compelled to leave him
much in solitude, by reason of the fact that both
had become merchants, and so must needs spend
the greater portion of the day in the counting
house. And then, one day it so happened, as this
sufferer was getting well on in years, that some
friends came to visit him, bringing with them a
young woman of comely appearance and a kind
and charitable heart. And when she beheld him
lying there she was filled with compassion and
solicitude, so that she begged to be allowed to
come and enliven his solitude from time to time,
and tend him, almost like a nurse. And this she
did, making that old man's days less lonely and
so happier, administering to his wants and com-
forts, until she became, as it were, indispensable
to him altogether. And then, out of gratitude, and
because she was kindly and comely and lovable,
that old man at length developed a romantic
attachment for her, as she also for him, out of pity
and admiration for his patience and nobility of
soul. But when these two sons, who were also
attached to one another in their brotherly way,
realised what had happened, they said : ‘ This will
never do, and what does our old father want
falling in love at *his* age, showing himself so
deficient in dignity? Moreover, people will talk
and indulge in objectionable gossip, for it is against

the conventions for an old man to have a young
and attractive woman about him, and alone with
him at all hours of the day. But, worst of all, who
knows but that he may not bequeath her his
fortune, or a part of it, and thus deprive us of our
rightful inheritance? So that we must certainly put
an end to this unseemly and dangerous state of
affairs without further delay.' Then those two
hard-hearted sons conspired together, and forbade
that young woman the house, giving strict orders
to the servants that she never be admitted on any
pretext whatever. But as a result, the light, as it
were, went out of that old man's heart, and because
of longing and grief and loneliness, and disappointment at the hard-heartedness of his sons, he
contracted a fatal illness, suffering tortures of
every sort, until he eventually died and went to
Elysium. And only on his deathbed, through the
kindly intervention of a benevolent old priest, who
expostulated with those hard-hearted and pitiless
sons, was he suffered to bid farewell to his
beloved, and so die in peace. But the hand of fate,
in the form of the law of sequence and consequence struck down those sons, separating them is
they had separated others; for the younger shortly
afterwards went to sea and was attacked by pirates
and killed, while the elder was left to mourn his
loss, living a life of solitude and sadness, for his

brother was his only friend in the world." And
Antonius paused for a moment and watched the
crowd; and then he said: " And now learn that
there are times to adhere to conventions and times
to go against them, as in the case of this story and
in my own case; for assuredly those . two sons,
though they did what was right according to the
ordinary ways of the world, committed a terrible
crime against the heart; so great indeed that the
hand of self-imposed destiny smote them without
further delay. Nay, seeing that old man had been
sorely afflicted enough by reason of his terrible
and incurable infirmity, to afflict him still further,
taking advantage of his helplessness, was an action
of cruelty, dastardly in the extreme. For to love,
and fall in love, is not a sin, but rather a virtue;
and to punish it, instead of to reward it, is a crime
in the eyes of God." And then he turned once
more to his judges, and said, with dispassion and a
smile of pity: " You, who condemned me, have
committed a crime against the heart also; but
seeing I bear you no ill-will, and you neither
awaken the pain-bearing emotions in me of resentment or anger, your crime can do me no harm.
Nevertheless, think well over what you have done
for the sake of those who follow, and stand before
you as I stand here to-day. And now, Citizens of

Marbletown, farewell, and may peace be with you!"

Then the soldiers took him away, but among the crowd there was a great uproar, for the people said : " He has been wrongly condemned, and he was no impostor, but a holy and just man. Did he not look noble and imposing as he stood there, and was he not a great orator? " And with such like expressions did they manifest their feelings until they dispersed.   But Antonius was escorted back to his own house, where by reason of a special favour he was permitted to say goodbye to his disciples and friends, though some of them never came, deserting him then and there, for they feared public opinion, and were loth to be seen in his company ever again.   Then when all were assembled, and they had crowded round him, giving vent to their love and admiration in soulfelt words, he said : " My friends, though I go, yet there are others who can not only discourse as I have, and better, but who can teach you and impart to you secrets I was not permitted to disclose.   And now my downfall here, though seemingly evil, is really good, since it has shown the true disciples from the false, and the steadfast in the pursuit of knowledge from the fickle-hearted and weak." So then the rest of that day they all spent in philosophical discourse, and arrangements for further instruction either from the lips of Petrius or Florian the Sage; but as the hours drew near to say farewell, some wept because of love and gratitude and sorrow at parting, not only from Antonius, but from Cynara as well.

XIX

AND in the morning the two wayfarers found themselves once more on the road; and this time it was for the very last part of the journey. And Cynara clung lovingly to Antonius as they walked along, calling him her hero and other fond names, expressive of tenderness and admiration and love. And they sometimes laughed together over the proceedings of the previous day, and yet at other times were a little sad because of compassion. For, said Antonius: " If it is so easy to condemn one man who is innocent, it is easy to condemn hundreds; and although in my own case it matters not a whit, for I, as also thou, have a happiness of the soul nothing can take away, yet others are not so fortunately situated, and may suffer unmentionable agonies as a result of their disgrace." But Cynara answered: " Although what thou sayest is true, nevertheless even the innocently condemned are not absolutely innocent in one sense of the term, for thou hast forgotten they are but suffering by reason of their former misdeeds, which although they may no longer recall them in any way, still bear result, according to the law of cause and effect. And so, my beloved, thou art forgetting thine own words of yesterday, and in one sense pitying those who are merely preparing the way to happiness by paying off their old debts." Then said Antonius, kissing her and laughing: "O, paragon of Widsom! thou art ever ready with an argument to dispel my sorrow, and so art an embodiment of the very quintessence of Consolation; for although many can cajole the mind into forgetfulness of its pains, thou dost banish the pains themselves with unerring dexterity. And yet one little pain thou art still loth to banish, and dost thou know what that is?" And she replied: "How should I know?" Then said Antonius: "By reading my thoughts, which I am well aware thou canst do." But Cynara answered: "Nay, that were not justified without thy permission." Then said Antonius· "But I give thee permission." And Cynara laughed, and looked a little embarrassed, and said: "Thy thoughts embody a question and a wish." And Antonius said: "Thy surmise is correct, and what is thy answer?" And Cynara replied: "I will give thee an answer at the end of the journey, when we are back in our own home, if we ever go back at all; but at present I will give thee a kiss instead, to seal thy lips."

And when he had received her kiss he said:
" Ah, at the mention of home I had a sudden and
ungovernable yearning to see Pallomides, my
beloved friend, once again; and his calm and
beautiful face arose before me like a divine
portrait, as he spoke to me across the great space.
Oh, truly it seems very long since I saw him for
the last time in his villa by the sea. And now, little
sorceress! I believe thou didst somehow conjure
up his image before me in order to divert my
thoughts from further questioning; was it not so?"
And she answered: " Nay, it was nothing of the
kind, and no doubt thy friend Pallomides was
thinking of thee at that moment, and thy mind
being like a mirror, reflected his image."

And just as he had finished speaking they
turned a bend of the path, along which they
walked, and lo, there in front of them lay a dog
which had injured its paw, and was in sore distress,
moaning and making a pitiful noise. And as immediately Antonius went up and petted it it wagged
the very end of its tail, and looked appealingly
up into his face. So then Antonius stroked and
caressed it the more, and talked to it, the while
examining its wound, which had come about by
reason of a large splinter having got embedded in
the flesh, causing thereby a festering sore. And
Cynara said: " Do thou search for and remove the

splinter while I go and seek a certain leaf, which
we will lay on, after having bathed the wound with
water." So saying she went into the adjoining
fields, first taking a little pot from her bundle
wherewith to bring water from the trickling
mountain spring. But Antonius, on his part,
plucked a big sharp thorn from a shrub near by
and said to the dog soothingly, as he proceeded to
work : " Old friend, with one thorn we make war
against another thorn, even as we set a robber to
catch a robber; " and the dog whined and yelped
and wriggled, but nevertheless it understood, and
was grateful. And when the thorn was extracted
it wagged its tail and licked the hand of its bene-
factor, until Cynara returned with the leaf and
some water in a little pot. And then she set to
and bathed the wound, finally bandaging it with
the aid of a strip of linen she took from her bundle,
tying it in such a manner as to fix the leaf upon the
sore. Then said Antonius : " We cannot leave this
younger brother of ours to starve upon the road so
far away from any habitation, and therefore we
must take him along with us, lest he be homeless,
having gone astray and got lost." So saying, he
lifted that sufferer in his arms very gently and took
him along.

And when it came to eventide those three way
farers, after much climbing, arrived at a village

high up in the mountains. And the snow was on
the ground, for the altitude was great, and it was
now winter, so that they were cold, and also hungry
and very tired; and the dog had proved no mean
weight to carry so long a way. And they found but
a very poverty-stricken and dilapidated guest-
house, seeing that few travellers ever came to so
remote a spot, especially in winter time.
Nevertheless they were able to obtain food and
drink, and warmth from a log fire burning merrily
on the hearth. And the innkeeper proved kindly
and full of solicitude for his guests, as also full of
inquisitiveness to know what possible enterprise
could bring them so far, and at so unseasonable a
time of the year. And Antonius, in response to
his enquiries, said : " Friend, we seek a monastery
situated near or on the summit of this very
mountain, and so to-morrow, at daybreak, we
journey forward without further delay." Then
that kindly old innkeeper put up his hands in
solicitous horror, and said : " Ye can never climb
that peak, and in the winter too, and one of ye a
lady at that; besides, what would ye with those
strange monks up there, who, it is rumoured,
practise all manner of unheard-of arts, and who,
to our knowledge, receive no visitors? " And
Antonius replied : " Nevertheless we go, and that
is assuredly our destination, unless we die on the

way." Then said the innkeeper, wringing his
hands: "Alas, alas, ye will surely perish in the
snow or fall down a ravine, or die of cold and
fatigue; and so, through mere foolhardiness, you
will go to your deaths, and never be heard of any
more." And Antonius said: "Friend, not so, for
we are extra strong and full of vitality; therefore
have no fear, and be not distressed on our
account!" But the innkeeper answered: "And
ye so young and so beautiful to lie frozen corpses
in the snow, with no human eyes, but only the
stars to behold you ever again." And Antonius
said: "Truly you have a tender heart, and will
not go unrewarded for your sympathy and well-
meant efforts to deter us from pursuing our
enterprise, but the sight of your compassion for
us awakens compassion on our part for you in
return, which we would gladly dispel, and, seeing
we know no other way, then go down into your
cellar and fetch a bottle of the best wine, that you
may drink with us and thus feel a little less
melancholy."

And then the face of that tender-hearted old
man lighted up, and, thanking Antonius, he
shuffled out of the room on his quest. And
Cynara said, when he was gone: "Thou seest the
Lords of the Left-hand Path are again at work to
deter us, but this time they work partly through

goodness and tender-heartedness and solicitude, using that lovable old man for their purpose, instead of scandal-mongers and unjust judges and the like, as heretofore. For truly the virtuous may be employed for evil purposes as well as the wicked, though no ill, but as thou didst say, reward will accrue to this our friend in return, seeing he is totally innocent of any evil design. And yet with him and his goodness, is it not as with the pure waters of a river, which quench the thirst of many a thirsty soul, thereby doing good, and at the same time prevent the wayfarer from pursuing his way, thereby doing evil?" And Antonius smiled with affection on his beloved: "But," he said, "little moralist! this time thy simile is somewhat lacking, for where do the Lords of the Left-hand Path come in with respect to the river?" And Cynara answered: "They so contrive that they lead the traveller to a place where there is neither a ford nor a bridge, or where the torrent is so swift that he fears to cross." So then Antonius replied with a laugh: "Thou hast scored thy point, and I on my part will pay my forfeit by giving thee a kiss."

XX

AND then, as bedtime approached, Antonius entered into his meditations, and in a little while he saw Petrius before him, radiant with love. And the Hermit said: " My disciple, thou hast done well, and yesterday thou didst sow good seeds, turning the occasion of thy trial into a sermon for the good of the populace, and making a defence which, though seeming to be one, acted as no defence at all, nor divulged any secrets according to our decree. And now, as a reward, thou shalt wander to-night, when thy body is asleep yet thy soul conscious, into regions of untellable loveliness and Bliss. And yet, be on thy guard, lest thou shouldst think to thyself: this unspeakable joy is all-sufficing, and now what need have I to go further and face the last and greatest ordeal? For learn, that until the End is attained there should always exist in the heart of man a Divine Discontent, ever murmuring, 'even this is not enough,' seeing that only when the End is achieved does Bliss become an Absolute and Eternal Consciousuess, never to leave the soul any more. Therefore, as I said, be on thy guard, and may my blessing go with thee! " And then Petrius suddenly disappeared.

So then that night Antonius went into a profound sleep of the body, but unspeakable consciousness of the soul, as his Master had foretold. But when the morning came he awoke and rubbed his eyes, refreshed in a way he had never felt before, yet at the same time feeling as if he had returned to a prison, or to a state of dream instead of waking life. And when he had arisen and dressed, and while, together with Cynara, he broke his fast, he said: "Beloved, last night, as I slept, I was together with thee in realms of unspeakable joy and light and colour, totally indescribable in any words whatsoever: and now tell me, hast thou also a recollection of so sublime a state?" And she answered: "I have, and yet I cannot tell thee of that state, for, as thou sayest, words cannot describe a condition which is beyond all experiences ever to be found on the dull planes of earth. But this I can tell thee, that the earth-consciousness seems like a dark shadow-land, born of unreality and delusion in comparison with that state from which we both have emerged. And now I understand full well why mystics and philosophers all describe their ecstasy and ecstatic vision in various and conflicting terms, so arousing the criticism and scepticism of the unenlightened; for those mystics, in attempting to achieve the impossible in the way of description, resorted to hyperbole and extravagant similes, relating of streets of gold and precious stones, which have no existence in fact, but constitute merely a feeble endeavour to convey some idea of the luxuriance and magnificence and radiance inherent in such exalted planes." Then said Antonius: "Beloved, in spite of what thou hast experienced, art thou willing to go forward?" And Cynara answered: "I am, and this very hour."

So then they furnished themselves with a supply of food and drink, for there were now no more villages on the way, and having arranged to leave the dog with the kindly innkeeper, who renewed his entreaties that they should remain, they set out in the cold crisp air. But that dog, out of gratitude, yelped and whined, trying hard to escape from the restraining hand of its new master, as it saw them depart; and they could still hear the sound of its lamentations as they went further on their way.

And Antonius said: "Gladly would I have brought that poor pitiful creature along with us had I not feared he might perish in the snow; and now, assuredly he must think to himself (if he can think at all, which I scarcely doubt): 'Strange are these humans, who do a kindness at one moment and then a terrible unkindness in the next, awakening my love for them by an act of charity, and then spurning it afterwards by going away and deserting me altogether.'" And Cynara said: "Nevertheless it is not only dogs who reason in this way respecting their masters, but likewise human beings respecting the Deity or His Agents. for when good luck attends them they say 'how

kind is God,' but when ill-luck comes in its turn
they say, 'now I am forsaken by God,' never
realising that the latter may be just as much a
manifestation of the Deity's benevolence as the
former. Nay, more so, even as thy apparent
desertion of that dog is a greater manifestation of
thy kindness, than bringing him to perish in the
snow. And yet the reason for men's miscompre-
hension of the Deity is not far to seek, seeing their
mistake lies in the fact that they regard everything
in part instead of in its entirety, thinking one
portion evil and the other good, and forever
asking why this should be so. For the unenlightened are ever ready to chide God and the
Laws of Nature, instead of chiding themselves,
forgetting that in whatever way the Cosmic
scheme might have been arranged, they would still
find fault, and deem things could have been
ordained to greater advantage." Then said
Antonius: "Truly thy practices have endowed
thee with eloquence, and seeing thou hast read few
or no books, more and more does the truth become
manifest that eloquence and inspiration come from
the heart, and not from the brain." And as he
spoke, suddenly they heard the dog coming
running along as best it could on three legs
through the snow. Then said Cynara: "Behold,
thou art outwitted, and this faithful creature has

broken loose from its moorings and escaped." And
the dog approached, wagging its tail and prancing
about and snorting and jumping up, first around
Antonius and then around Cynara, in an ecstasy of
joy, so that neither had the heart to send it back.
And Cynara laughed and said : " See, this dog is
more faithful to its Deity than man to *his*, for it
says, ' Even if thou dost seem to forsake me, yet
will I not forsake thee.' " And she patted its
shaggy and ill-kempt coat and kissed its head.

So then those three plodded on all day through
the snow, on which the sun shone with a brilliancy
blinding to the eyes, and yet warming to the heart.
And the ascent was very arduous, and time and
again Antonius needs must ask himself the way.
And around them on all sides arose innumerable
white peaks and mauve and azure valleys tinted
by the blue sky and shadows, while the air was like
the choicest sparkling wine. But as evening
approached it began to grow icy cold, for the sun
sank in a great vermilion disc, deserting as it were
the earth, and leaving it like a great heart voided
by love, and light and comfort, and everything
which sustains life. And Antonius said : " We can
see no more, and we are too weary to proceed any
further, so with our hands we must dig a hole in
the snow to shelter us from the icy wind, and so
rest. But let us beware that we go not to sleep, for

to fall asleep in the snow means never to wake any more." And so they did as he said, and rested a long while, until the cold cynical moon arose and gave of its ghostly light, looking like a mask suspended aslant in the deep unfathomable lapis sky. And then at lenght they plodded on with increased difficulty for another few hours, until, by reason of utter weariness, they were compelled again to dig a hole in the snow and recline, sheltered from the wind. And so they passed the entire night, which each succeeding hour rendered more and more difficult, until at last they felt they must perish. But when finally the sun rose they rose also, beginning again the awful ascent, which seemed to get more formidable at every step. And the dog grew so weak and weary that Antonius needs must add to his difficulties by carrying it on his shoulder; for, said he, " I would as lief die myself as leave it to die." But Cynara said : " The time will soon come when thou must leave us both to die, for in a little while I shall be able to go no more." And he looked at her with a terrible anxiety, and saw she had grow haggard and ill, so that his heart almost wept as it were for pity and love. And he tried to cheer her with inspiriting words, saying the way could hardly be much longer, seeing they had gone so far already; but as time went on her strength ebbed lower and lower,

so that she could scarcely make any headway at all.
And then at last, as once more the sun descended
and the icy chill of evening came over the earth,
she sank down, utterly incapable of moving another
step. Then Antonius was well-nigh overcome with
despair, and totally at a loss what to do, for to
return were as useless and fatal as to proceed, while
to carry her in his arms had become impossible,
seeing his own strength had all but ebbed away.
And so he began to chafe her hands, and her face,
and her limbs, and to press her to himself and
whisper soothing words, while the dog nestled
close to them both, making demonstrations of
affection, and licking her face and hands as best it
could in the utter extremity of its weariness. And
Cynara whispered : " Do thou go on alone, my
beloved, and leave me to sleep, for now I know
what the Masters meant, and the attainment for
the goal for me is not to be in this body, but on
the further side of death." And Antonius answered,
kissing her with the lips, as it were, of his very
soul: " Then for me also attainment is on the
further side of death, for leave thee now I could
not, even if the whole universe were my reward."
And she began to beg and implore with the last
flicker of her expiring strength, saying : "How
can I go to my happiness, knowing thou hast failed
through me?" And he said : " To die with thee

is to have triumphed, and not to have failed; for truly I believe this is the last ordeal, and the last test of the heart, which is to renounce life, that we may in reality gain it and emerge from these prisons of bodies, so as to be eternally free." And she answered faintly : " Not so, for thou hast still strength to reach the goal on earth, so that it seems the Masters have ordained that death be only for me, and not for thee." And again she began to entreat him he should go on, and leave her to sleep in the snow.

Then all at once her voice ceased and her eyes closed, and her face took on the pallor of death, and Antonius, as he pressed his lips to hers in his agony of suspense, could feel no breath. And he cried in his transport of despair : " Will nothing on earth save her? And where are our Masters? And where is the happiness of my soul? " And for moments, which seemed to him hours, he shook in a paroxysm of weeping, moaning to himself : " Now I am utterly forsaken and alone."* But his faithful companion licked his hands, and pressed its muzzle into his face, and nestled closer against his body, and then whined, and then wagged its tail, and then yelped, and then licked again, and nestled still closer in a transport of

---

* This agony of desolation precedes attainment in all mystic literature.

sympathy and consolation, almost every whit as
intense as his master's despair. Then all of a
sudden it stopped and lifted its head and raised its
ears and listened; and then it barked, and then
sniffed, and, finally, as if for a moment it had lost
all its weariness, scampered off on three legs and
disappeared behind a great boulder of snow that
stood like a tower on the edge of the slope. And
Antonius uncovered his face, and looked up
wondering; and instantly from behind that boulder
came two tall figures, with the dog prancing and
barking at their side, as if to hasten them on. And
they were dressed in a strange monkish garb of a
dark colour, and had long pointed beards, though
Antonius was too overcome to notice anything
save that they were men. But as they came nearer
he recognised their habiliments, and so knew them
at once to be the monks of the Brotherhood, for
the moon had now risen and lighted them up with
its pale beams. And when they were quite close,
in the extremity of his anguish, he prostrated
himself at their feet and cried : " O, Masters, you
come too late, for my beloved is dead." And then
one of them, who was the tallest and most
imposing, lifted him up with the gentleness of a
woman, and said in a voice of ineffable tenderness
and encouragement : " Not so, my brother, for she
does but swoon." And immediately the other

produced a small phial containing a dark liquid, and, raising her head, opened her lips and poured it down her throat. Then in a few moments, while Antonius looked on in a transport of suspense and hope, she opened her eyes. Whereupon that same brother lifted her up in his arms as if she were but a child, and said: " I will take her hence, for it were not well to linger here any longer—do you follow me as soon as you can; " and so saying he moved away. But Antonius faltered: " My limbs refuse to stir, and my head swims, and I am totally undone." Then the tall monk knelt down beside him, and stroked his hand for a moment, and smiled lovingly. And he said: " Thy woes are over, my brother! and thou hast come through thy severest ordeal with nothing worse than an exhausted body, which will soon be restored. And now drink this, for it will revive thee as nothing in the world has revived thee before." So saying, he also produced a phial, and held it to Antonius's lips. And he drank, reposing his head against the monk like a comforted child. And then very soon he began to feel refreshed and strengthened, so that every sensation of ill and dizziness faded like magic away, while in his soul he felt an indescribable relief, so intense that he was almost fain to cry for joy now, as abandonedly as a moment ago he had cried for grief. But instead, he said at length: "Now I am ready to go, and indeed glad to walk once more, for my clothes are frozen, and I would fain reach our destination, which I hope 's now not very far away."

And the monk said: "Nay it is close at hand, and in a very short time we shall be there." So saying, he rose, and gently raising Antonius as well, they began to move away. But when they had gone a few steps, suddenly Antonius stopped and said: "But the dog, why does it not follow?" And he looked round to see that faithful companion lying immovable on the snow. And he said, with compassion in his voice: "Alas, if that old friend be dead my heart will surely burst with pity; and yet perhaps he also merely swoons, and may be revived." And immediately he went back and knelt by the dog, and patted and stroked it, and tried to rouse it, but to no avail. And he said to the monk: "I pray you give me of your elixir to refresh this unfortunate dog." And the monk replied: "What, waste my precious elixir on a mere dog?" Then Antonius cried: "Ah, would that I had not taken the precious fluid, that this poor creature might have had my portion instead." And the monk said: "Why waste your grief over one who is oblivious to pain, being unconscious, and therefore contented? Moreover it is not well to linger here, so come away to where warmth and comfort, and food, and, still better, your beloved await you." Then Antonius exclaimed : " Never will I come and leave this poor faithful dog here until I know he is utterly past all help, and if you will not give me of your elixir then I will carry the dog to the monastery, in order to see if warmth will revive him, for certainly I will not leave him to die in the snow." Then that monk said in a voice suddenly charged with approval and sweetness and love : " My brother, thou hast indeed learnt the true compassion,* and now I see thy evolution has been, as it were, along the Way of Mercy, and thou art fitted for a Helper of Mankind. But in any case I would have saved thy faithful hound, not only for thy sake, but because of love for a younger brother in evolution." And then once again he produced that life-giving phial, and after administering its precious contents to that all-but expiring dog, lifted it gently in his arms, and thus carried it home.

XXI

So then Antonius and the monk, whose name was Pasimunda, instead of ascending the mountain summit, walked along a projecting ledge some

---

* The true compassion is beautifully set forth in the Mahararata—
the story also centring round a dog which Arjuna refuses
to desert.

considerable way below the top.   And when they
had come round to the further side, there, not far
away in a valley, sheltered from all winds, lay the
monastery, illumined by the white light of the
moon, while from its little windows gleamed forth
yellow beams, tinting the snow.   And Pasimunda
said : " Behold our destination, and does it not
look like an embodiment of welcome, with every
window lighted up as if for a festival?   And now, if
you look beyond it, you will see the lights of a
village glimmering in the circumjacent whiteness,
for we are not so isolated as you supposed; and he
who knows the right path can reach the world of
men without difficulty at all, as you will see, when
the time comes for you to go home." And Antonius
answered : " Truly my home has now become the
whole earth, and I feel myself no longer a denizen
of any one city, nor an owner of any one house, nor
a native of any one country; and yet some day I
will gladly return to my own home for the sake
of reunion with a friend I love; for not only do I
love him, but owe him a debt of gratitude I can
never repay." And Pasimunda said : "And of what
nature was his service? "   And Antonius replied :
" He opened my eyes to that Great Science, and
although he lent me but a few books and so
awakened my interest, yet had it not been for him
and his kind action, I should have wasted the whole

of my life." And Pasimunda said : " Only the wise know what incalculable effects may accrue from the most trifling acts of benevolence; and yet methinks very soon you will learn that your debt is of even greater magnitude than you supposed. But now, walk warily, for the descent is steep and the path slippery, so take care lest you fall." So then in a little while Antonius at last reached the end of his journey, and as he entered the great monastic hall, lit by lamps and a blazing log fire, Cynara came forward and embraced him long and ardently. And the dog, now perfectly restored, sprang from Pasimunda's arms and jumped up around his master and mistress, while the other inmates of the monastery, who had collected awaiting the evening meal, stood round looking on, and smiling with their wonderfully benevolent eyes. Then one of the brothers led Antonius to a room, where he found everything prepared for his comfort and refreshment, telling him to make a little haste, as suppertime was at hand. So he bathed, and put on the warm dry clothes that had been laid out for him, making all possible speed, for he was very hungry after so long a fast. But as at length he walked along the narrow long corridor towards the refectory, he thought to himself : " Somehow I have a premonition that I stand on the verge of a great and joyful surprise, and yet I know not what it can be, for surely the entire scale of the unexpected is exhausted, save that of the realms of spirit which are illimitable, and can only be brought about within my own soul, and not by any exterior thing. And then, suddenly as he turned a corner of the corridor, he beheld the open door of the refectory, and lo! there, standing just a little way inside, and talking to Cynara, he saw Pallomides. And in a moment they had embraced each other with the ecstasy of two long parted souls re-unified, while Antonius said: " Little did I dream that the cup of my happiness could be filled like this to the very brim; and yet the unexpected sight of thee, my beloved friend, has brought it about as nothing else in the world could have done. But tell me, how camest thou here? " And Pallomides laughed gently, and said: " Nay, this is a retreat to which I often come, accounting it as much my home as my villa down yonder by the sea." And Antonius said in astonishment: " Then thou art also a brother, but since when? And why wouldst thou not come with me when I asked it of thee? " And Pallomides laughed again, and said: " Nay, seeing I had come the way thou didst come already, it was not necessary to make the same journey again, and especially for thy sake it had been inadvisable."

Then suddenly Antonius divined the truth, remembering the words of Pallomides. And he said, with love and reverence: "Master, I owe thee everything, and now I believe thou it was who sent that old sage in the disguise of a mendicant to urge me to seek the Path, and so thou wast all the time the unseen power, as it were, behind the throne, directing me to my various teachers." But then suddenly a bell rang for the evening repast, so that for answer Pallomides merely smiled, and led his pupil lovingly to the table, the head of which he took himself, putting Cynara on his right and Antonius on his left, while the rest of the brothers occupied the many seats along the two sides. And the discourse during that meal was light-hearted and happy, the gentle laughter of those care-disburdened monks falling like music on the ears of their two newly arrived guests. And Antonius thought, "Wonderful indeed is the modesty of the Great, for it is now obvious that Pallomides is the Chief of the Brotherhood, seeing he occupies the seat of honour; and yet all these years have I known him, and never once did he breathe a word of so momentous a fact." But after the meal was over, and the brothers had dispersed, Antonius and Cynara and Pallomides were left alone. And Antonius said: "Master, tell us now what it all means, for although I divine much, yet

I would gladly hear everything from thine own lips." And Pallomides said : " My friend, call me not Master, and I will tell you both all that you wish to know; for learn that your journey, though actual, was also, as it were, symbolical, being as the journey of the soul to Divine Knowledge, as well as that of the body to its attainment. And although I could have instructed you in my own villa by the sea, yet nevertheless without that journey and its hardships and its bitter experiences, my teaching would have proved barren, or at the most very tardy in result. For the long way is often the shortest way in the end, and to teach (as thou didst, in Marbletown, Antonius) is to learn, by reason of the merit acquired, which allowed the opening of the gates to further knowledge. And now, up here where the air is pure and rare, and also untainted by the impure thought-vibrations of the city, you can both progress in a way which were well-nigh impossible elsewhere. And yet, although there is an easy ascent to this place, which I and my brothers take, nevertheless the more arduous one was necessary to you as a test and an experience to purify the heart, as now no doubt you realise for yourselves. But all the same, the very end of the journey is your own home, seeing it were fruitless to remain here for ever, and there is yet something to be done for the good of the world. And that

home-coming will be again a symbol as well as a
fact, for just as you will then have made a
circuitous journey, so does mankind itself, going
forth in search of happiness and knowledge, finally
to learn they can alone be found within the soul."
And Antonius said: "Much did I read in thy
books of the years of arduous strife and terrible
deprivations necessary to the attainment of Divine
Initiation, and yet were I to look back, save for that
final agony, when I deemed I had lost all, the way
has not seemed so very hard." And Pallomides
said: "Know my brother, that thy ascent did not
begin in this life at all, as thou wilt soon see when
memory of thy past lives comes once more; and
although the beginning of thy present one,
steeped as it was in the pleasures of the senses,
seemed remote from, and totally incompatible
with, the Path; yet appearances are ever deceptive,
and he who seems to be the furthest away is often
nearest to the goal, as was also the case with
Cynara, thy faithful and selfless helpmate and
friend. For truly it happens times without number
that what the world calls a sinner is often merely
divided by so minute a thing as the breadth of a
hair from a Saint, or at least a *potential* Saint, and
his vices are therefore but the last flicker of the
expiring flame of the lower self, ere it dies never
to live again." And then Pallomides paused, and

looked lovingly on his two pupils for a moment, saying at length : " And now I must go for a while to my meditations, and must leave you alone, but I will return shortly, ere we retire for the night."

And when he had gone Antonius took Cynara's hand and said : " Beloved this is the end, and yet it is but the beginning, for hitherto we have been as mere children learning to walk, and unable to act, because of our limitations, aye, even unable to feel and unable to love. For now I know what the uninitiated call love, in comparison to the ecstacy I feel for thee is hardly love at all, being a capricious admixture of desire and sadness, and fluctuating joy and apprehension and jealousy, and many other unstaple things as well." And Cynara smiled and said : " As to love, thou sayest true, but as to the end, it is so for thee, but not as yet for me; for know that I have not gone through the terrible desolation which leads to the final goal." And Antonius looked at her with the very essence of loving compassion in his eyes, and said : " Aye, I would I could spare thee that moment, for its agony is indescribable, and like the very aggregate of all agonies concentrated in one. But shall I tell thee how it came to me ? " And she answered : " Tell me!" And he said : " Know that out on the mountain yonder I thought thee dead." And she squeezed his hand, and looked into his face with an ocean of eloquence in her gaze, but for a moment uttered no word. And then she said: "Yet had I been dead, thou knowest full well, that were no separation." And he answered: "I know it well, and yet that was my ordeal, since for the last time the awful illusion of separateness overwhelmed my soul, leaving me like one utterly forsaken, and deprived even of Love itself. And yet, this I will tell thee, never is Succour so near as when it seems totally beyond all reach, and therefore remember this when the time comes for thy last ordeal. And now answer me something." And she said: "What is thy desire?" And he said: "Didst thou hear the Master say there is yet something to be done for the world?" And she answered: "I did!" And he said: "The limitations of space and time and fatigue having departed for ever, and the helping of the great orphan Humanity being the joyful delight of every brother, which he accomplishes by reason of his added capacity, then the work to which Pallomides referred must be related to the physical plane." And she answered: "Maybe that is so; and what then?" And he answered: "Know that as these bodies last but a short while compared with Eternity, and the brothers to carry on the work are few, so that the complete climax of our earthly lives were only reached if we provided a vehicle for an exalted soul: May I now ask of thee two things? Give me a wife in the shape of thy beloved and beautiful self—and a son." And she answered: " I will."

So then, after a while, those two united ones returned to their native place, and in the course of time a son was born to them; and because of the purity of their love and the exaltedness of their souls, they attracted to themselves an entity so lofty that he became a great sage, leaving the world an enrichment in the form of a divine philosophy. But as for his parents, in the Autumn of their lives, though still looking young and beautiful, they quitted the body, and are now working together in the highest spheres of Bliss, until the time comes for them to be reborn once more as an aid to the further enlightenment of Mankind.

Cyril Scott (1879-1970) has been described as "the father of British modern music," and an eminent composer; his work has been performed thoughout England, Europe and the United States. As a young man, Scott pursued studies in Yoga and unorthodox medicine, joined the Theosophical Society, and contacted a number of gifted seers and occultists. His best known work is *Music: Its Secret Influence.* He wrote the *Initiate* trilogy as an account of his spiritual quest—*The Initiate, Initiate in the New World,* and *Initiate in the Dark Cycle.*